RUDE AWAKENINGS

'What glorious breasts you have, Ailsa,' said Gerald as he unclipped her bra. The cups fell away to bare her big creamy mounds. With a finger and thumb he pinched a large pink nipple while she tried to avoid his gaze.

'Don't be ashamed,' said Gerald. 'I can feel you trembling. You're trembling because you're excited. These nipples give you away, they're begging to be sucked. You want me to suck them, don't you?'

'Do what you like,' muttered Ailsa, trying to suppress a moan as he began to kiss the upper slopes of her breasts, 'like you always do . . .'

Rude Awakenings

Lesley Asquith

Delta

First published in 1997
by HEADLINE BOOK PUBLISHING

A HEADLINE DELTA paperback

10 9 8 7 6 5 4 3 2 1

ISBN 0 7472 5464 8

Typeset by Palimpsest Book Production Limited,
Polmont, Stirlingshire
Printed and bound in Great Britain by
Mackays of Chatham PLC, Chatham, Kent

HEADLINE BOOK PUBLISHING
A division of Hodder Headline PLC
338 Euston Road
London NW1 3BH

Rude
Awakenings

Chapter One

Coming Attractions

Sleep was impossible in her over-excited state. A hand fondled and cupped one firm breast, tightly squeezing the ivory-smooth swollen mound, thumb and forefinger plucking at an erect nipple. The other hand stroked and fondled the moist outer lips of her sex which parted in arousal to allow fingers to explore and titillate the soft inner flesh. New sensations drove her to spread her legs as never before.

Her *own* hands and fingers, not someone else's, Manda ruefully acknowledged as she gave in to temptation. Despite contempt for her weakness, she continued to prolong the delicious feelings coursing through her nubile young body. It felt so wonderfully *good*, another part of her conscience reasoned, so how could it be so wrong?

Come morning she'd be sailing on her first cruise, an exciting prospect that made the night seem endless. She told herself she needed to masturbate to hasten the long hours. An honest girl, she also had to admit the urge to give herself relief had been overpowering since that afternoon. The wonder was that she had held out until night and the privacy of her bedroom before seeking the needful climax.

That afternoon her mother had been absent on a last-minute shopping expedition to buy clothes suitable for their Caribbean holiday voyage, and St Boniface's School for Senior Girls was quiet, closed for the summer vacation. Blushing at the thought on a bright July afternoon, Manda had resisted the urge to go to her room and pleasure herself. Instead she

1

had restlessly wandered into the teaching staff's rest room and library, seeking a book.

There she found Myra Starr, the school secretary, comfortably settled in an armchair, smoking and drinking a glass of sherry she'd helped herself to from the sideboard. The woman made no attempt to rise on being discovered, calmly awaiting the reaction of the daughter of the school's headmistress and owner. Too timid to show signs of disapproval, Manda merely excused herself and said she was looking for something to read.

'It's holiday time, join me in a sherry,' Myra had invited casually. 'They won't miss it. I presume you're excited about the cruise, even if it is an academic one?'

'You suggested the trip and booked the tickets,' Manda reminded her.

'On your mother's strict instructions to find an educational experience,' Myra said. 'Don't worry, I'm sure it won't be lots of dull classroom lectures. The ship will visit some outstanding tropical islands, smaller ones off the usual tourist route. You'll have a lovely time and make new friends. That will be fun – especially for a pretty young girl like you.'

Manda found herself blushing at the older woman's words. 'Trust my mother to insist on an educational cruise,' she said, trying to cover her embarrassment. It had been the way Myra had expressed the compliment that had disturbed her. She spoke like a male admirer, flattering her for an ulterior motive.

'My dear girl, why are you blushing?' Myra laughed. 'Are you so unused to hearing compliments? If that mother of yours allows you a little freedom for once, you'll be the most sought-after girl on the ship.'

'I hope it *will* be fun,' Manda said, annoyed with herself for appearing so naive. 'I can't wait for tomorrow,' she added as Myra rose to pour the sherry, refilling her own glass as well. 'This day has seemed endless.' She accepted the drink nervously, wondering what her mother would say if she could see them.

2

Myra Starr wouldn't care, she knew. Nothing seemed to worry her at all. Manda had long found her fascinating. Myra was an attractive and self-assured individual in her late thirties, with a curvaceous figure. She lived-in on the premises but was notorious for returning late at night or sometimes not at all. She had been married, it was known, and was no doubt very sexually experienced. The virgin Manda was in awe of her as they touched glasses. No doubt her mother would have fired Myra long before had she not been so good at her work.

'Want to see a film?' Myra had asked, sliding a cassette into the video recorder set below the television. 'It's called *Basic Instinct* and is supposed to be rather sexy. How old are you, Miss Craig? Would your mother allow you to watch it?'

'She's not here to say, is she?' Manda pouted, aggrieved her mother still vetted what she could view. 'I'm almost eighteen, I can see what I like. I'm a big enough girl, don't you think?'

'From where I'm standing, yes,' Myra observed slyly, noting how the flushed girl's school blouse was filled out by an impressively thrusting bosom. The plain white cotton was stretched to contain two big shapely breasts. Below, the short black skirt was moulded to firm curvy thighs and a pertly rounded bottom. 'Big enough and old enough undoubtedly,' the older woman said meaningfully. 'Are you sitting comfortably? Consider this as part of your education, my dear. I'd say the time was ripe – you certainly are.'

The film had soon set Manda's pulse racing, her imagination running riot and her sex throbbing. As she played with herself in her lonely bed that night, she dwelt on the explicit sex scenes in the film. She recalled the beautiful blonde female star being interrogated by detectives while seated before them. During the questioning the actress had crossed and uncrossed her legs, short skirt hitched up to reveal a taunting flash of pubic hair and the fact she wore no panties.

The very thought was terribly exciting, wantonly erotic, making Manda thrill at the wicked idea of showing herself off before a male audience. She threw back the duvet to admire her body, neck craned to peer between uptilted marble-firm

3

breasts to the raised tufty mound being fingered below. Lost to all but the erotic sensations created by her hand, her bottom jerked wildly up and down from the bed. Ecstatic moans escaped her lips as her climax neared, then she froze in utter dismay as her bedroom door was opened.

'It's only me – Mrs Starr,' Manda heard with relief as the school secretary entered the room. 'I was passing on my way to bed and saw your light shining under the door. Can't you sleep?'

She approached closer, seeing the girl naked and prostrate, the duvet thrown aside. In the glow of the bedside lamp she noted Manda's hands: one still clutching a breast and the other between her thighs as if frozen there in fear. Myra's short emphatic chuckle had the girl cringing in dire humiliation.

'Well, well, Miss Craig?' her intruder asked teasingly. 'Are you having fun? Giving yourself a really good come?'

'I was *not*. It isn't what you think,' Manda began desperately. 'It was hot, so I pushed back the duvet and took off my nightie—'

'You were hot,' Myra agreed. 'I can see that. So carry on what you were doing.'

'I told you I was doing nothing,' Manda weakly defended herself.

Myra smiled. 'There's nothing to be ashamed of, young lady. I do it all the time myself when I need relief. You'll find a vibrator adds greatly to the pleasure if you're going to make a habit of it. It's quite natural. Why do you protest so much?'

'I thought you were my mother,' Manda blubbered, her eyes brimmed with tears. 'You have no right to enter my room and say such things.' She tried to pull the duvet over her naked state but Myra was grasping it firmly to prevent her. '*Please*,' she cried. 'It was my first time, honestly. Why are you looking at me like that, Mrs Starr?'

'Because you are a very beautiful young creature,' Myra said. 'Lovely and enticing. Such full breasts you have for such a slim girl, almost as large as mine. And that little

4

pouting quim with its wisps of hair adorning quite a naughty thrust-out mound. Men would love to kiss it.'

'Don't *say* such things,' Manda implored her. 'It's not right. I'm not like that.'

'You could have fooled me,' Myra said, amused. 'Your dear little pussy's still pouting and twitching. You're a little fibber. So what if you've done it before? Who on earth hasn't? Why does your mother keep a vibrator in her underwear drawer, for example? Does she use it to polish her nails? We're all at it, honey, including you.'

'I want you to leave,' Manda pleaded in her turmoil. 'Why won't you?'

'Because you arouse me,' Myra stated, 'and because you don't really want me to go, do you?' She sat on the bed beside the trembling girl, the tapering fingers of her right hand lightly brushing Manda's nipples. 'How stiff they are,' she said, her voice low and seductive. 'That's a giveaway sign of your need to be pleasured, little minx. Allow me this time, won't you? Two is much better than one.'

'But you're a *woman*!' Manda gasped, any further protest stifled as Myra leaned over to kiss her. A moment later a warm wet tongue probed inside Manda's mouth. 'No! Please, no!' the girl stammered as the fierce kiss ended. Her lower stomach churned and she found the sensations of her earlier arousal returning. 'Mrs Starr, you're *seducing* me,' she protested. 'Please don't. My mother is just two rooms away. She'll hear us.'

'The walls of this old school are thick,' Myra reminded her, pecking light kisses to her eyes and mouth while cupping Manda's breasts. 'I caught you masturbating and now you act like Miss Goody-Two-Shoes. But that's not the real you, is it, Miss Manda Craig? At heart, my dear, you are a naturally sexy trollop, a baggage, a randy young tart. Didn't I hear that one of the authors of the hand-written pornography circulating in the school was you? I'm told your stories were the most imaginative and lewd. Deny that you feel horny now?'

5

'It was the film,' Manda sniffed to excuse her lapse. 'It made me feel strange, *unusual*.'

'Randy is the word you mean,' Myra said mercilessly. 'And what about those dirty stories?'

'All the girls wrote them and exchanged them,' Manda pleaded. 'Honestly, do you think I'm that kind of girl?'

'Yes,' Myra said. 'You were diddling yourself when I walked in. You need good come. I can give you as many as you like. Do you still want me to leave?'

'I – I think so,' Manda said uncertainly.

'Then I'm wasting my time,' she was told sternly. 'If you deny your feelings you'll end up a frustrated woman. And you want it all the time, that's obvious.'

'No, no I don't,' Manda said. 'It's you who makes me want to.'

'That amounts to the same thing,' Myra informed her, about to reluctantly rise from the bed. 'You want it and I'm willing to give it. You silly little bitch, don't fight your nature. No doubt you've been raised to think our basic urges are shameful but that's cruel for someone as highly sexed as you. Did mummy tell you these are nasty dirty feelings that should be suppressed? Stupid girl, I'd like to spank that harmful nonsense right out of you.'

'You wouldn't dare,' Manda said, resenting the lecture but the thought of being spanked exciting her. 'You wouldn't dare try to beat me,' she repeated as if making it a challenge. 'I'd tell my mother.'

'Tell her what you like,' Myra said, ignoring the squeal of surprise as she flipped the girl over and pinned her with a firm grip at the nape of her neck. 'I'm leaving tomorrow anyway. I'm getting out before the school folds. You can inform your ma the lack of pupils are her fault. Who'd send their daughter to a school run by a frigid, puritanical bitch? It's a great pity, as your mother is a good-looking widow. Her years are passing and she's missing out.'

'Let me up,' Manda screeched, struggling. 'Don't even think about spanking me, you beast!'

The first smarting crack of Myra's hand across the girl's wriggling buttocks made her soft cheeks flinch and redden. And despite her sobs and pleas the punishment continued, a repeated flurry of sharp smacks making Manda at last lie still as ordered. Crying for mercy and her eyes full of tears, Manda found her humbling unbelievably stimulating. The heat in her spanked bottom seeped through to her already burning cunt, increasing its throb.

At last fully contrite, she sighed as Myra's palm rested on her inflamed cheeks. The cooling touch on the hot flesh made her feel entirely wanton, desperate for satisfaction. In her struggles she had rubbed her mound hard into the bed, adding greatly to her need for relief.

'You're – you're horrible,' she sobbed to her tormentor. 'And you have no right to say things about my mother.'

'It's all true though,' Myra said, leaning over to press kisses to Manda's ravaged behind. 'She's a good woman wasted. Celibacy doesn't suit her. Don't think I haven't wanted to make love to her. I've given the signals, but they've been ignored. You've inherited that lovely figure from her. You have such a pretty bum, girl. It makes me want to do more to it than just spank it.'

'You enjoyed it, you *wanted* to do it,' Manda accused, giving a shudder as Myra ran her outstretched tongue over the cleave in the girl's bottom. 'You smacked my bare bum because you like doing that, not just because you said you would teach me a lesson. You enjoyed beating me. It gives you pleasure smacking girls' bottoms.'

'And men's too, let's not be sexist about that,' Myra laughed. 'Oh, yes, men love their backsides thrashed, believe you me. One day I've no doubt you'll do that yourself. It can be great pleasure for both parties, giving and receiving. In your case, you needed it.' She smoothed her palm over Manda's silky smooth cheeks, hearing a suppressed sigh from the girl. 'For my part, I admit, I couldn't resist smacking such a gorgeous girlish botty.' She bent to kiss each cheek reverently, alert to Manda's low moan of pleasure. 'Remember, you are a lovely young woman on the verge of life,' she said. 'Don't waste any of it. I'll say goodnight to you now as you obviously wish me to leave. Sleep tight and pleasant dreams, my dear.'

'What would you have done if I'd wanted you to stay?' Manda asked shyly, turning her head.

'Made love to you like only another woman can,' Myra said tenderly, pressing kisses to the girl's fiery bottom. 'Give you the relief you obviously want, and as many times as you could stand before begging me to stop. You sweet child, you must know women do such things.' She gave a friendly pat to the rounded cheeks of Manda's rear. 'Of course you do. Admit it, or do you need another smacked bum?'

'I've heard,' Manda began, her voice throaty with emotion. 'I've heard some of the senior girls at the school say they—'

'Satisfy each other's needs,' Myra finished for her. 'I've often looked in when returning early in the morning to see girls sharing beds. Never once did I report it, they're doing what comes naturally in the absence of boys.' The fingers and thumbs of both her hands splayed Manda's buttock cheeks wide, bringing a gasp to her throat.

'You shouldn't look in *there*,' she muttered feebly. 'I'm sure it's not very nice.'

Myra laughed at her concern. 'I find it utterly delightful. I see a pretty little virgin cunt and just above it the unsullied ring of your dear bottom-hole. Both right under my very nose and all the better to kiss and lick.' She dipped her face, running an outstretched tongue-tip in a sweeping movement up the length of Manda's swollen sex lips, continuing on to momentarily titillate the crinkled anal orifice. She inhaled deeply of the girl's aroused scent, saying, 'Such a pity that you want me to leave.'

'I can't force you to go,' Manda whimpered, her arousal agonising. 'Not if you insist. Ooh, *aaagh*, what are you doing there, Mrs Starr?'

'Going down on you, sweetheart,' Myra informed her, delving with nose and mouth into the cleft of Manda's cheeks, probing a snake-like tongue beyond the swollen outer labia and seeking the girl's highly responsive clitoris. Manda gave out a series of low mewing sounds, the intruding tongue throbbing in her inner channel like a heartbeat, its wet warmth adding to the oiling of her already-burning cunt. Her bottom buffeted Myra's face, jerking and rotating as the long-desired climax shook her to the toes, continuing for a second and third series of spasms in a multiple orgasm. Manda collapsed forward limply on her face and belly, feeling gloriously drained and sated as never before.

In time she recovered sufficiently to brush aside strands of long blonde hair from her flushed face and gaze in wonder at the woman who had given her such incredible pleasure with her tongue. 'I didn't know it could be so marvellous, dear Mrs Starr,' she breathed, still dazed. 'It was heaven. I want more.'

Myra was standing beside the bed naked, hair down to her shoulders, clothes at her feet and magnificent in the thrust of her large pendent breasts and the white columns of her thighs with the forest of hair between. Manda helplessly held out her arms to receive her as the older woman got on the bed. Their lips met in a long and passionate kiss as they embraced.

'You have so much to learn, so many delightful pleasures to be taught,' Myra said as she drew the girl closer: bare breast to breast, belly to belly and cunt to cunt. 'It will be my pleasure to initiate you tonight. To teach you for others too, for it's in your nature to love and be loved.'

'I want to learn everything. I'm sorry you won't be with us on tomorrow's cruise,' Manda whispered, nuzzling into Myra's ample breasts, her mouth seeking a proffered thick nipple, suddenly madly desirous of nursing on it. 'It would be nice.'

'Yes, wouldn't it?' Myra cooed, tilting up the teat being so greedily suckled. 'As it so happens, I booked a ticket for myself.'

Chapter Two

Marriage Guidance

'It's more than a year since you married Nigel,' said Gerald Marsh, thinking what a glorious fuck his daughter-in-law would make. 'I've been his father for twenty-three years and never figured him out. Don't blame yourself, my dear, for him being a complete flop as a husband.' The professor of science and tutor to the senior girls of St Boniface's, crossed the room to where Dorothy sat attempting to stifle her sobs. He pressed a large brandy into her hand, raising the drink to her lips to make her swallow deeply.

And what lips, he considered lewdly, ruby red and moist. Made for kissing, or, even better, to be clamped around his dick, which always stirred at the sight of his well-built daughter-in-law. He perched on the arm of her chair, putting a consoling arm around her waist, glancing down the neck of her dress and ogling the creamy upper swell of her plump breasts.

'Drink up,' he ordered kindly, giving her an affectionate squeeze, enjoying the pliant feel of girlish flesh. 'Nigel must be mad,' he added as if speaking his thoughts aloud. 'A hot-shot lawyer in court but a no-no in bed. It doesn't make sense for a young wife like you to claim you're ignored. You do mean sexually?'

'*That* and in every other way,' Dorothy admitted tearfully. 'We hardly speak.' She drained the remains of the brandy as if to brace herself, trying hard to stifle her sobs. 'We're going on that cruise tomorrow and he doesn't want to come with us. It's going to be obvious to Mummy and Manda.

11

Mother suspects we're not getting along and now she'll learn the truth. Nigel doesn't love me or want me any more. He has even moved into a separate bedroom. What can I do?'

She burst into a fresh outbreak of tears as Gerald tut-tutted and took the opportunity to hug her closer. 'He's always been a brain-box without a real life,' he announced. 'I blame his mother. Years ago I couldn't stick the pair of 'em ganging up on me and walked out. The wonder is that a pretty girl like you ever married the creep, or that his darling mummy allowed him to. No doubt he's with her tonight. One thing you can be sure of, my dear, he hasn't got a girlfriend on the side as you suspect.'

'But we *never* make love any more,' Dorothy wailed. 'What else could I think?' She lowered her tear-stained face as if bitterly ashamed. 'I must blame myself too. If he goes elsewhere for *that*, isn't it my fault?'

'Jesus, when he's got you at home?' Gerald marvelled, still admiring the deep cleave and alluring swell of her full breasts. 'He goes to see his mummy,' he assured her, the soft warmth of her body increasing his arousal and lust. 'Bet on it, young lady. He's still under her thumb as always. If he didn't visit her daily I think she'd still cane his backside like she did when he was a boy.'

He held her even tighter, the wrist of the arm encircling her stomach bearing the delightful weighty mass of an impressive right breast. The Craig girls, Manda and Dorothy, who now sat beside him as an unhappy Mrs Marsh, had both been blessed with the shapely big tits of their mother Ailsa, headmistress of St Boniface's and his employer. 'I can hardly believe it's your fault if the marriage isn't working,' he soothed craftily, pecking a soft kiss to her cheek. 'Not a stunning wife with a figure like yours. I take it you want sexual relations to continue? That you encourage him?'

'Ye-yes,' Dorothy muttered, an admission almost shamefully disclosed. 'I still love Nigel. I truly want us to act like man and wife. I do try.'

'Of course,' Gerald nodded, choosing his words sympathetically to draw her out, eager to get her defences down and – hopefully in time – her knickers. There's nothing like getting a frustrated female to talk about her sex life, or lack of it, to get her aroused, he considered. 'I presume you make that plain?' he added very seriously, as if having nothing but her best welfare at heart. 'Do you initiate an approach at any moment you feel like making love? Would you like good regular sex?'

'Yes,' Dorothy said almost too quietly to be heard.

'Good. And therefore do you tempt him in the right way? Don't be too shy to tell me. Get it off your chest.'

Some chest too, he pondered looking down at the creamy cleavage below his nose, wondering if he dare cup a luscious tit. *Don't rush it,* an inner voice of experience warned, *get her weak at the knees and yours for the taking.* 'I need to know just how hard you try,' he said, switching to a stern tone. 'If you use all a woman's wiles, the blame must be his.'

'I'm not very good at using a woman's wiles,' Dorothy admitted sadly. 'Mother brought us up to be so – circumspect – not forward. I'm too shy to ask Nigel outright to make love to me,' she said, swallowing as if to force out the words. 'But I do things like wearing nice underwear, even letting him see me undressed – naked – after a bath or preparing for bed. But it does no good, he looks away. And now he sleeps in the spare room.'

What *is* the world coming to? Gerald thought bitterly, envisaging his daughter-in-law nude and eager to be fucked. His hand moved up and clasped her right breast, giving it a suggestive squeeze. She turned in surprise to face him and he kissed her open mouth. For a long moment their lips clung and his tongue entered her. He held her close, kissing passionately.

Then, to Gerald's great frustration, Dorothy tore herself free. She leapt to her feet, looking at her father-in-law aghast, wiping her wrist across her mouth. He in turn felt cheated – the girl had been a whisker away from surrendering. Never was he more sure that for a lingering few seconds she had welcomed his advance.

'Why did you do that, Professor Marsh?' she asked nervously.

'For your own good,' Gerald stated, seething at being denied. 'You act like a coy spinster instead of a married woman, and a discontented one at that. Do you want the plain truth?'

'I came here for help and advice,' Dorothy began feebly.

'And I'm giving it to you straight,' Gerald said. 'If you can't get Nigel to screw you, when you're patently panting for a good going-over, then grow up! With those big boobs and curvy thighs you could give a corpse a cockstand. Use your potential, girl, that's why you were given tits and a fanny. When my son gets home tonight, seduce him. Rape the silly bastard if you have to. If he doesn't come across then, let his mother keep him. Get the picture?'

'I think I had better leave,' Dorothy said faintly, shocked by his language. 'Would you bring me my coat, please?'

'Steady yourself with another brandy,' Gerald insisted, going to the sideboard, 'then I'll drive you home.' She swallowed the drink almost gratefully, still shaken. In the car she sat beside him silently as he drove through the town, drawing up in a quiet lane as they approached the village where his son and daughter-in-law lived. He made a great show of putting on the handbrake.

'Please, drive on,' Dorothy said, growing alarmed. 'Thank you for driving me but I really am late already.'

'Don't be alarmed,' Gerald assured her, returning to his caring approach. 'I need to explain my manner this evening. If you think I spoke crudely, it *was* for your own good, believe me. Being a nice quiet shy girl all the time won't save your marriage. Feeling guilt about wanting sex is an entirely wasted emotion, even harmful to health in a young frustrated woman. That's what you are, dear, and a bundle of nerves with it. If I may speak plainly, you are in need of satisfying sexual

14

intercourse. You almost gave in to the urge when we kissed, didn't you?'

'For a moment,' Dorothy admitted in a shamed whisper. 'It's been so long, I was tempted. It felt nice. But it wouldn't be right.'

'To hell with right,' Gerald said grimly. 'It was what you needed. I only did it for your own sake.'

She flinched as his large palm cupped her breast but she made no attempt to pull away. His fingers closed firmly over the pliant mound, the taut nipple tingled as he massaged the swollen flesh. Below, her lower stomach fluttered in a surge of arousal, her cunt seeming to pulse as if on cue. 'Let yourself go, girl,' she heard Gerald urge as he pressed kisses to her mouth. 'Do you deny that you're bursting for a fuck?'

'Professor Marsh,' she began, her protest fading as her resolve weakened. His next kiss left her even more breathless and her lips parted willingly to accept the hot tongue which probed her mouth. Unresisting, she thought fleetingly of her husband as she clung to Gerald and crushed her mouth fiercely to his. 'Oh, yes, do it then. Do it to me,' she heard herself say as their lips parted. Regardless of the consequences, the urgent throb in her cunt demanded deep penetration by a rigid prick. 'Yes, do it!' she repeated hoarsely. 'I want to be fucked. Fuck me, Gerald!'

She could hardly recall the last time Nigel had made love to her, unsatisfactory as it had been. Nor could she remember ever telling a man to fuck her. Bottled-up desire now made her wantonly eager, her hand reaching down to the prick she so desperately craved. Gerald had opened his pants and the cock reared mightily as she clasped its throbbing heat. 'It's so *huge*,' she murmured, amazed by its length and thick girth. 'Nigel's is a big one too, if only he'd get it like this with me.' She rubbed the stalk in her hand, marvelling at its steely hardness, suddenly bereft as Gerald disengaged her massaging fingers.

'Don't say you don't want to,' she complained bitterly. 'Now that you've made me want it so badly.'

'Nothing of the sort,' Gerald said smugly, elated with

his success, but intending to make the most of this rare opportunity to fuck his daughter-in-law. 'It's roomier in the back of the car. You didn't expect me to jump on you like an over-excited kid, did you? That's not my style, or what any woman should expect.' He kissed her fiercely again, fondling her breasts to maintain the momentum. 'You've heard of foreplay, haven't you? Well, maybe not with Nigel. Into the rear seat with you.'

Dorothy hesitated, once more her conscience warning her it was wrong, even if it was what she so badly wanted. But Gerald opened the rear door and bundled her into the back. She sat quivering and in a stupor as Gerald joined her. At once he resumed his assault, his hands seeking her breasts. Her mouth parted for his tongue and more of his passionate kisses.

Her hand went down to seek his standing prick again and she wondered almost fearfully what that monstrous weapon would feel like thrusting its length deep inside her. She made no attempt to resist him, between each kiss begging him to *fuck her, fuck her!* When he pushed her coat from her shoulders she found herself helping him. She leaned forward as he unzipped the back of her dress, allowing him to pull it down to her waist.

Her bra was next to go and she reached behind to aid him as he fumbled to unhook it. She heard his gasp of admiration as he tossed the garment aside and her big young breasts were bared to be kissed, fondled and sucked. Sucked especially, she hoped. It was something she longed for her husband to do, once timidly requesting him only to be rebuffed. Now she could not help herself.

'Do my breasts,' she pleaded. 'Hold them, feel them, kiss them, Gerald. Suck them, please. Suck on my nipples.'

'You don't have to ask, darling girl,' Gerald told her, his leg pressed hard between her thighs. He made a show of kissing her throat, drawing down his wet tongue into the tight cleave of her uptilted breasts, then cupping each one in his hands as he sucked avidly from nipple to nipple. Whimpers and soft

16

moans escaped her lips as she delighted in the pleasure of being suckled, thrusting her crotch forward to feel the hard muscle of his thigh against her mound, unable to prevent herself bucking up to it.

'Such glorious tits,' she heard him say as he switched from nipple to nipple. 'How often I've dreamed of having them bared for me. Lie back along the seat, my love. This is the stuff dreams are made of. I want to see every part of you.'

'Yes, and all of you,' she answered huskily, raising her hips and bottom for him to draw her dress down over her feet. Her panties, stockings and shoes followed until she lay before him completely naked. He stared at her in the faint light, for once silent as his eyes went from the beauty of two superb breasts to the soft curling growth of pubic hair adorning the pretty split mound between her thighs.

Dorothy lay back, scarcely daring to breathe while she waited to be entered, hopeful it would be everything she had fantasised about. Gerald, naked too, kissed her mouth, breasts and inner thighs while she yearned to be penetrated by the big cock she gripped in her hand. To her surprise, using his palms to part her upper thighs wider, it was his tongue that forced a passage beyond her cunt lips, going in deep.

She froze as she was licked and lapped by his tongue. 'How dirty, dirty,' she moaned as the persistent probing took effect, making her jerk in response and automatically grasp his head to pull his face closer to her source. To Gerald, the channel he so expertly tongued felt narrow and tight through lack of use, but as pulsating and moist in its arousal as any he had known. He sought the enlarged nub of her clitoris to stimulate it further, delighting in the moans and gasps forced from her throat and the frenzied bumping of her bottom on the car seat as she climaxed.

'Oh, please, Gerald,' she begged, her body wracked by her spasms. 'What are you doing? Oh, God, it's too much. I'm done. I've never felt like this before.'

'You're not done by any means yet,' the grinning Gerald

assured her suavely. Tickled by the inexperienced girl's response, he asked her how she had liked it.

'I did, you must have been aware how much,' Dorothy said shyly. 'I would never have imagined. You made me *come*. I can't believe I did.' She emitted yet another low moan as Gerald slipped a finger in her cunt to continue titillating her engorged clitty. 'I never thought I'd be brought to a climax, not by a man,' she confessed. 'Oh, I want to have that lovely feeling again. It was so *good*.'

'You just didn't have the right partner,' Gerald said smugly, proud at making her squirm so on his exploring finger. 'There's nothing wrong with your plumbing, young woman. You juice up beautifully. So what is it you want next? Speak up and name it.'

'I – I'd like you to put *this*,' she began falteringly, reaching for Gerald's prick again and relieved to find it still rearing, 'into me. Please.'

'You can do better than that,' Gerald suggested.

'I want you to push your big hard prick into my cunt and fuck me,' Dorothy said, forcing the words. '*Please*. Fuck me. Fuck my cunt.'

'Now you're talking,' he said. 'It will be my pleasure.'

Gerald was determined this fuck had to be special, some-thing she would recall with excitement and pleasure so she would return for more. Her need was so urgent, only his best effort would do to overcome the repressed nature instilled in her by her mother and the added problem of a deficient husband. It was a challenge that Gerald felt necessary to meet for his daughter-in-law's sake as well as for his own future prospects.

He smiled into her apprehensive face to reassure her all would be well and positioned himself comfortably in the cradle of her wide-apart thighs. With care he directed the plum-sized knob of his prick to the lips of her cunt, hearing her sharp intake of breath as he eased in the first few inches. Motionless, he let her get used to the bulbous head parting her cleft. Gradually Dorothy's tenseness lessened, her bottom wriggled and jiggled and she lifted her pelvis as if ready for more than the fat knob he had so far inserted.

'Go on, Gerald, go on,' he heard her say. He gave her another inch or two, looking down on a face contorted with pleasure as his thick girth forced its inward passage. He felt her warm, wet cunt channel was ready for all he could give. One little yelp and a shudder was all she uttered as he slid the final inches into her. He leant over her on his elbows, buried to the hilt.

'It's all in, isn't it?' Dorothy panted, enjoying the feel of being so full. 'It's all right, I can take it all. Push into me now, Gerald. Please.'

'That's my lovely girl,' he encouraged her, starting with a slow movement of his hips, his arse muscles clenching. Her next cry was one of distinct delight, thrusting back hard to meet his inward shunts, widening her thighs to get as much of the prick as she could. Without instruction, she curled her legs around his waist, the ankles locked, hands reaching down his back to grip his buttock cheeks and haul him ever closer. Her agitated jerking grew wilder by the moment.

'God, *yesss*,' Dorothy cried out, her bottom pounding the car seat. 'Fuck, fuck, fuck it all into me, Gerald. Don't stop! It's so good, good – keep fucking me!'

Gratified by such complete abandon, Gerald realised that the girl beneath him was a highly sexual creature awaiting fulfilment. He crouched over her, thrusting his prick up her, balls bouncing against the cushiony moons of her bottom, now fearful of not lasting out with such an insatiable partner. 'Fuck me, fuck me harder, faster, deeper!' he heard her cry.

He fucked like a man inspired, thrilled to know from her convulsions that she was in the throes of a multiple climax. His hands cupped her arse-cheeks, a finger infiltrating up to the second knuckle in the clenching tightness of her rear hole, making her squeal and buck against him even more frantically. It was, he decided, more than a man could stand.

He felt his balls boiling over and his juice spurted, drenching her cunt. He shouted out in his lust as the climax shook him and heard her scream too, her heels drumming on his back as a last climax in a series shook her.

She felt his hot juice in her pussy channel as, completely spent, she lay bearing his weight, her entire body throbbing deliciously.

'Better get up and dress,' Gerald said at last, breaking the spell. 'No doubt Nigel will be wondering where you are. You'll admit nothing of this to him, of course.'

Guilt overcame Dorothy as she sat up fumbling for her discarded clothes. What kind of wife was she? she thought, her conscience returning to plague her. To be fucked in the back of a car – and by her father-in-law of all people. In her troubled state, she heard Gerald repeat that she was to tell no one.

'I would die first,' she said woefully. 'How could I? What came over me? I blame myself for giving in to you, you beast.'

'Enough of that,' Gerald said. 'You needed it and went at it like a proper little whore. Just remember how good it was.' He shook his head as Dorothy began to sob. 'Oh, no, not the waterworks,' he complained, struggling back into his trousers in the cramped space. 'Grow up. A fuck is a fuck, girl, not the end of the world.'

'Take me home,' Dorothy insisted, dabbing her eyes. 'You've said and done enough for one night. How can I live with myself after this?'

'You'll survive,' Gerald told her gruffly, starting the engine. Outside her cottage he leaned over to push open the car door on her side. 'I presume you are on the pill?' he asked as an afterthought. 'Just in case.'

'As if *you* cared,' the distraught Dorothy cried as she got out. 'You took advantage of me. You – you fucked me.'

'Stop complaining,' Gerald said as she turned to walk away. 'From the way you take the dick, it's what you need. Regularly – otherwise you'll self-destruct. Now go indoors to your husband and jump his bones. I'll be interested to hear how you get on. Tell me all about it in the morning when we leave on the cruise.'

Chapter Three

Between Sisters

Manda awoke in sunlight. She was alone in the bed. At once the memory of the night shared with one of her own sex – hours spent indulging in uninhibited lust with an older woman – returned to haunt her. Her face coloured as she recalled the intimate caress of Myra Starr's hands and mouth on her body. She remembered how willingly she had embraced the other woman, how she had enjoyed Myra fondling and fingering her. Then she groaned aloud at the thought of Myra's mouth *there*, between her legs – and how right it had seemed at the time.

Manda's nipples and virgin quim still tingled from Myra's skilful ministrations. Glancing down at purplish love-bites on the slopes of her ivory breasts, she hurriedly covered herself with the duvet as her mother walked into the bedroom. As ever, Ailsa Craig, a mature version of her daughters Dorothy and Manda, was smartly dressed with not a hair on her head out of place. Full-figured, her heavy breasts bobbing beneath a purple silk blouse, her grey skirt stretched tightly across her shapely hips, moulding the ripeness of her rounded buttocks.

'Aren't you well, Amanda?' she asked, pressing a hand to her youngest daughter's brow. 'You look so hot. Whatever is the matter?'

'Nothing,' Manda said irritably. 'I'd like to shower. Leave me, mother, for goodness sake.'

'That's a fine attitude to take on the day we're going away,' Ailsa complained. 'I thought you'd be up, excited, and here you are hardly awake. You look awful, your hair's matted and

21

your eyes are dull, as if you haven't slept.' She took hold of the duvet to pull it down but Manda gripped it fiercely. 'Are you getting up?' her mother demanded.

'As soon as you leave, I promise,' Manda said, willing her mother to go. 'And I *am* excited about the cruise, it's why I couldn't sleep.'

'You'll have to get your own breakfast,' Ailsa told her. 'Remember, the minibus to take us to Southampton will be here at eleven sharp. See that your case is down in the foyer with the others by then.'

Left alone, Manda went into the adjoining bathroom. She studied herself in the mirror over the wash-basin, noting how her thick nipples were a darker red than usual. Her breasts felt swollen and heavy to her hesitant touch. Below, on the fleshy mound at the join of her thighs, the soft thatch of curling pubic hair lay flat and damp. Under the cooling spray of the shower, she felt a thrill as she thought of Myra's hairy mound pressing against her own as they had jerked frenziedly in their throes.

Manda could hardly count the number of times her seducer had made free with her body. Myra had employed a variety of licentious techniques to bring the untutored girl to many climaxes. Manda had to admit she had behaved like a randy slut and had actually begged for more. Soaping herself vigorously, her finger probed her sex, experimentally touching the distended nub of her clitoris. The inner flesh of her cunt was soft and yielding, oiled and pulsing as if prepared for penetration.

'No,' she told herself hoarsely, but the finger continued working, the feeling she gave herself was too delicious to stop. She desired a repeat of the ecstasy she had experienced the previous night. Her wrist worked faster as she brought herself off and she fell back against the tiled wall of the cubicle as her spasms faded.

She went down to breakfast feeling ravenous and wonderfully free of guilt. She cooked scrambled eggs and bacon, made a pot of tea and was sitting down to eat at the long table when she was joined by her sister Dorothy. The two girls greeted each other as if both had their own private thoughts to dwell upon, having much more than the impending cruise on their minds.

'I've just seen Professor Marsh arrive. I rushed in here to keep out of his way,' Dorothy said, pulling a face. 'I'm only sorry he'll be with us on the ship.'

'Why do you still call him Professor Marsh?' Manda asked. 'Isn't that rather formal? He is your father-in-law after all.'

'Because I can't stand the sight of him,' Dorothy said heatedly, the memory of their previous evening's session still rankling. 'He's a pig.'

'He is a bit of an arrogant creep,' Manda agreed. 'Handsome, I suppose, but doesn't he know it. Every time he sees me I feel he stares the clothes off me. All the girls in the school say the same: he undresses them with his eyes. They call him the lecherous lecturer.'

'He deserves whatever they say about him,' Dorothy said vehemently. 'I don't know why mother employs him.'

'Because I'm an excellent deputy head, science tutor and administrator,' Gerald Marsh said as he glided silently into the kitchen. 'Indispensable, in fact,' he added cheerfully, lifting a crisp slice of bacon from Manda's plate and munching it. He grinned at the shocked pair. 'Say what you like about me, girls, I undoubtedly deserve it. Right now I'm looking for your mother. Any idea where she could be?'

'Try the garden,' Manda offered. 'No doubt there'll be last minute instructions for the gardener. You know mummy.'

'Not as much as I'd like to,' Gerald smirked. 'And what's up with you two beautiful creatures on this fine day? You both look miserable. Is all well with that son of mine, Dorothy?' he asked slyly. 'I assume he's saying a tearful farewell to his mumsy before he joins us.'

'Everything's just fine,' Dorothy said, her voice showing her contempt for her father-in-law. 'Why shouldn't it be?'

'Glad to hear it,' he grinned. 'Nigel's so lucky to have a

wife like you, my dear. I'd better go and seek out your mater. Don't do anything I wouldn't do, girls.'

'If I hear him say that once more, I'll scream,' Manda vowed. She looked at her sister for agreement and was surprised to see Dorothy fighting back the tears. 'Hey, don't let that creep upset you, Dorrie,' she begged, rising to hug her consolingly. 'I know things aren't brilliant with Nigel. Have you had a row? Whatever's the matter?'

'It – it's not Nigel, not entirely,' Dorothy sobbed openly, clinging to her sister. 'It's *him*, Gerald. You don't know what he did—'

'Nothing he'd do would surprise me,' Manda said. 'Has he been interfering between you and your husband?'

Dorothy lowered her head, stifling her sobs, twisting the handkerchief in her hands. 'He – he's – I can't tell you,' she blubbered. 'It's too awful.'

Interest greatly aroused, Manda took the handkerchief and dabbed at her sister's eyes and cheeks. 'Poor Dorrie,' she commiserated, dying to know the secret. 'You can tell me all about it. Whatever could he do to upset you so?'

'He had sexual relations with me,' Dorothy blurted out, raising her tear-stained face to her sister.

'I can't believe it!' Manda exclaimed amazed. 'You let him do *that*?'

'It's true,' Dorothy said, hurt to note the way her sister's eyes lit up. 'And it's not something to look pleased about. How could you, Manda? I hate him for it.'

'I wasn't looking pleased,' Manda protested while striving to suppress the wicked giggle in her throat at the surprising admission. 'You really mean, you went *all* the way?'

'Every inch,' Dorothy confessed sorrowfully, at once regretting her choice of words. 'The dirty swine had me good and proper.'

'Your father-in-law forced you?' Manda queried, hugging her sister closer, intent on learning all. 'Poor Dorrie. You mean he raped you?'

Her questioning brought on a fresh outbreak of sobs. 'It

– it was worse than that,' Dorothy admitted. 'He seemed so sympathetic when I said things weren't working out with Nigel. He held me and kissed me. He touched me. He *made* me let him. I – I – *wanted* him. Wanted him to do it.'

'You mean he seduced you?' Manda gasped, a surge of excitement at the thought making her cunt throb. 'Was it good? Did – did you come?'

'So many times I lost count,' Dorothy admitted tearfully, unable to completely hide a note of pride in her voice. 'He made me come and come.'

'There's a brutish attractiveness about him. He's very manly,' Manda conceded, still digesting the astounding revelation that Gerald had fucked her sister. 'But he's so old, mother's age.'

'Not that old,' Dorothy said defensively, straightening in the chair. Having confessed, she didn't feel so guilty. 'Whether I hate him or not, he's very virile,' she added as if to excuse her lapse. 'He certainly proved that. Of course I should never have let him, but he was so – so—'

'So good at getting you all worked up,' Manda finished for her, her excitement showing in her eyes and flushed face. 'He was doing his son's job for him,' she added as Dorothy smiled wanly at her. 'Well, it's done, so forget it, sis. I don't blame you one bit if he made you horny. Where did you do it?'

'On the back seat of his car,' Dorothy said, drying her eyes and discovering that talking of the experience was strangely pleasurable. 'He didn't rush things. He insisted on taking off all my clothes as well as his own.' While wanting it to appear that Gerald had forced himself on her, she was keen to continue the telling. 'The beast did something to me I'd never experienced. When he licked me I lost all control.'

'You mean he used his tongue on you?' Manda said delightedly. 'I've heard men love to do that to a girl. The girls talk about it at school. Was it as good as they say?'

'I should be ashamed to admit it,' Dorothy confessed, 'but it was heaven. I couldn't stop him. I didn't want to. Then he put his big stiff thing right inside me and made me come. That

25

was marvellous too. Don't look so happy about it, Manda, I'll die of embarrassment. It was disgraceful but I couldn't help myself. I loved it.'

'But being made to come *is* lovely,' Manda said, surprising her sister by stating it so openly. 'Your body goes all shuddery and weak. There's no other feeling like it.'

'You've only ever brought on a climax by yourself,' Dorothy said, feeling superior. 'Wait until you experience the real thing. I mean a man deep inside you, huge and hard. Thrusting it into you, filling you right up. That's very different from giving yourself a thrill.'

'You don't know everything,' Manda retorted, the sisterly rivalry making her bold. 'I *do* know what it's like to have someone else make me come over and over, so there. You're not the only one who misbehaved last night.' She paused and giggled. 'Misbehave. That's hardly what mummy would call it. She'd have kittens. But like you, I couldn't help myself. There's no stopping when someone gets you really worked up, is there?'

'You mean you're no longer a virgin?' Dorothy said, shocked by her young sister's frankness. 'You've done it with a man?'

'Not exactly,' Manda had to admit, her face flushing but determined to match her wayward sister's confession. 'You can talk about having a sexy fling, why shouldn't I?'

'It was *not* a sexy fling,' Dorothy denied. 'I was seduced by a brute of a man. As for your supposed sexual experience, I've no doubt it was with some other girl like yourself.' She smiled to show she understood. 'It's not the same, believe me, Manda. I went to school here too, remember? We all had harmless crushes on each other. Monica Beale and I used to kiss. It was nice but just girl stuff.'

'Mine was no girl,' Manda said defiantly. 'I had a real grown-up woman – a proper lesbian with loads of experience. The things we did! Her mouth and hands were *everywhere*. My nipples and pussy are still sore, but nice sore. She made me come over and over. I did things to her as well, and she came a lot. You can't have stronger climaxes than what we had. We slept together naked too, only we didn't get much sleep.'

'I bet it was Mrs Starr,' Dorothy said. 'I know, I know!' She looked down before raising her face with a deep blush on her features. 'You too. I've often wondered if she'd made advances to you now that I've left.'

'So she had you too!' Manda exclaimed delightedly, enjoying the pained expression on her sister's pretty face. 'And I always thought you were such a goody-goody. It seems we are all at it. How did she get you? She's so clever at seduction, isn't she?'

'It was almost blackmail,' Dorothy said. 'She caught Monica Beale and I together under the shower. Under pressure I went to her room as she suggested, fearful she'd inform mother. The awful woman got me to strip. She – she put me over her knee and smacked my bottom so hard I cried. It was the same every time I went to her room. She played with my breasts and sucked on my nipples until they hurt. She had an object, a sex-toy shaped like a big penis and made me use it on her to bring her to an orgasm. Sometimes she used it on me.'

'And did you come?' Manda asked expectantly, her arousal mounting.

'I couldn't help it, the way she used it made me feel so excited,' Dorothy said as if saddened by the memory. 'I knew it was wrong but I went back each time almost looking forward to her doing things to me. It was shameful. The dildo or vibrator, whatever it was, became like a drug to me. She told me mother had a similar one in her bedroom. I couldn't believe it of mummy, but I can see why women have one. They can always make you come.'

'And you like that, don't deny it, Dorrie,' Manda said challengingly. 'Poor you, so used to having a nice come from a vibrator and now you never get one with your husband. You must miss it. Is a dummy cock so good you come every time?'

'It's so lifelike,' Dorothy said. 'Myra Starr had one she could strap about her and use on me like a man. When she

27

was – doing it to me she used the crudest words. Gerald too, he called me a whore and a slut when he was – was—'

'*Fucking* you,' Manda continued for her, enjoying uttering the forbidden word. 'We might as well say it. That's what he was doing.'

'Fucking me,' Dorothy agreed, submitting. 'And saying such things about me while he was fucking me. That I was hot and loved his big thing up me. It made me terribly excited. Nigel never does the stuff his father did to me, or says anything to arouse me. From the start of our marriage I wanted him to say rude words to me. I shouldn't be telling you this but I wanted him to fuck me and suck me, to do what he liked and say what he liked. I must be a whore. I think it's my true nature.'

'Then it's mine too,' Manda supported her sister. 'Mrs Starr warned me guilt over enjoying sex is a wasted emotion. I believe her. In future I won't feel any shame over wanting sex or having it. To think I almost made Myra leave my room. I'm glad she didn't go. Do you know she said she fancied mummy and had always wanted to make love to her? Can you imagine that?'

'I can believe anything of that woman,' Dorothy said.

'Well, I don't blame her for how she feels, you can't help fancying someone,' Manda defended her. 'Even if you think Gerald Marsh is a lecherous beast, he must have fancied you. I'll bet you're glad he fucked you so hard and gave you lots of comes. From what you've just said, Nigel never does.'

'I've tried,' Dorothy said wistfully. 'I'll try even harder on this cruise. Nigel had better try too, or we'll be finished. He's so frustrating at times that I feel like hitting him, beating him.'

'Maybe you should,' Manda advised, smiling wickedly. 'Myra Starr spanked my bottom too, really hard like she did yours. It made me awfully randy thinking about someone smacking my bum. The heat of it seeped through to my – I'm going to say it – my cunt. It made it throb and want to be satisfied. Try it with Nigel, order him over your

28

knee. If it doesn't make him horny, at least you can enjoy thrashing him.'

'I don't think I would spare the belt,' Dorothy said thoughtfully. 'What a lewd girl you are, Manda, thinking of something like that. We've never been close or talked like this before. I'm glad we have done. Perhaps we're two of a kind.'

'You should admit we are, and no false modesty about it,' Manda said, pressing a kiss to Dorothy's cheek and linking her arm with her own. 'Sisters and friends. I'm glad we'll be together on the cruise. Who knows, perhaps the sea air will cure Nigel's reluctance to be a proper husband?'

'I doubt it,' Dorothy said sadly. 'It would take some kind of miracle. However, they say stranger things have happened at sea.'

Chapter Four

Up the Garden Path

Gerald strolled towards the girls' mother as she finished giving instructions to the gardener. Ailsa Craig pointedly ignored his approach until he came behind her and casually fondled her rounded bottom. She turned in anger, slapping at his hand.

'Do you have to do that?' she complained icily. 'In future I'll thank you to keep your hands to yourself.'

'No thanks necessary, I find it quite impossible to refrain,' Gerald returned easily. 'So I felt your bum, big deal. You ought to learn how to relax, woman. Forget the school for once. I run this place for you and do my level best to keep it from folding, which is not easy. There's no need to always be so uptight.' He attempted to slip an arm around her waist but she drew back and held up her hands to ward him off.

'No, not now,' she said, 'I know what you want and I'm not letting you.'

'You poor soul,' he told her. 'You wouldn't recognise a good time if it strolled up whistling Dixie and kissed your lovely arse. Like I will every time I get the urge. Have you got something against enjoying yourself?'

Ailsa raised her hand to smack Gerald's face but he intercepted the blow, grasping her wrist and shaking his head at her impotence. Watching from the kitchen window, Dorothy and Manda gasped at the scene. Dorothy was first to find her voice. 'The beast,' she said in horror. 'Do you think he and mother—?'

'No, not mummy,' Manda said. 'You saw how furious he

31

made her, and she tried to slap him.' The sisters, watching with growing interest, saw their mother facing Gerald, obviously disputing what he was saying. They wished they could hear.

'I wouldn't put anything past him,' Dorothy said, speaking from recent experience. 'He thinks all women are fair game and mother is still very attractive.'

Gerald stood beside the ornamental pond admiring the breathless rise and fall of Ailsa's superb breasts. 'You look even better when you're worked up,' he said evenly. 'Now go to the potting shed and I'll join you. Don't make a fuss. You know you want to.'

'You really are just one step away from a savage,' Ailsa said bitterly, standing her ground. 'I won't go.'

'You will because you love it,' Gerald said. 'You love the idea that I'm forcing you. Love a bit of rough in your repressed life. I won't tell you again.'

'If you can't control your lust, why not seek out Mrs Starr?' Ailsa said cuttingly. 'You've never needed to force her, I'm sure. Or is it that you prefer your victims unwilling?'

'Either way, I'm easy,' he assured her. 'Don't knock Myra, she's everything I like in a woman: lewd, promiscuous and willing. She's also been more than useful helping me keep the school in business since you gave up trying.'

'It was only after my husband passed away that I couldn't cope,' she murmured in excuse.

'Then it's as well for you I was around,' Gerald reminded her, tugging at her arm. 'By the way, Myra has gone, bag and baggage. What if I quit on you too? Shall we take that stroll to the potting shed?'

'Under duress,' Ailsa complained, disengaging her arm and walking on as ordered. 'I shall always hate you for this. It's sexual harrassment—'

'So sue me,' Gerald said. 'D'you think I'd waste my energy on you if I wasn't sure you liked it?' He followed, admiring the seductive sway of her rounded buttocks, each plump cheek jiggling under the tight skirt. Unable to resist, he felt her bottom again, making her hurry ahead. 'What a fine arse,' he whispered in her ear. 'What a lovely fuck you'd make.'

'I will not allow it,' she insisted over her shoulder, made wary by his words. 'I won't. Not with you. *Never* with you.'

'One of these days I'll screw that fine arse off you,' he promised. 'I can wait. Until then we'll settle for our usual routine. Don't tell me you don't enjoy it.'

'I do not,' she denied hotly. 'I *don't* enjoy it.'

Her two daughters watched from the window as their mother entered the wooden hut. Gerald followed a few moments later, looking around to see if they'd been observed as he closed the door. 'Oh, God,' Dorothy muttered, staring as if willing herself to see into the shed. 'I don't believe this. Why would mummy go in there with *him*?'

'I'm going down to find out,' Manda said. 'You could see she didn't go without an argument. I want to know what's going on.'

'And I'm coming with you, I know what he's like only too well,' her sister said angrily. 'If he tries anything, I'll kill him.'

Inside the dusty potting shed Gerald had guided Ailsa to a rough wooden table, her bottom pressed against the edge as he faced her. 'There isn't time for this,' she protested as his fingers unbuttoned the front of her blouse. 'My girls will be wondering where I am.'

'Manda's having her breakfast in the kitchen and Dorothy is with her. There's plenty of time,' Gerald said as he pushed the blouse from her smooth white shoulders. 'Nigel hasn't arrived yet either, so relax.' He eyed her lacy bra, overflowing with rounded breast flesh. 'You really have marvellous tits, Ailsa,' he said. 'Two big beauties just ripe for sucking and titty-riding.'

'How crude you are,' Ailsa said, her face flushing deep pink.

'Your breasts are worthy of an epic poem,' he teased her. 'You passed 'em on to your girls too. They're bulging in all the right places like their mother. You're all splendidly hung in the tit department.'

'Don't you dare talk about my daughters in that way,' Ailsa said spiritedly. 'You may think you can use me as you wish with your threats, but if you ever—'

'Ever what?' Gerald asked genially, thinking what a glorious fuck her daughter Dorothy had already proved. He reached behind Ailsa to unclip her bra. The cups fell away and her bare breasts thrust out, creamy white with a faint tracery of light blue veins beneath the satin skin. With the finger and thumb of each hand he tweaked her large pink nipples while she tried to avoid his gaze.

'Ashamed, Ailsa?' he asked her. 'Ashamed because you're trembling already? The feeling you're fighting is arousal. These nipples give you away, sticking out like thimbles begging for a good sucking. You want me to suck them, don't you?'

'You'll do what you like with me as always,' Alisa said, her voice hoarse and eyes lowered. She tried to control an anguished moan as he dipped his face and fastened his mouth to a thick nipple. '*Please*,' she groaned. 'You musn't.'

'Oh, but I must,' Gerald said, moving his mouth to the other nipple while Ailsa tried to feign indifference. He suckled on her gluttonously, drawing breast flesh into his mouth before withdrawing his lips to grin up at her. 'Play the cold bitch if you like, but at least *they* respond, don't they?' he goaded her. 'I'll bet you're already soaking down below too. Shall we find out?'

'No, not that,' she pleaded, shuddering as her skirt was hitched up to uncover supple thighs and lacy briefs that matched the unfastened bra. 'You musn't touch me there,' she appealed in a strained voice. 'Please, Gerald.' But even as she protested, Ailsa raised her bottom from the table, allowing him to pull down her briefs.

'Hah!' he said. 'You say one thing and do another. You want it, that's for sure.'

'I know you're going to do what you like and I just want it over with,' she responded. 'Don't think I'm helping you.' He had pushed up her skirt so that it was held up under her

34

bottom, her thighs and crotch now open to his gaze. 'Don't stare so,' Ailsa said as he knelt before her, his face at eye level with the mass of thick hair on the cleft mound at the fork of her thighs. 'It's too embarrassing.'

'But very tempting,' Gerald insisted. 'It's a beautiful cunt, just begging to be usefully employed. One day I swear I'll fuck it. I can wait. You'll come around in the end.'

'Never,' Ailsa swore, the knot in her stomach tensing as he prised her upper thighs apart with his thumbs, pushing his face into the cleave, breathing in her female scent.

'Nectar,' he mumbled lewdly. 'Cunt Channel No. 5 – my favourite perfume.' He reverently kissed the pouting sex lips peeping through the bush of curling hair, first tenderly and then with increasing passion until the crinkled outer folds were sucked deeply into his mouth.

As his stiff tongue worked its way inside, the knot in her tense stomach melted, replaced by a wave of excitement she had not sought. 'No!' she moaned weakly, the unstoppable surge within gaining in strength as his determined tongue continued to probe. 'Oh, God, no,' she repeated, resistance feeble as he delved, swirling the intruder around the bud of her sensitive clitty, now standing stiffly erect. Helplessly she widened her stance on the bare planks of the floor as Gerald sucked on the responsive nub of taut flesh. Her hands reached to pull his head in closer, burying his nose in her pubic thatch as he lapped and licked the moist inner folds of her cunt.

Approaching the hut, Dorothy and Manda exchanged enquiring looks, aware of the grunts and moans originating from within. A dusty side-window allowed them a view of the interior and the sisters bent low to peer in with eyes aligned barely above the sill of the window to avoid detection. Both girls stifled cries at what they witnessed. Their prudish mother, the woman who had brought them up in fear of men's carnal intentions, was deep in the throes of sexual gratification. Her head was thrown back, her mouth agape, as she uttered formless sounds while she was being pleasured. Leaning back against the rough table, her legs widely parted and her knickers lying on the floor, she was obviously approaching orgasm. Her large bare breasts jiggled and bounced as her body undulated and her pelvis jerked as she thrust into Gerald's face. On his knees before her, his head bobbed rapidly between her thighs as he tongued her to distraction.

The girls exchanged disbelieving looks as Gerald pulled his face away and their mother cried out in despair at being denied. He stood up, his features wet with her sex juices and grinned broadly at her obvious dismay. To the watching pair's further astonishment, he drew out his engorged prick and placed Ailsa's right hand around it.

'Can you feel it throb?' he asked as she swayed before him, weak in her heightened arousal. 'Think how good that hot rod would feel up your cunt, Ailsa. Imagine that thickness buried up your hungry snatch. I said I'd wait until you begged for it. All you have to do is ask.'

'I – I won't. I won't give you the satisfaction,' Ailsa groaned tremulously, resisting the urge to let him. 'However much you make me want to. I've that much pride.'

'And I've that much patience,' Gerald said, forcing her to stroke the rigid bar of flesh in her hand. 'You'll come around to it. Maybe on this cruise. It's what you obviously need.'

'If you've quite finished,' Ailsa said, mustering all her dignity, 'I'd like to adjust my clothes—'

'And leave you like that, trembling on the brink?' he said. 'Even I am not so sadistic. Rub me up nicely and I'll do the same for you. That's fair enough, surely, if I can't fuck you?'

'I'm quite able to contain myself,' Ailsa said coldly, attempting to pull her hand away from his prick but unable to. 'I can resist my urges, despite what you think. We're not all beasts like you.'

'You could have fooled me,' Gerald said. 'You're still on heat from that tonguing I gave you. A normal woman would order me to finish her off. I can see you really want me to. I'll be kind and do it anyway.'

Still clamping her fingers on his rearing cockstand, his free right hand went between her parted thighs thumb upward and penetrated the swollen outer lips. 'Swine,' she uttered, even as her cunt opened to his caress. 'You're unspeakable.'

'How true,' Gerald announced smugly, the thumb now buried deep within her, the downsloped curve of her cunt pressed hard to the side of his hand. 'You're soaking,' he added, his wrist working rhythmically. Ailsa was helpless to refrain from responding, grinding her mound down against the heel of the pleasure-giving thumb. She swirled her hips, directing the stubby intruder to the parts she wished titillated, altering its angle of penetration. Strangled cries issued from her throat, even calls for him to push, push.

'Go on, work that big arse,' he taunted her. 'Give yourself a good come, woman. It's what you need.'

He released the hand holding his prick and noted with a satisfied growl that she continued to rub him up vigorously in time with her own frenzied jerking. Then both cried out simultaneously, Ailsa's body shuddering under the power of her climax. Her hand was almost a blur as she rubbed Gerald's thick tool, until a series of spurts shot his hot spunk over her belly and breasts. She leant against him, breathless, slowly realising the enormity of her lapse. Regaining her senses, she let go of his limp dick and struck Gerald a stinging slap on his grinning face.

'That's the thanks I get,' he laughed, unperturbed by the blow. Producing a large handkerchief, he proceeded to mop up his come from her stomach and between her breasts while she scowled at him. Snatching it from his hand, she used the handkerchief to dab off the residue. When done as best she could, she deliberately let the soiled square of cotton drop to the floor for him to retrieve.

'You astound me, Mrs Craig,' he said formally. 'Why don't you join the human race and admit you get as randy as the next woman? I like you. I think I could love you if you'd give me some encouragement. I'd even considered marriage. With the school to run, we'd make a good team.'

'And have a bully and a lecher for a husband?' Ailsa said acidly. 'No thank you!'

'Bully and lecher?' Gerald said, astounded. 'If I appear to you that way it's only because you need a strong hand, preferably across the bottom when over my knee. I'm asking you to marry me, Ailsa. Let me change your life.'

The girls watching at the corner of the window saw their mother shake her head, as they turned to creep away. Overcome by what they had seen and heard, they were unable to voice their thoughts until they reached the deserted quiet of the school foyer, piled high with luggage. Even then they could only speak in whispers.

'He made mummy *come*,' Manda said in wonder. 'You saw what he did and she was loving it! He had her breasts out, and her knickers were on the floor. She came off like a steam train!'

'He *forced* her, like he forced me,' Dorothy defended her mother.

'He seduced you,' Manda reminded her, still shocked but undeniably aroused by what she had witnessed in the potting shed. 'And he seduced mummy too. She was willing once he got her worked up. After all the advice she's given us about avoiding men, she should talk. She was *horny*!'

'Seducing is the same as forcing. I know,' Dorothy said, still anxious to reassure herself about her own indiscretion with Gerald. 'Don't make excuses for the brute. He used his filthy tongue and his finger to make her helpless, then he could do what he wanted with her. I don't blame mother. At least he didn't – didn't put his thing into her.'

'Like he did with you,' Manda said to the embarrassment of her sister. 'I wonder why he didn't?'

'I don't know,' Dorothy said. 'It's not like him.'

'You heard him say he would one day. Fuck her, I mean,' Manda said. 'He even told her she would come begging for it.' The thought made her giggle irreverently. 'And did you see the *size* of his cock? Of course you did, you've even tried it.' She gave an involuntary shudder, a mix of wonder and future anticipation. 'It was so big and fat, stiff as a poker. No woman could take that huge thing without knowing what was up her.

I'm not surprised it made you come over and over when he put it in you, Dorrie.'

'Don't go on about it,' her sister said irritably. 'I sometimes think you'd like to try it yourself. I suggest you keep yourself pure for your future husband.'

'A fat lot of good that advice did you, ending up with a wimp like Nigel,' Manda retorted. 'I shall try before I buy, and I wouldn't mind one like Gerald. At least he's a real man, and knows how to turn on a woman. If mummy wasn't such an absolute prude and would admit she needs sex like everyone else, she should beg him to fuck her. She could do a darned sight worse.'

Chapter Five

Room With a View

Gleaming in a new coat of white paint, the Motor Vessel *Aphrodite* looked sleek and shipshape berthed alongside the dock at Southampton. Once a passenger ferry plying the Inland Sea of Japan, now refurbished and converted, she was a modern medium-sized cruise ship. At the foot of the gangway, a tall young man relieved Myra of her suitcase and welcomed her aboard.

'Mrs Starr, undoubtedly,' he greeted her warmly. 'I've looked forward to meeting you in the flesh, as it were. I recognise you from the sex education videos you've appeared in.'

'Then you'll have seen all of me there is,' Myra smiled, returning his gaze and thinking that here was a handsome hunk she could definitely do something with. Stepping aside to allow her to board, his eyes followed the seductive jiggle of her amply rounded buttocks encased in the tight skirt of her smart grey suit. 'I'm at a disadvantage,' she remarked, amused by his ploy to ogle her rear. 'Who are you? American, obviously. Are you staff or crew on this love boat?'

'Calvert,' he offered. 'Dexter, but Dex will do. Like you, a hired hand, a member of the revered Dr Leo Weissbinder's research team. You come very highly recommended, by the way. The boss is delighted you were available. He insisted on having you.'

'Well, he should know, he's had me before,' Myra said wickedly. 'Being in that electrified wheelchair with all its microchip gizmos didn't stop the old ram. It's the kind of work I most enjoy, curing people's sexual hang-ups. Bring on the repressed and impotent, I'll uninhibit 'em.'

'You do it so well – as those videos proved,' Dex Calvert laughed, ushering her across the spotless deck to her cabin. Once inside, he set down the suitcase, awaiting her reaction. 'You'll do some of your work in here,' he said. 'Is it okay?'

'Fabulous,' she said, admiring the chintzy feminine decor and the out-sized waterbed. 'A veritable love-nest,' she added slyly, looking directly at Dex Calvert. 'No expense spared, obviously, to fit out a seagoing surgery for the sexually impaired. Is that the politically correct term for Doc Weissbinder's suckers?'

'Close enough,' Dex grinned. 'Of course, he prefers the word "patients".'

'I have to admit he's exceeded himself,' Myra conceded. 'The last survey of his I worked on was conducted in the cramped quarters of an unheard-of university in California.'

'He owns that now,' Dex informed her. 'It's the Weissbinder Clinic and making big bucks as a rehab centre for movie stars hooked on everything you could name. Things have improved considerably since his early forays into sex counselling and psychotherapy. The published surveys have made Weissbinder's name as a respected sexologist and researcher in the field of human sexual desires and repressions.'

'A scholar, a gentleman, and a fine judge of arse,' Myra laughed irreverently. 'I know him, remember. Does he pay any better, or still expect the help to work for the fun of it? Not that I'm saying it isn't fun, fucking for scientific reasons, but evidently he does okay out of these surveys. Last time I was lucky to come out of it with my fare back to England. Not that I'm complaining about a stay in sunny California and all the screwing one could ask. Just the same, this time I want some of the loot. Hazarding a pretty rough guess on his past record, the devious doc is an old skinflint.'

'Your estimate is a little generous but otherwise correct,' Dex agreed genially. 'Take the old bastard to town, he can afford it. His surveys have been published worldwide. The books and videos alone have made him rich. To top that, institutions of note and famous universities are lining up to offer financial grants to further his so-called research.'

'Enough to charter this floating palace dedicated to fornication,' Myra observed wryly. 'I like it, it's a stroke of genius. A Caribbean cruise should help get his paying customers in the right mood to let their hair down.'

'And they pay through the nose to be here,' Dex affirmed, 'so I guess the old fraud is a genius. Since I've been aboard I've had my doubts about him, but I'm only along for the ride. Or for the riding,' he added mischievously, 'for I don't think my career prospects will benefit. He'll grab all the glory. I'm bound hand and foot by contract.'

'So enjoy the trip,' Myra advised. 'You look willing and able.'

'Give him his due,' Dex said. 'Money has poured in and all the facilities are purpose-designed, the latest technology utilised throughout. They tore the guts out of this ship in Hamburg to my designs, all done in the name of Weissbinder. He intends to make this voyage the most in-depth survey on sexuality ever conducted. We've an interesting bunch of mixed specimens due on board – or list of passengers, more correctly,' he amended, grinning. 'Not the least the school people you've arranged to sail with us. On your recommendation, Weissbinder is charging them so little they must wonder what kind of cheapo cruise they're taking. How come?'

'I booked for them and told the headmistress there were empty cabins that had to be filled. She's hard-up and has two daughters she wanted to treat,' Myra said. 'It was too good an opportunity to miss at the price so she went along with my suggestion. Of course, they've no idea what the object of the cruise is. I considered the risk worth taking.'

'Will they fit in?' Dex asked. 'They're not exactly volunteers like the others, are they?'

'Not exactly,' Myra agreed, 'but their potential is excellent. They're a really fouled-up group of individuals – good-looking intelligent people but all suffering varying complex sexual hang-ups, the two men as well as the three females. I can't wait to see them get straightened out.'

'Doc Weissbinder will relish the challenge no doubt,' Dex said. 'I'm to take you along to his control centre for coffee and a preliminary briefing. He's looking forward to seeing you.'

'Not like this,' she said. 'I need time to freshen up and change, make use of that luxurious bathroom. I think I'll take a shower.'

'You look great to me,' Dex said, eyeing the large breasts bulging her jacket. 'By far the sexiest female therapist Weissbinder has hired.'

'Thanks,' Myra acknowledged, 'but I've been working all night, doing advance research on one of the female subjects arriving today. It proved very pleasurable. Manda Craig is a sweet young thing and shows promise. You'll no doubt enjoy continuing the sexual therapy I've begun with her.'

'How selfless of you,' Dex said, tongue in cheek. 'Nice work if you can get it.' His eyes followed her as she slipped off her suit jacket and draped it over a chair. With her eyes fixed steadily on him, she unbuttoned her blouse and tossed it aside casually, revealing the tight cleave of the ample breasts that had strained the crisp white cotton material. Kicking off her shoes, she shimmied her hips and her skirt slid to her feet. Stepping free of it, her eyes still on the young man, she posed in the overfilled black bra, matching panties, suspender belt and sheer black stockings.

'Should I be the only one getting undressed?' she enquired, unhooking the bra.

'Not from where I'm standing,' Dex agreed readily, 'and I use the term "standing" in its proper context. Watching you undressing, Mrs Starr, has given me a boner hard as blue steel.'

'Call me Myra,' she invited, pushing down her knickers and kicking them off her feet, showing her plump cunt and its forest of hair. 'No doubt we'll soon be on intimate terms in our association. And I do use the term "intimate" in its proper context, don't I?' she copied him.

44

'Nothing surer,' he promised, peeling off his shirt. 'I'm not complaining, but you don't waste any time, do you?'

'I'm not getting any younger,' she joked, giving a luxurious shake to the large teats freed from their confining cups. She admired the broad masculine chest Dex had revealed. 'I like what I see so far, young man.'

'So do I,' he replied, unbuckling his belt. 'You've got what I call great tits. Such good size and shape and a delightful lift. The big nipples to go with them too, ones you could hang coats on. Myra, in strict medical terminology, you got the boobs. Jugs, fun bags, knockers, bazookas—'

'I take it you approve,' she laughed at his exuberance. With an appreciative nod she watched him shed his jeans and briefs to join the shirt and sandals hurriedly cast aside on the cabin's deep-pile carpeting. Broad of shoulder, narrow of waist, athletically built and muscular, most of all she approved of the monumental stalk of rigid flesh rearing upright from his big balls.

'I can see why Weissbinder sought you out too,' Myra said, greatly impressed. 'That's what I call a prick. Seeing a beauty like that always makes me go weak at the knees.'

'You should take something for it,' Dex advised, his cock in his hand and pointing it at Myra. 'This, for instance.'

'Yes. The poor thing looks so stiff and inflamed I'm sure it must be painful,' she said. 'I just happen to have the very thing made for relieving that. It's called a cunt. Or, in strict medical parlance, a quim, a snatch, a pussy – you want me to go on?'

'Welcome aboard,' he laughed. 'Lie on the bed. Allow me some quick relief before we put on our saddles and report to the sawdust ring. He who must be obeyed awaits us.'

'Stuff him. Who mentioned *quick*?' she warned, lolling back on the bed, breasts tilted and legs overhanging the bottom edge. She reached behind her head to pull a pillow under her bottom, raising her crotch and angling her hairy cunt at him. 'Okay, show me why you were selected as super stud on this trip,' she challenged him.

'It will be my pleasure,' he murmured, leaning over as his mouth sought a taut nipple. Moving his muscled thigh between her legs, hard to her mound, he felt her lift and thrust against him as his lips found the other nipple, nipping and sucking teasingly. His mouth slid down over her stomach, lips remaining in contact with the soft flesh. At the fork of her thighs he lifted her legs over his shoulders, getting an unobstructed view of her tilted cunt. Eager to kiss, suck and tongue it, his face went in drawn by the sight and pungent scent of her pouting sex.

'Not a bad start,' he heard Myra say, her hands reaching for his head to draw him closer if possible. 'I do like a spot of nipple sucking and a licking out to get me lewd. It's the only way to fuck, to be made lewd and desperate.'

'My sentiments exactly,' Dex growled, pausing for air before returning to the assault. 'I'll get you so lewd and desperate you'd fuck a doorknob. How do you like this?'

This was his stiffened tongue snaking in among her warm wet cunt folds to swirl around an enlarged clitoris. 'Oooh, you've eaten cunts before,' she grunted, squirming her bottom and bucking to his face. 'Stop! Stop now before you make me come. I want to savour this lovely feeling of being brought to the brink. It's absolute torture but I love the delicious throb and ache that stays in my cunt. It makes coming later even more marvellous. Talk to me now, tell me what you're going to do with me.'

'Fuck you,' he said gruffly, raising his sodden face, elated with Myra's responses and uninhibited nature. 'Fuck you front, back and sideways, because you're built to suck and fuck with those big tits and a great ass I'll get around to later, believe me. All that and a juiced-up greedy snatch I've already enjoyed eating and intend to give every thick inch of my dick. But that will only be after I've got you so goddamn horny you'll be on your knees begging for a fuck.'

'Promises, promises,' Myra said. 'You'll be the one to beg.'

'Maybe,' Dex countered. 'Meantime, I didn't mention your

mouth.' Shuffling forward over her, he settled with his knees dug into the bed under her armpits, his buttock cheeks resting on her cushiony breasts. 'Wet its head,' he ordered, rubbing the bulbous knob against her lips. 'Deep-throat it for poppa,' he said. 'Past the lips and over the gums, look out when the jism comes. Give baby a nice suck.'

'I never give any other kind,' Myra said flatly. 'The best you'll ever get, buster. I'll suck your balls up through your dick. You'll beg for mercy.'

Cupping his heavy balls and licking wetly up the extended stalk, she probed the eye of his knob before opening her mouth to cover half its thick length. Gripped between her tongue and palate, she suctioned strongly, drawing in the final inches of his prick. Bobbing her head, flicking her tongue around the stem and probing the eye between concentrated sucking, she heard him groan at being so tormentingly pleasured. With an effort he withdrew quickly, his inflamed and saliva-glistening stalk dragged out from her pursed lips.

'Finding that too much?' Myra taunted. 'Couldn't hold out any longer—?'

'You're good,' he allowed, 'but I can stand it, I'll see you off. Right now I've a strong letch to fuck these big tits I'm sitting on.' Easing himself backward, his slippery prick trailed over her chin and throat and came to rest between the deep separation of her splayed breasts.

'You really know how to sweet-talk a girl,' Myra laughed, pressing her breasts together from their curved sides, making a tight channel for his prick to shunt back and forth as he rocked his hips over her. 'As to seeing me off, you'll be first to cry mercy. I'll wring you out like a wet rag.'

'Don't bet on it,' he told her grimly, thrusting between the cushions of her breasts. 'You make a great tit-ride and an even better fuck, I'll guarantee. When I get around to screwing you with my big dong, baby, you'll stumble about like a zombie afterwards, outta your mind. Fucked to a frazzle.'

'The trouble with you is,' Myra said, determined to meet and match his verbal challenges despite the mounting arousal

47

a hot throbbing prick between her breasts produced, 'you confuse the size of your sexual prowess with the size of your dick. I've rejected bigger ones, had longer and thicker specimens shoved up my arse. Talk is cheap.'

'We are seeing two supreme artistes at work,' Dr Leo Weissbinder announced satisfactorily to his nurse. Helga Dietrich stood obediently beside his electronically operated wheelchair in the large cabin designed as his private control centre. Together they viewed the continuing sex-play Myra and Dex displayed on the banks of closed-circuit screens arrayed in a semi-circle set before them.

'Should we be spying on them, Herr Doktor?' Helga asked nervously, made uncomfortable by the increasingly persistent arousal she felt. 'They are members of your staff, not subjects of your survey.'

'All sexual activity conducted on the *Aphrodite* is of interest to my project,' he informed her, aware that his pleasantly plump bespectacled young nurse had a strong desire to be noticed by Dex. Her infatuation for him was hard to hide and she felt darts of physical pain seeing his activities with the newly-arrived stranger.

'That woman is a whore,' she said, despite a resolve to hold her tongue.

'No,' Weissbinder admonished her. 'What we have here are two sexual experts trying each other out and giving no quarter. Members of my team,' he said proudly. He pressed a button, one of an array situated on the console set into the right arm of his wheelchair. At once the images of Myra and Dex loomed in close-up on every screen, clearly showing the film of sheeny perspiration caused by their exertions.

'*Gott in Himmel,*' Helga gasped. 'What are they doing?'

'Seeing who will submit first, trying each other out both verbally and physically,' Weissbinder said affably. 'This is an excellent opportunity to sample the efficiency of the video cameras concealed in every cabin. Simple security-type scanners which will prove invaluable in our research. It will let us know how our patients behave after undergoing our

48

counselling and therapy when in the privacy of their cabins. How well they've been helped to face their repressions.'

'It could be seen as an invasion of their privacy,' Helga said timidly, hardly bearing to watch Dex's muscled buttocks flex as he sensuously tit-fucked Myra, her mouth capturing the glistening red knob projecting from her cleavage on each upthrust. The dampening of Helga's crotch, an inner sensation that went from her cunt to her swollen breasts and stretched her nipples against her white nylon nurse's overall, made the viewing more agonising. 'What goes on in people's own time in their own cabins is surely private?' she felt forced to say, wishing he would terminate the showing.

'Everything on this cruise is my business,' Weissbinder said curtly. 'And while working for me, so are you, Nurse Dietrich. You will undoubtedly witness every sexual act and position possible while attending to me. Your infatuation for Dr Calvert will not be allowed to affect your contribution or his. Is he aware of this obsession?'

'No,' Helga said miserably. 'I would die first.'

'That won't be necessary,' he said, 'instead learn how to control your emotions. I know you find it difficult to watch the sexual activity on the screen. Rest assured any inhibitions you have I will remove, as I do for all my patients. You say that's what you want and I'll do it. You will obey my orders, of course.'

'I wish it so, Herr Doktor,' she murmured, lowering her eyes. 'Only you must be strict with me.'

'As much as is necessary,' Weissbinder said, lolling back in his wheelchair and unzipping his fly. 'Do you know what I expect of you now?'

'Yes, Herr Doktor,' she said in a tiny voice, kneeling before him and fumbling in his trousers, unable to control her trembling. She brought out his flaccid prick and balls, and produced a bottle of sweet-scented almond oil from the pocket of her white overall. 'Massage?' she whispered, her excitement mounting. 'Or?'

'Massage for now,' he said, his prick stirring into life.

'Meanwhile, get used to my survey being twenty-four hours daily, in or out of the lecture or therapy sessions. Forget the secretive use of surveillance cameras, they are a tool to tell us how successfully sexual repression is being resolved among our patients. We're doing essential work here.'

'That I'm understanding,' Helga agreed, the prick in her massaging hand now rearing long and thin. 'I try, I do try.'

'Then look at them now,' he said, ordering her to turn her eyes to the screens. 'Tell the truth – you wish you were there with him, don't you? Or even with *them*?' he added, feeling her hand tighten on his stalk, suspecting he had uncovered a dark secret. 'Have you had many men, Helga?' he asked casually. 'Surely, a fine well-built girl like you has had admirers?'

She was unable to answer, swallowing deeply.

'Okay,' he continued. 'I know you fancy Dr Calvert, so you're no lesbian, at least not a true one. But have you ever made love with another woman? I know you are a trained masseuse and that in Germany you gave massage exclusively to members of your own sex. Did you give them sexual relief if required? Did they return your caresses?'

Still getting no reply he shook his head, not diverted by her increased rubbing of his prick. 'You don't answer, so I must take that as a yes,' he said to add to her discomfiture. 'I really will have to be strict with you. Look at the screen and take a lesson from what you see there. There are no inhibitions with those two. They've enjoyed the rapture of mutual embraces for fully half-an-hour and are still at the foreplay stage, taunting each other with lewd talk. It looks at last as if both are agreeing to proceed to the ultimate and fuck wantonly. He to give her the prick and she to take it. What uninhibited sexual animals they are.'

'Dr Calvert was told to bring Mrs Starr to you as soon as she arrived,' Helga reminded him, envying Myra as Dex positioned his hugely rampant prick at the mouth of her proffered cleft. 'She's a big woman. I can't see why he finds her so attractive.'

'All that there is of her is choice,' Weissbinder said, thinking

50

there was even more succulent flesh on his nurse. 'Don't let your feelings for Dr Calvert spoil the pleasure of seeing two sexual athletes performing. Take note, Helga. See how he prepares to mount her at last, how she widens her thighs and tilts her pelvis for the penetration, guiding it in for him. This will be some fuck.'

'I don't think I can watch,' Helga said, her voice hoarse. 'It disturbs me.'

'As it would any normal person,' Weissbinder said, 'yet it disturbs you in a different way. Nurse Dietrich, if you weren't such an interesting case, I'd order you off my vessel right now. I take your presence here as evidence of your desire to rid yourself of a restrained nature, so watch the screen. Use what you see as fantasy material. Picture Dr Calvert doing the same to you when you next masturbate.'

'Why do you think I do *that*?' she asked, mortified.

'Of course you do,' he said shortly. 'Your type more than average. The video tape of this will be used as an example to encourage others. The time they can last out interests me, to learn how long such a lusty pair can endure the pleasure and who will succumb first. My God, watching them does have an effect.' He looked down at the kneeling Helga stroking his prick, reaching for her head and drawing it into his lap. 'Now,' he said simply. 'Now.'

In Myra's cabin it was as if the lovers had unanimously agreed their prolonged foreplay had run its course. In all their wordy preparation for working the other up to submit, this final act was unspoken as they both positioned themselves, desperate to fuck.

Guiding Dex's hardness with her hand and directing the egg-sized knob to her swollen outer lips, Myra lunged upwards at the exact moment he thrust. It was what she urgently desired – deep penetration. With the whole of his thick prick embedded, she curled her legs around his back and urged his buttock cheeks forward with her dug-in heels. Her bottom jerked, rising and falling with each thrust and withdrawal of his big stiff prick. 'Fuck me, fuck me,' she shouted, unaware

51

of anything but her desire to climax repeatedly. 'Fuck me to a frazzle like you promised.'

Above her, Dex revelled in riding such a spectacular mount. On each out-stroke, Myra's experienced cunt gripped vice-like on the retreating bar of flesh. Aided by the abundant juice of their desire, he was able to withdraw to the bulbous knob before ramming in to the farthest recess of her channel. He sought to bring her off first in their battle of wills. Both his hands were in use cupping the bouncing cheeks of her arse, hauling her to him to increase the power of his thrusts. The middle finger of his right hand was buried to its second knuckle in the tight puckered ring of her rear hole, adding to her squeals and cries.

It could not last. Both of them were out of control, humping wildly with bellies slapping, coming off simultaneously. Maintaining their close embrace, the couple fucked without pause until their final spasms ceased. Then they lay together almost insensible, weakened by the violence of their climaxes, and regaining breath gradually. Then they laughed, hugging each other in the sheer elation of the moment.

'Quits, I think,' Dex said. 'That turned out to be the mother of all fucks, Mrs Myra Starr. You're some woman. I was about to give in to you.'

'And you almost had me,' she admitted, leaning up on an elbow, her sweat-glistened breasts seductively pendent. 'When we both made our move together, I was ready to beg you to fuck me. I've no doubt you'll excel as Weissbinder's resident stud.'

'You'll do the same in tutoring the men,' Dex said. 'Lucky fellows.'

'It will be too much to hope they'll be hung like you,' Myra laughed.

'There'll be other times,' Dex said. 'Part of the treatment for the repressed of both sexes is for you and I to stage exhibitions of screwing to give 'em some ideas. I can live with that,' he grinned, rising from the bed, admiring her nakedness. 'Guess we'd better shower. Maybe we could stage another rehearsal while under the spray. Then I'd better take you to see the illustrious Dr Weissbinder.'

'Who no doubt is wondering where we've got to,' Myra smiled.

'I hardly think so,' Dex grinned in return. 'No doubt he's been drooling over the action in his private viewing centre. He's not above that.'

'Why else is he so eager to conduct these sex surveys?' Myra said. 'To further the interests of science? I doubt it. He's a lecherous old devil, but he gets away with it and even makes a profit. We should be so smart.'

Chapter Six

Bikini Girls

Manda returned to her bedroom with Dorothy to complete packing, both sisters in turmoil at the sight of Gerald making free with their mother. Above all, they were amazed by her response and her obvious strong climax, despite her initial reluctance to allow Gerald such liberties. The girls seriously discussed the issue. They concluded that it was impossible for a woman not to reciprocate once she had been sufficiently worked up.

'Myra got me so excited I allowed her to do whatever she wanted to do,' Manda told her sister. 'Then I did everything she wanted me to do to her. Don't take on so, Dorrie – I'm not ashamed of it. It was lovely sleeping with her, and I'd do it again. I don't blame mummy for coming off with Gerald like that. It's the same as you letting him fuck you after getting you so aroused. I would have done it myself.'

'That doesn't make me feel any better about it,' Dorothy said glumly.

'Come on, sis,' Manda tried to cheer her, 'it's happened, so just accept it. It's time we faced facts and forgot all that stuff mummy drummed into us about men. You saw for yourself how horny she gets. And what about the vibrator she keeps in her bedroom? She must do it to herself. So Gerald had you – it's not the end of the world.'

'He said that too,' Dorothy remembered. 'The beast seduced me. As a married woman I'm ashamed of myself, even if I do need sex so much.'

'Then you got what you wanted,' Manda said cheerfully.

'What are you complaining about? You're not the first wife to turn to other men.'

'I detest him for using me, all the same,' Dorothy said. 'Not just because he made me give in to him, I accept that I wanted to. It's because the arrogant swine thinks he can have anyone he fancies. Me, our mother – you too if given half the chance. He needs to be taught a lesson, one that would deflate his huge ego.'

'And deflate his big cock, just when he thinks he's going to use it on one of us,' Manda giggled at the thought. 'Let's make a pact to ignore him on the cruise. Let's tempt him, then treat him with the contempt he deserves when he tries it on.'

'As I'm sure he will,' her sister said knowingly, 'even with Nigel there if he feels he's got a chance to have me again. A little thing like my husband's presence won't deter him. But tempting him would seem like offering ourselves, wouldn't it? He doesn't need encouraging.'

'It would offer *us* the chance – to slap him down,' Manda said deviously. She held up the two scanty pieces of a crimson bikini she was about to pack in her case. 'Wearing this should get him going. Make him drool at the mouth.'

'I just wish it would do the same to my Nigel,' Dorothy said wistfully. 'I've almost given up on arousing him. You're not going to wear that, surely? That bikini could fit into a spectacle case.'

'With the two others I've got,' Manda said proudly. 'A gold one and a white one. Why not? Other girls wear them, some even go topless.'

'Those itsy-bitsy things barely cover the essentials,' Dorothy frowned. 'Gerald would love that, and mother will have a fit. Does she know that you bought them?'

'I didn't give her the chance,' Manda declared. 'She'd have said no. If you haven't got a bikini, Dorrie, you're welcome to wear one of mine.'

'Nigel wouldn't like me to be seen in so little,' Dorothy said, 'but it's tempting to find out if it does anything for him.

I feel there's far too much of me to appear in public in such a skimpy costume. My breasts and bottom are so big.'

'Hardly bigger than mine,' her sister argued, 'and I'm game. If it makes the lecherous Gerald goggle and go hot under the collar, I'll wear a bikini just to frustrate the horny hound. And there'll be other men around to appreciate us. You'd look great in one, Dorrie. You're right, it may make Nigel forget his mother and see he's got a fabulous wife. It could give him ideas.' She held up the miniscule bra and briefs. 'Try this on, there's just time before we leave. I want to see how gorgeous you look. Go on, I'll put one on too, I've tried them all. You'll find they make you feel terribly sexy.'

'It seems it doesn't take much to make us feel that way,' Dorothy admitted. 'Not with all that's happened since yesterday. I feel I'm becoming obsessed by sex whether I like it or not. You're even worse, there's not an ounce of shame in you. I think you even enjoyed seeing poor mother being ravished.'

'I bet it made you all randy too,' Manda challenged. 'You won't admit a thing, even if you feel the same way. It's all our previously repressed feelings bubbling over, I'm sure.' She began to unzip the back of her sister's dress. 'Come on, help me undress you. I bet going nude is even better than a bikini. I'd love to try it.'

'I suppose there is a certain excitement about revealing one's body,' Dorothy said hesitantly. 'I know it's awful of me, and you must never repeat it to a soul, but at times I have the feeling that I'm a frustrated exhibitionist. I've fantasised about wearing a very brief bikini and being ogled by all the men on a beach. Once, when we were first married, I even suggested to Nigel that we might try the local nudist colony.'

'There's hope for you yet,' Manda enthused. 'How wonderful that would be, showing off our titties, pussies and bottoms to others – especially men. And think how we could compare their cocks. I'd love that. What did he say?'

'Nigel went berserk, said I was going mad. After that I

didn't like to suggest anything he might disapprove of,' she said sadly.

'It's high time you put your foot down with him and do what you like,' Manda said. 'No husband of mine will tell me what to do. I shall keep him begging for favours, and take all the lovers I choose. I wouldn't marry one who turned down the chance to go with me to a nudist club, anyway.' She began to undress beside her sister. 'Myra told me last night to always be my own woman and to use men. They are there to serve us and they like a really stern mistress. She told me she'd actually smacked grown men's bare bottoms, and they'd loved it.'

'I can believe that of her,' Dorothy said. 'She's a strong woman.'

'Then you be the same,' Manda said. 'Nigel is a mummy's boy, so you should be strict with him. I bet he'd love that.'

'What have I got to lose? I'm running out of ideas,' Dorothy sighed, shedding the remainder of her clothes while Manda did the same. The nude sisters giggled as they eyed each other and compared bodies. Manda was the first to move, taking Dorothy's hand and leading her to the full-length mirror on the door of her wardrobe. 'Oh, I can't bear it,' Dorothy said, shocked. 'Look at me. I'm all breasts and bottom, and such a growth of hair on my – between my thighs. I wouldn't dare wear a bikini.'

'Nonsense,' Manda told her. 'You're gorgeously built in all the right places, just like mummy. It's what men adore. I'll bet Gerald had an eyeful of you. What a sense of freedom there is in being naked. In the buff is the only way to make love, so Myra said. Skin to skin and no inhibitions about anything.'

'Gerald insisted upon that too,' Dorothy remembered. 'I feel strange standing here like this with you. It's quite shameless of us.'

'It's turning you on, isn't it?' the forward Manda laughed accusingly. 'That's how I feel too. If a man came into the room right now, I'd let him! Let him feel me up and fuck me. I'd want him to.'

'Oh, Manda, what's become of us?' Dorothy said, 'I feel

so – so mixed up as to what I am or what I want to be.' Manda took her in her arms, crushing their breasts together. 'Really, you are beyond belief,' Dorothy told her sister, trying to put on a brave face. 'It wouldn't surprise me if *you'd* corrupted Myra Starr, instead of the other way round. Give me that indecent bikini and I will try it on.'

Manda grinned. 'I'm just beginning to enjoy life. Not before time. It would pay you to think the same. Here, put on this bikini.'

As if in awe of her younger sister, Dorothy obeyed. Wearing the two tiny parts of the scarlet swimsuit, she studied herself in the long mirror while Manda looked on approvingly. Her splendidly shaped full breasts overflowed the half-cups, making them look even more voluptuous in their scant covering. The big orbs nestled tightly together, rounded flesh swelling out to the front and sideways to her arms. Her nipples were barely concealed, stiffly erect and pressing against the flimsy material. She turned to Manda, the slight movement setting her breasts jiggling in their captive cups, threatening to burst free.

'How does that feel?' her sister asked. 'Wicked, isn't it? You look awesome.'

'It makes me feel lewd and immoral,' Dorothy said. 'That's what you want to hear, isn't it? I might as well be wearing nothing.'

'That's the object of the exercise,' Manda said. 'Think how it will be, parading before the men, showing off your goodies. What fun. Even dull old Nigel should get the hots for you. Maybe he'd get a thrill knowing other men are ogling you; some do, you know. I can't wait to flaunt myself.'

'You talk like a loose woman,' Dorothy complained, but her voice was hoarse with the arousal she could not contain. A persistent throb in her cunt unsettled her. Her taut nipples rubbed tormentingly under the bra cups. Although she had made up her mind not to wear it, the thought of exhibiting herself in the negligible two-piece was thrilling in the extreme. It was too much to bear without getting relief from the torment she felt.

'I want to get dressed now,' she murmured weakly, struggling to ignore the tremors in her lower abdomen. Looking down at the join of her thighs, the plump mound between seemed all the more prominent under the tiny triangular patch which barely covered the curved bulge. It was held in position by two scarlet straps that led over her hips and joined at the back to make a single thong, running down between her buttock cheeks. It revealed so much of her bottom, her arse was to all intents and purposes completely bare.

'You look a knockout, Dorrie,' Manda complimented her. 'Drop-dead gorgeous.' She watched intently as her sister took off the bikini and sat trembling visibly on the edge of the bed. 'You've got that nice feeling inside you, haven't you?' she alleged slyly. 'When you want it badly, bursting for relief with nobody to give it to you but yourself. Why don't you then? I won't mind. I do it myself often enough. Go on, do it.'

'How could you?' Dorothy whined. 'What an awful thing to say.'

'Don't act the innocent,' Manda said. 'I'm sure you do it lots, since your husband's such a dead loss. Just lie back and play with yourself. Use your fingers to have a really lovely come. There's no need to be shy with me. You'll feel better for it.'

'I – I couldn't,' Dorothy said feebly, allowing Manda to lower her across the bed, eager to urge her on. 'I admit I do it to myself, but I couldn't with you here. How can you suggest such a wicked thing.'

'Who says it's wicked?' Manda insisted, drawing up a chair to the bedside and looking down at the anguished Dorothy. 'I know you're dying to, even with me here. Maybe even more so with me here. You didn't mind opening your legs for Gerald, did you? You wanted your father-in-law to fuck you and you let him. Even begged him for it, I'll bet.'

'If I did it was because I couldn't help myself,' Dorothy replied, wishing her sister would be more understanding. 'He – he aroused me so, and wouldn't leave me alone. He kept on

60

to me when I was vulnerable, just like you are doing. I wanted it so badly.'

'Wanted what, sis?' Manda enquired. 'You can tell me, we've no secrets now.' She bent over Dorothy, sitting forward in her chair, smiling affectionately. 'Tell me and ease your conscience. What was it you needed so much?'

'To be *fucked*,' Dorothy shouted, her voice almost a screech. 'There, did you hear that? I begged him to fuck me, to thrust his big prick up my cunt. That's what I told him – the actual words. Why are you torturing me so?'

'You're torturing yourself, denying the urge that's unsettling you,' Manda accused. 'Why not let yourself go? Just think if Gerald could see you now, laid back desperate for it, stark naked with your lovely big breasts and pussy on show.'

'Please,' Dorothy appealed. 'It's you. I am *not* desperate for it.'

'You admitted that you're frustrated and obsessed by sex,' Manda said. 'If he walked in you'd let him fuck you again. Let him shove his big brute right up you and give you the satisfaction you're dying for right now. Doesn't it make you go all hot and shivery remembering his stiff cock inside you, thrusting away? How you must have loved it.'

'So what if I did?' Dorothy whined. 'And you – you just want to make me more excited so I'll do *that* to myself. Well, I won't, not with you going on about it.'

'I thought we had an understanding,' Manda said impatiently. 'We agreed we'd do as we liked from now on without false modesty. What a hypocrite you are. You weren't so reluctant when Gerald was getting across you. I can tell by your nipples that you're aroused, like mother's were in the potting shed. Your titties are just like hers, so big and round. Did Gerald fondle yours too, suck hard on the nipples? Tell me, please.'

'I asked him to, my husband never does,' Dorothy moaned. 'Why are you doing this to me, Manda? It's not fair. You know very well how I'm feeling.'

'On heat,' Manda nodded, 'but I need to know. I want to

61

find out what to expect when a man does the things Gerald did to you. You're my married sister, you should tell me,' she added artfully. 'Mummy never would. After sucking on your nipples and playing with your breasts, what did he do next?'

'He – he – parted my legs and did things to me *there*.'

'You mean he put his finger inside you?' Manda demanded to know. 'Before getting you so worked up you begged to be fucked?'

'Among other things,' Dorothy admitted. 'There was something else.'

'Hah! You mean he licked your pussy!' Manda said in delight. 'That must be absolute heaven. Did it make you come?' She shook her sister physically by the shoulders. 'Lucky you, what was it like?'

'Please don't go on,' Dorothy begged. 'Don't you know this is torment for me? Yes, he used his tongue and made me come. Then he fucked me. How many times must I say it? Fucked me and I came, over and over. I was so helpless, madly aroused and didn't know what I was doing, only what I wanted. I was boiling over.'

'Like you are now,' Manda reminded her heartlessly. 'Your bottom is writhing about on the bed, you're so horny. Why don't you give yourself a nice come and be honest about it?' She trailed her fingers lightly over the soft reddish fleece covering Dorothy's plump mound, circling the swollen outer lips of her cunt. 'Go on, forget everything except what you really want to do. Give yourself a lovely strong climax thinking how Gerald's big dick poked you crazy. It would be our secret.'

'You little bitch,' Dorothy groaned, removing Manda's hand from her groin but letting her own remain there. 'I know what you're trying to make me do. *Making* me do,' she added in a wavering voice, long slim fingers commencing to stroke the pouting sex lips. 'I shall never forgive you for this, you wicked creature,' she whined. 'Getting me to play with myself.'

Giving up the struggle completely, Dorothy slipped two

fingers into the oily interior, flicking around the stubby clitoris, her buttocks thrashing and contorting on the bed. Lost to all but her own self-induced pleasure, she garbled out unintelligible sounds, in a world of her own as her wrist and hand worked frantically.

She came almost immediately, gasping in her throes, the violent spasms causing her body to undulate wildly even as she continued for further climaxes. When the frenzied contractions finally subsided, she lay still, gathering her wits and breath. Beside her she saw her sister lolling back in the chair, legs parted widely and with a triumphant grin on her face. 'Me too,' she said, bending forward to give Dorothy a loving hug. 'Wasn't it great? Watching you made me so horny I had to do it too.'

Dorothy tried without success to wipe the blissful look off her face. 'You're a bad influence,' she attempted to scold her sister. 'I never thought I could do such a thing with someone else present, but you made me want to, damn you.'

'So what? I don't suppose we'll be eternally condemned for what we did,' Manda said lightly. 'It was lovely and don't you deny it. Your nature is the same as mine.' Using a fingertip, she traced a circle playfully around one of Dorothy's erect nipples. 'The best way to meet temptation is to give in to it. I'm sure there'll be plenty of opportunities on the cruise.'

'We'd better dress and go downstairs,' Dorothy said, removing Manda's hand and trying to ignore what her sister said. 'Thank goodness mother will be there to keep you in check on the cruise and I'll have Nigel with me.'

'Poor you,' Manda sympathised. 'Mummy or not, I shall do my own thing. That's unless someone else wants to do it for me,' she giggled as an afterthought. 'I'm intent on losing my virginity and I've gone on the pill just in case.'

As they began dressing, they were startled by an urgent knocking at the door. 'Dorothy, Amanda, are you in there?' said a man's voice. It was Nigel. 'Your mother says it's almost time for the minibus to arrive. She wants you both downstairs at once. Are you ready?'

'Ready and willing, Nigel,' Manda called back cheekily, glancing at her sister to note her reaction. 'Come in, there's something we want you to see.' She silenced Dorothy with an uplifted hand, ignoring her anxious plea to behave. 'This is your big chance if ever there was,' she said. 'If the pair of us standing stark naked can't get him going, there's no hope for him.' She pushed Dorothy in front of her, directly facing the door. 'What is a sister for but to help out?' she giggled. 'He's in for a treat. This must be every red-blooded man's dream.'

Nigel entered and then staggered back as if he had been struck as he was confronted by his wife and sister-in-law standing naked before him, breasts thrusting and pubic hair on show. 'No, no,' he managed to stutter out. 'Have – have – you both taken leave of your senses? Have you no shame at all?'

'Not any more,' Manda affirmed, advancing on him as she saw he was about to turn and flee the room. Her breasts bobbed enticingly as she grabbed at his arm, urging Dorothy to grasp the other and hold him. Emboldened by her sister's brazen assurance, Dorothy took hold of Nigel's arm. Together they dragged him protesting to the bed, throwing him down on his back as he struggled to rise.

'Don't you dare try to leave. Now, you listen to me for once,' Dorothy surprised herself by saying sternly. 'It's time you did your duty as a proper loving husband. I'm not standing for being neglected any more. Any real man finding his wife waiting for him naked would have her on her back by now, eager to – to fuck her.'

'And me as well for seconds,' Manda whooped. 'Have you two fucks in you, Nige? Can you manage us both?'

'You *are* mad, the pair of you,' he screamed. 'How could you parade yourselves so? Where did you learn such disgusting language? Let me go. I demand to be released!'

'He hasn't even got an erection, not even with the two of us flaunting ourselves before him,' Dorothy said dejectedly, her hand grasping his crotch through his trousers. 'I give up. We may as well let him go.'

'Let's punish him for insulting our womanhood,' Manda announced dramatically. 'Don't let him off, Dorrie. Give him what for. Beat him like the utter wimp he is.'

'He deserves it,' Dorothy agreed, slapping his hands away as he tried to prevent her loosening his belt. 'Over with him,' she ordered and Manda helped her roll the outraged Nigel on to his stomach. As if in unspoken accord, both girls hauled down his trousers and underpants, revealing a lilywhite backside jerking about in anguish.

'Nigel, lie still!' his wife threatened. 'It will be the worse for you if you don't.' Manda handed her a silver-backed hairbrush from the dressing table. 'Thank you, sister,' she said gravely. 'Now do something to stop him wriggling about so much. Sit on his head.' She raised the hairbrush above her head. 'This I'm going to enjoy.'

'Whack him with the back, then the bristly side,' Manda recommended, climbing over the squealing Nigel to sit with her crotch firmly planted on the back of his neck. His attempts to prevent suffocation, the agitated side-to-side motions of his face buried in a pillow, made her cunt rub tantalisingly against the nape of his neck. Her pleasure increasing, she ground the fork of her spread thighs into him. 'Oooh,' she sighed happily, straddled above him. 'Make my day, Nigel. Struggle all you want. I like it.'

'He won't like this,' Dorothy said grimly, her right arm striking down with the hairbrush which landed with a startling *whack* across both cheeks. His howl, muffled by the pillow and the weight of Manda sitting on him, was followed by further squeals and yells as his wife laid on the strokes. Each resounding smack of embossed silver-plate reddened the target area. Gradually his howls turned to cries for mercy.

'Yes, beg, beg!' Dorothy shouted, elated by the thrashing she was meting out. 'Beg like I was so often tempted to do when I needed fucking.' One tremendous blow sent the head of the brush flying from the handle. It shot across the room, breaking the girls' concentration.

Nigel summoned all his strength and thrust Manda aside,

rolling over on his back with trousers and underpants around his knees. In doing so he revealed a prick in a high state of arousal, inflamed and straining. At that instant it jerked, jetting out arcs of thick creamy come that splattered over his bared stomach. Leaping from the bed, Nigel fled into the corridor. The sisters collapsed across the bed, hugging each other, their derisive laughter following him.

'Well,' Dorothy declared at length. 'Bad influence you may be, Manda Craig, but that proves he can be aroused by something. Obviously I've been wasting my time being passive where he's concerned.'

'There's a good cock on him,' Manda observed, wiping away the tears of mirth from her eyes. 'When he pushed me off and rolled over, did you see how big and stiff it was? And what a load he shot, the dirty devil, enough to give you that baby you want.' She giggled at a thought. 'When you whacked his bum, the design on the back of my hairbrush was embossed on both his cheeks. No wonder it broke.'

'He'd have got more if it hadn't,' Dorothy said, allowing herself a giggle with her sister. 'Who would have thought I would ever do such a thing? I enjoyed it.'

'With the right treatment, I believe you could make Nigel be more of a husband to you,' Manda observed. 'Even if it means spanking him. Why not? You like it and so, obviously, does he.'

'Hmm,' Dorothy said thoughtfully. 'We'll see what happens on the cruise.'

'I'll help if necessary,' her wayward sister offered cheerfully. 'I'm looking forward to this holiday. I wonder what the others on the ship will be like? What will they make of us?'

Chapter Seven

Carnal Knowledge

What others would make of Manda and Dorothy, plus the remaining members of the group due to arrive from St Boniface's school, was a subject of discussion between Myra Starr and Dex Calvert. Showered and dressed, they made their way to report to Dr Weissbinder somewhat delayed by their sexual dalliance. Entering the control room, Dex announced that Myra had arrived.

'Yes, over an hour ago,' Leo Weissbinder noted, greeting Myra with a welcoming handshake. 'You forget, Dex, sitting here in my wheelchair I know everything that goes on. Helga and I watched you and Mrs Starr on the closed-circuit TV. You're first to be caught by your own idea of having it installed throughout the *Aphrodite*. Intriguing, the way you two immediately had it off. Perhaps I should rephrase that,' he added, smirking. 'I meant hit it off, of course. Anyway, it's a good start to your professional contribution to our survey. Didn't I tell you Myra would prove an asset to our projected programme?'

'In any position you want to use her,' Dex said, meaning exactly that. 'She's also been instrumental in bringing a very interesting group for us to study. According to what she's told me, they badly need therapy of the kind we aim to provide.'

'That's what we're here for,' Weissbinder said, rubbing wizened hands at the thought. 'The more hung-up the better. Well done, Myra. We've already a good mix of volunteer patients in need of our treatment. Married couples, singles of both sexes, closet lesbians who want to come out and meet soulmates, you name them we've got them, all desiring guidance and example to straighten out their sexual inhibitions. They will all make a contribution to the research which goes into our instructional manuals and videos to guide the afflicted at home.'

'All certain to prove best-sellers,' Dex said laconically.

'Money isn't everything,' Weissbinder said, annoyed at the laughter his sanctimonious words caused. 'I find your attitude disrespectful and frivolous at times, Dex. Watch it. Now, Mrs Starr, what of your interesting group?'

'They're not exactly volunteers,' Myra said, 'but with clever handling I'm sure they'll conform. I consider them ripe for the plucking – and fucking, if your methods work. The mother is the one you'll have to work on. She's turned herself into a one-woman crusade against the evils of sex, but she's got potential.'

'We've got ways,' Weissbinder said cunningly. 'The cruise will be conducted in a party atmosphere. To put passengers at ease over nudity, for example, a mixed group of naturalists are joining us. They'll no doubt go naked and unashamed around deck or at the swimming pool, which should encourage others to do the same. Then there are our lectures, of course, video screenings and demonstrations on the techniques of sexual enjoyment. Live shows to get them in the mood, with surrogate lovers on-hand for those who desire some hands-on training. I don't think we'll have any problems with your group.' He smiled ingratiatingly at Myra. 'Tell me more about them.'

'Mrs Ailsa Craig is a beautiful woman in her early forties, widowed and very sexually repressed,' Myra began. 'Her upbringing was undoubtedly in a puritanical family with parents who considered sex almost a mortal sin. To compound this, the man she married was not highly sexed. The lady was never satisfied by his efforts. I suspect she thought it could have been much better. This gives hope for bringing her out. Her husband died, leaving her with the responsibility of running her school for girls single-handed for years. During this time all her energy and effort has been expended on the school and raising two daughters. She's a good woman wasted.'

'Interesting,' Weissbinder observed, his pale eyes lighting behind the thick spectacles he wore. 'So, she has never been fulfilled as is a woman's right, and therefore needs to be. We look forward to treating this Mrs Craig. What of the others with her?'

'The daughters have been strictly brought up,' Myra reported. 'However, I know from personal experience both girls are highly sexed by nature. This despite, or because of, the mother imposing her own strict rules of chastity and decorum on her girls. The elder, Dorothy, is twenty-two and married. She has the worst possible husband imaginable for a pretty young wife yearning for sensual excitement yet she remains faithful to him. Nigel is still very much under his mother's thumb and is negligent of his marital duties. Whether this is because of a low sex drive or hidden homosexual tendencies is not known. What turns him on and arouses this young man is for us to discover.'

'This gets better,' Weissbinder said elatedly. 'What of the other daughter? Amanda, isn't it? Have we a problem there?'

'Only in keeping her satisfied,' Myra smiled, recalling the passion of the previous night. 'Manda is repressed, yes, but raring to go. Both girls are beauties, just like their mother. And like their mother, they are also frustrated. Manda is eighteen, blonde and blue-eyed, curvy in all the places men like. Women too, I must add. She's a cock-virgin at present. Is that a problem?'

'Not where I'm concerned,' Dex Calvert commented. 'Be glad to help out. There's one other male arrival you mentioned – Professor Gerald Marsh.'

'He could be a problem,' Myra stressed. 'He thinks he's God's gift to the female species and would fuck anything with a pulse. He's the assistant head at the school. He's boasted to me he'll screw Mrs Craig and her two daughters, even though Dorothy is his daughter-in-law. Nigel the deficient husband is Gerald's son.'

'Sounds quite a character,' Weissbinder said. 'Was he merely expressing a wish or being serious? He sounds the opposite of his mother-fixated son.'

'Two more different men you couldn't imagine. Gerald was being quite serious about having the mother and daughters,' Myra affirmed. 'He's macho, tall, good-looking in a raffish way and altogether too much of a good thing. I didn't want him on this cruise but he wanted to come. Gerald usually gets his way. He's well endowed and no slouch at satisfying a woman.'

'He sounds unbearable, a confirmed libertine,' Weissbinder stated, unable to hide the malice in his tone. 'What's his relationship with the Craig females, mother and daughters? Is it close?'

'Hardly,' Myra said. 'Mrs Craig barely tolerates him and I know rejects his advances, but he is vital to the running of her school. As for her daughters, he ogles them but their mother has them well warned, no doubt. I'd say he's considered a necessary pest.'

'He should be taught a lesson,' Weissbinder noted vindictively. 'We have a programme for that too – a strict regime which instils proper respect and appreciation of the female sex. You've experienced him, Myra?'

'Of course she has,' the listening Helga found herself saying. '*She'd* experience anything with a penis. Look how she threw herself at Dr Calvert to have sex with him as soon as she arrived. It was on the screen.'

'Taped purely as an instructional video, no doubt, Dr Weissbinder?' Dex said. 'We were quite good, I thought. Did it make interesting viewing?'

'It was enjoyably spontaneous,' Weissbinder agreed, unabashed. 'Helga is only jealous she wasn't the one on the receiving end. She failed to hide her excitement behind her protests about Myra's promiscuity.'

'Just who is this big-titted bitch?' Myra enquired, staring daggers at Helga.

'My personal nurse,' Weissbinder informed her. 'An experienced masseuse I discovered in a Munich health spa and invited to join our team. She's new to the research work we do, but I'm sure she'll try to do her best to fit in. Her wish is to be as free of sexual inhibition as the rest of us. I'm afraid an infatuation for Dex has complicated her situation somewhat, but she'll cope.'

'Then she'd better wise up to the facts of life,' Myra declared. 'There'll be a whole lot of fucking going on aboard this shagging ship. It's a project dedicated to sexual therapy and the erotic education of the inhibited. That's the name of the game, Helga dear. If I let Dex fuck me it was because I wanted to try out one of the resident studs, as well as fancying a good screw. He had no complaints.'

'Dr Calvert is not one of the resident studs,' Helga defended him stoutly.

'You could have fooled me,' Myra laughed. 'With his equipment and ability to give a woman multiple orgasms, he'll do until a stud comes along. Who the hell *are* you then, Dex?'

'He's a qualified doctor and psychiatrist, the top of his class at Harvard, a Rhodes scholar at Oxford, a sex therapist and counsellor – you name it,' Weissbinder answered for his assistant. 'We're fortunate to have Dr Calvert with us, just as he is fortunate to study under me. He's got more degrees than a thermometer, and qualifications as long as your arm, as well as the huge equipment you mention, Myra. Having our project at heart, of course he agreed to stand in as a stud as well. For that I'm sure his female patients will be truly grateful.'

'Someone's got to do it,' Dex said modestly, stifling his grin. 'It's purely in the interest of advancing scientific research, of course.' He smiled at Helga who regarded him with awe. 'It's just a job.'

'Sure, helping the needy and greedy,' Myra observed wryly.

'I'll go along with that, only I'm not having Fraulein Fatso making bitchy remarks about my sexuality. If she can't stomach seeing people she fancies fucking, she's on the wrong boat. Didn't you vet her before signing her on, Doc?'

'Thoroughly,' Weissbinder said emphatically. 'Such a repressed nature as hers has presented an immediate challenge. She needs help to overcome her phobia which prevents her regarding sexual activity as normal, natural and pleasurable. In her work as a masseuse at the Munich clinic, her clients were exclusively female. No doubt some wanted sexual relief during the massage. I have the feeling that Helga provided it and is bi-sexual although she can't admit it. So far she won't tell me about her past experiences with men, but all will come out. I count her as a patient as well as my nurse. We must use all our talents to free her of years of denying her true self.'

'Why not right now?' Myra suggested bitchily. 'Let's get the prude nude. I want to see if those tits are for real. They look bigger than mine. Order her to strip and let's have some fun.'

'My research is not fun but has a serious therapeutic application,' Weissbinder said pompously. 'However, your idea is sound. Because of her obvious dislike of you, Myra, you may kiss and fondle her to judge her reaction when she is undressed. Helga, you will allow this to show willingness to accept the treatment I prescribe. Take your clothes off, Helga.'

'I *can't*,' Helga pleaded, mortified. 'Not with *her*. Don't ask me to, Herr Doktor.'

'I'm not asking, I'm ordering,' Weissbinder told her sharply. 'Your very reluctance makes it imperative that I do for your own sake. Off with your overall, Nurse Dietrich, and everything else. To make you feel more at ease, Myra and Dr Calvert will undress too. Your panic is unnecessary.'

'You could be doing this since you've got the hots for him,' Myra taunted her, unbuckling Dex's belt and drawing down his jeans, revealing an already impressive bulge in his pants. He peeled off his shirt, kicking away both sandals and jeans, advancing on Helga. 'Lower his underpants and see what's in there,' Myra invited her. 'It won't bite.'

'Do it,' Weissbinder ordered the chastened young woman. 'I know you want to.'

'Only because you are making me,' Helga whined. Trembling hands fumbled at his waistband hesitating. Drawing Dex's briefs down allowed his engorged prick the freedom to spring upright, quivering in its rigid state. She stared at it as if mesmerised. 'It's – it's—' she began.

'Beautiful,' Myra finished for her. 'Big and thick and begging to be sucked from the look of it. Why don't you order Helga to take it in her mouth, Doctor? If she won't, I'll gladly show her how.'

'One thing at a time,' Weissbinder instructed. 'She hasn't stripped as ordered and neither have you, Myra. Let things take their course.'

'You're the boss,' Myra said, pulling the loose-fitting dress she had changed into over her head and slipping off her shoes. She wore no bra and her breasts thrust out, the nipples proudly erect. Standing in only the tiniest of lacy briefs, she nudged Dex aside and stood facing Helga. 'See, there's nothing to be ashamed of,' Myra said, aware of the nurse's deep blush as her eyes stared at the bared breasts and went down to the bulge between Myra's thighs. Myra pulled her panties down her thighs to show off the thick triangle of hair on her mound, the cleft parted in arousal.

'Touch me,' Myra said. 'Don't say you're not turned on.' She took Helga's right hand and held it to her breast, moving it around with the palm rubbing the stiff nipple. Then she took it to her cunt. 'Feel. I know you want to.'

'I *don't*,' Helga wailed, pulling her hand away as if burnt. 'Doktor, please, tell her to stop. She's a woman—'

'Her supposed outrage may be taken as a protest against her latent or actual bi-sexuality,' Dex considered, moving behind Myra and inserting his erect prick snugly between the tight cleft of her bare buttocks. 'That's my professional opinion.'

'It did not escape my observation,' Weissbinder replied, not to be outdone by his assistant. 'I was aware of her arousal when you fucked Myra, her reason then being you. Helga is such a mass of complexes worthy of research that it is not unlikely she's bi-sexual, hence the guilt syndrome.'

'Never mind the psychological mumbo-jumbo, you pair of trick-cyclists,' Myra said impatiently. 'I want at her tits. Let's see how her bloody guilt syndrome reacts when she's getting her nipples sucked in my warm wet mouth. Get her to strip.'

'I don't want to, Herr Doktor,' she whimpered.

'Nonsense. We are all scientists here. Do as you are told. You want to remain on my staff, I presume? There's still time to put you ashore.'

Without further protest, glancing at Myra and Dex with burning cheeks, Helga began to undress. The onlookers were eager to see such a voluptuous young woman naked, her reluctance adding to their enjoyment. Unbuttoning the white nurse's overall with unsteady fingers, she draped it over a swivel chair beside Weissbinder. Her white cotton bra bulged with her outsized breasts, the nipples prominent under the cups. Both Myra and Dex murmured their astonishment at their size and firmness. The flesh that overflowed the bra was creamy white and satin smooth, with the weighty mounds pressed together so tightly that the dividing cleave was a mere thin line.

Below the curvature of her breasts was a pale rounded belly with a deep navel. Sensible white knickers and white cotton stockings held up by elastic garters completed her ensemble. Where the stocking tops ended, several inches of splendidly rounded ivory thighs were revealed. At her crotch, the cotton of her knickers curved into a noticeable bulge, behind which the outline of a pubic forest darkened the white cotton.

'Hurry, *liebchen*,' Weissbinder ordered, his interest aroused. 'We want to see the rest of you.'

Helga falteringly unhooked the bra, uncovering two large trembling breasts. Freed, they appeared to defy gravity, standing out from her chest like full-sized rugby balls. Dex's interest

74

was so confined to the magnificence of her teats that his prick, embedded up Myra's cunt from the rear, ceased to plunge into her hot core – until a waggle of her bottom reminded him to keep it moving. Helga's breasts fell forward as she bent to slip down her knickers. The round pointy tits became enlongated, their mass and weight swinging them apart, thimble-sized nipples pointing to the floor.

Both Myra and Dex gasped in admiration, eager to fondle such beauties, to stroke the pliant flesh and suck upon the thick nipples. Helga stood in just her stockings. Between the ample thighs was the hairiest cunt Myra could remember seeing, a light-coloured heavy thatch on the prominent mound which disappeared as thickly between her legs. Her armpits showed the same hirsute growth.

'You may keep the stockings on, Helga,' Weissbinder instructed, his voice thick. 'That wasn't so bad, was it? You're a very shapely woman. I can tell that Myra and Dex are impressed.'

'She must have had lovers,' Dex said, easing his prick gently up and down Myra's receptively lubricated cunt channel. 'Do you want me to fuck her?'

'Never,' Weissbinder declared. 'I want you to keep your minds on your work, not romance. But I'm sure Helga has had admirers and we'd like to hear about them. Come here, Helga, let me be your confessor. Call it therapy, it's what you need to rid yourself of your mental burden.'

Helga shuffled over to him, unable to disobey, her breasts trembling, until she stood before the wheelchaired psycho-therapist. 'Can – can I dress now, please, Herr Doktor,' she begged of him. 'I am ashamed. The others are staring at me. I feel so strange.'

'Learn to enjoy being admired,' he told her. 'As for that strange feeling, is it not a pleasant one if only you'd admit it? What superb breasts you have,' he said, lifting each one in his thin hands. 'Firm as marble yet soft and warm. Observe how your nipples are hard and erect. Are you truly not aroused, Nurse Dietrich?'

'I – I don't know, Herr Doktor,' she said in a low whisper. 'I have tried not to be. Not with others to witness my shame.'

Weissbinder snorted in disdain. 'Stupid girl,' he said. 'Part your legs.' With long fingers of both hands he prised open Helga's outer cunt lips. Myra watched with interest, Dex too from over Myra's shoulder as he shunted his prick almost imperceptibly within her. Weissbinder held both folds of flesh apart, revealing the glistening pink interior of Helga's sex. 'Your labia is swollen with excitement, Helga, and that which I see is not a virgin's cunt, is it?' he said sternly. 'The truth now. No false modesty.'

'N – no,' Helga quavered in shame.

'Who was the first?' he persisted. 'Was it a man or a woman?' He inserted a crooked finger inside her, making her take a sharp intake of breath. She shuddered and would have overbalanced had Myra not gripped her arms from behind to steady her. 'The first?' Weissbinder repeated. 'Someone must have been.' His finger circled the hypersensitive clitoris, causing her to moan and squirm. 'One thing you can't deny,' he said, 'is how wet you now are. Talk to me. You'll find it's a great relief to unburden yourself.'

'It was – while at the academy,' Helga groaned, in an anguish of shame mixed with helpless mounting arousal. 'At school. I was seduced,' she pleaded. 'I was young, innocent, afraid. Believe me, I did not want him to . . .'

'But he did and you let him,' Weissbinder said in a kindlier tone. 'There's no shame in that at all. You must learn to admit it was what you really wanted. How old were you and who was the fortunate man?'

'I was sixteen. A virgin,' she told him, her agitation increasing, striving to prevent herself working her pelvis against his hand. 'It was such a shock to know a girl could have such strong feelings. He made me have them, the things he was doing to me. My best friend's father too. One night after visiting her, sitting in her bedroom playing tapes and discussing boys and what sex would be like, he drove me home in his car—'

'I know the scene,' Myra laughed. 'A boyfriend's dad couldn't keep his eyes off me too. He fucked me in his car but he wasn't the first. His son was. I was also sixteen. I have to say the father was better at it.'

'How did you manage to stay a virgin that long?' Helga found the will to say in her ordeal. 'You would encourage the man, I did not. He – he – did those things to me until I could not resist any more.'

'The end result was the same,' Myra taunted her. 'We both got fucked. It was the best thing to happen to me, having an experienced man show me how.'

'Quite so, Myra,' Weissbinder said. 'But it's Helga we are discussing. Which reminds me – turn around, face the other way.' He withdrew his finger from Helga's cunt, smiling as she uttered a drawn-out sigh. 'Don't worry, it will go back in soon. Turn, I said. Place your feet apart.'

Helga moved around as ordered, facing Myra with Dex's face looking over her shoulder. 'What gorgeous big tits,' Myra said lewdly, her hands unable to resist grasping them. 'How full and firm they are.' She cupped them both, her mouth greedy to surround and suck on a thick nipple. 'Let me have her, Doc,' she pleaded. 'I'll give her relief. She's panting for it.'

'Just her breasts then,' Weissbinder allowed. 'Do what you wish with them while I continue to explore the subject's past sexual history. Your girlfriend's father?' he demanded of Helga. 'Was it only once or did you continue fucking in his car over a period of time?' He smiled, hearing Helga's low moan as Myra began suckling avidly on one of her nipples, admiring the plump bare buttocks presented before his face. 'Speak up,' he commanded, his hands parting the splendidly rounded moons of her arse, admiring the downhung bulge with its moist split and surround of soft downy hair nestling in the deep cleave.

'In his car, in his house, in his bath,' Helga stuttered, the effect of Myra's suction on her nipple and Weissbinder's finger resuming the probing of her rearward directed cunt making

77

her lose all resolve. 'I – I – was a wicked girl, going to him whenever he wanted me, even suggesting meetings myself, phoning him at his office to say I needed him. It went on for over a year, until one day his wife caught us in bed at their house. I never lived down the shame. My parents disowned me, made me leave the house. I left school and trained as a nurse.'

'That's all water under the bridge, Helga,' Weissbinder said charitably. 'You must put that behind you. Never think of yourself as wicked for obeying a natural impulse. You are shaking like a leaf. Is that arousal? I think so, I feel you are drenched inside and working against my finger. Admit that you like it.'

'It – it's what you and that woman are doing to me,' she whined. 'It is too much, I can't help it.'

'Neither you should,' Weissbinder said. 'I can guess what Myra's doing to you. What's going on with you, Dex?' he enquired. 'I don't like to think you've been left out of it.'

'I didn't intend to be,' Dex called over Myra's shoulder. He stood with his arms around her, cupping her breasts while she dipped her back and presented her bottom for the full penetration of his prick. Moaning her pleasure through lips clamped to Helga's other nipple, she thrust back as Dex thrust forward. 'I'm fucking Myra slow and easy,' he announced. 'Carry on with your interrogation of Helga. I'm all ears.'

'She has such a perfect rear-end that I cannot resist it,' Weissbinder said suddenly, overcome by its proximity and flawless rounded cheeks. 'It's made for using to the utmost, it would be a crime not to. Has it been thoroughly spanked, young woman? Put to the cock and entered? Buggered? I need to know. Tell me!'

Her answer was mumbled so hesitantly in her embarrassment that she was made to repeat it clearly. 'Both, both!' she shouted, the gyrations of her backside now becoming frenzied. 'Don't make me talk of such things. What will Dr Calvert think?'

'That you've given me an idea,' Dex shouted back. He

withdrew his prick, sliding it up the cleft of Myra's bottom until the inflamed knob paused at the tightly puckered entrance to her back passage. The first press inward parted the crinkled ring, the egg-shaped crown gripped snugly as Myra gasped and eased her cheeks apart to accept the long thick prick in her anus. Going in her to the balls, Dex shunted his length in to the tight tunnel while Myra met each stroke by grinding her bottom back against his belly. She found her face lifted in Helga's hands and a fierce kiss pressed to her mouth. The two women clung together as they climaxed violently, the spasms continuing until they were both drained and barely able to prevent each other from collapsing.

'She came, we both came,' Myra said breathlessly on recovering somewhat, feeling Dex drawing out of her, his hot emission deposited deep inside her arse. 'We all bloody came. My God, that was good. How do you feel now, Helga?' she asked affectionately. 'Dr Weissbinder is right, you've nothing to be ashamed of any more. You're with friends here, all of us admire you for admitting what you are. And for coming like that. On just a finger too! I can't imagine what you'll be like when it's a big prick instead.'

'A start has been made,' Weissbinder announced in his professional voice, sparing Helga's blushes and not preventing her reaching for her clothes. 'It has been quite promising. She did well and will do better.' He leaned back in his wheelchair thoughtfully. 'Helga will learn to reveal all in time, without shame and embarrassment, in our open therapy sessions. She can be an example to the other patients. Now I suggest we prepare ourselves to receive our paying guests who will be the subjects of our research. They should be arriving on board any minute now.'

Chapter Eight

In Camera

'It's not on, it won't do,' Gerald Marsh complained to the attractive receptionist, pushing his way back through the queue of other passengers waiting to be allocated their cabins. She stood smartly uniformed behind the desk of the purser's office in the foyer of the *Aphrodite*, attempting to hide her annoyance behind a smile. Aware of Gerald's eye on her trim figure, she had already concluded there was one of him on every cruise. He silenced her polite request that he wait his turn by interrupting her, saying with an ingratiating smile, 'You cannot be serious about the accommodation I've been given.'

'Sir,' she answered, curbing her aggravation, 'I gave you the correct keys. Your cabin is on the upper deck, designated first-class and with *en suite* bathroom. It's the best there is and I'm most surprised you find it unsuitable.'

'Well, I do,' Gerald insisted. 'Not about the cabin *per se*, but the fact that I'm having to share it.' He gave the girl a knowing grin. 'It could cramp my style, don't you think? A romantic cruise, the tropic moon, an available single man like yours truly.' He added a sly wink which made her groan inwardly as he read from the disc pinned to her lapel. 'What if I wish to entertain a lady, Miss Ellen Jackson, Assistant Purser? It's been known. And here I've been made to share with a Mr Nigel Marsh, who happens to be my own son. What's more, he has a young wife on this same ship and should be with her. That's a foul-up, you must agree.'

'Dr Weissbinder decided where passengers would be accommodated,' Ellen Jackson replied coolly. 'He's the cruise director and has chartered the *Aphrodite* specifically for a research project he's conducting. This is an educational cruise and has been advertised as such. I presume you were aware of that. If you're unsatisfied with your cabin arrangement, you must take it up with him.'

'Rest assured I will,' Gerald promised, turning away surprised that the pretty girl had not been more impressed by his presence. The rakish yachting cap, blazer and white trousers were clothes eminently suitable for a voyage, he considered. He cheered up immediately as he eyed the variety of good-looking females around. There were no end of likely candidates to charm in his opinion and, as for this guy Weissbinder, he'd personally straighten him out. The name seemed vaguely familiar and he wondered where he'd heard of it. A cabin of his own was a top priority considering what he had in mind. Apart from the bevy of female passengers, there were his plans for all three comely Craigs for starters – singly, or together in a gleesome threesome, he fondly imagined the thrilling scene.

'One can almost read his lustful mind,' Weissbinder said to Dex Calvert, monitoring the scene at the purser's desk on a screen in the control room. 'Such arrogance and conceit – typical behaviour of such a type. As Myra has reported, he thinks himself God's gift to women. Oh, but we'll have fun with him. It's pay-back time for the Craig ladies who have had to suffer his insolence.'

'Just what have you in mind?' Dex asked, thinking that the doctor's jealous streak was showing. Gerald, he thought, although flamboyant, was not that different in his outlook from himself. 'Going to get the business, is he?'

'Mr Macho Marsh will be taught a lesson on how to respect the opposite sex,' Weissbinder said, unable to disguise the venom in his voice. 'I have in mind a short sharp shock to teach him to regard women not merely as objects of his licentious desires. My putting him in a cabin with his son was

82

deliberate, a ploy intended to cramp his style. Together with his weak-kneed boy, Nigel, we have a unique opportunity to counsel them accordingly. To knock the cockiness out of the father and discover what makes his son tick. You, Dr Calvert, will aid and abet me without question in this research. I can assure you those two will end this cruise different men.'

'Nice touch,' Dex thought he'd better say. 'So to cut Marsh down to size from day one, you put the Craig sisters in a cabin together and their mother in one on her own. I've spoken to them and there's no complaints about that so far. The married girl called Dorothy doesn't seem to object to not being with her husband. From what we know of their marriage, it's no wonder.'

'I'm giving the boy a chance,' Weissbinder said cynically. 'I want to learn if absence from her bed will make him approach her for sex. Let's see if he really isn't interested or finds it too challenging. Possibly he's afraid of failure with a woman, among other possible permutations.'

'He must be impotent or gay not to want to fuck that lovely young wife of his hard and often,' Dex declared. 'I saw her arrive. Sweet face, burnished chestnut hair, great body. Big boobs too, a fine tight ass and amply rounded thighs. As she came on board I couldn't help thinking there'd be a sweet little quim tucked in between those long shapely legs, rubbing together nicely. I felt like falling on my knees and kissing her ass.'

'Hardly a professional medical man's description of the female anatomy,' Weissbinder reprimanded, 'but I have to agree with your assessment.'

'All the Craig women are worthy. I can sympathise with Gerald Marsh having a letch for them,' Dex said. 'The young blonde Amanda is a perfect example of youthful beauty. She's got a great pair of tits. The mother is a superb specimen of ripe femininity, maturely attractive, bound to be sought after.'

'And all of them no-go areas for Marsh,' Weissbinder warned. 'Shall we allow ourselves to see how they are settling in? It's all part of our research, of course.'

'Of course,' Dex agreed, hiding his grin at the devious character of his boss. 'The hidden cameras and mikes in the cabins will pay dividends.' He watched as Weissbinder touched a button on the arm of his wheelchair. 'The things we do to further knowledge and scientific research. It's a tough job but I guess it must be done.'

'I believe you're being facetious. It does not become you, Dr Calvert,' Weissbinder said, frowning. 'Believe in the importance of our work or we can terminate your employment now, before we sail. Of course, being under contract, I should sue you for breach of that agreement you signed. We do not use the closed-circuit system to pry, merely to gain valuable insights into those we seek to help.'

'Sure, and with no chance of our clandestine viewing being uncovered,' Dex said. 'Not with the scanners concealed in any one of the air-conditioning ducts over their heads.' Before them the crowded scene at the purser's reception desk faded on screen to be replaced by Dorothy and Manda busily unpacking in their shared cabin. In the early afternoon heat both were dressed simply in their bras and tiny briefs, putting clothes into a wide built-in wardrobe. Giggly Manda was as happy as a schoolgirl on holiday while Dorothy looked serious.

'I've left a little something for them to find,' Weissbinder said. 'Just to get them in the right frame of mind. I had Myra leave an interesting item or two in the top drawer of their dressing table. We've done the same for Nigel in his bedside cabinet. It will be instructive to note their reactions on discovering what they'll assume was left by the previous occupants of the cabins. Meantime,' he continued, his hand poised over the remote control panel on the arm of his wheelchair, 'shall we see how their mother is doing? A particularly fine woman this Ailsa Craig. Smart, attractive, truly a good sexual prospect wasted unless we use our professional talents to overcome her reticence.'

'I'd prefer you'd keep the camera on the daughters for now,' Dex suggested. 'What an unusually gorgeous pair, and I don't just mean their exceptional tits. I'd say Amanda is a go-er, she looks a sexy little piece. She slept with Myra, so is undoubtedly bi. Dorothy is obviously a different type, or appears to be. Myra claims she's had her too. Can't we stay with them until they discover whatever you've left in their dressing table?'

'It will be recorded,' Weissbinder said, and on the screen appeared Ailsa in a satin dressing-robe unpacking a suitcase laid on her bed. The German nurse, Helga, entered the control room and touched Weissbinder's shoulder lightly to divert his attention from the viewing. 'What is it, Dietrich?' he asked snappily. 'Can't you see we are engaged in research?'

'And such a lovely woman,' Helga said, unable to contain her spontaneous admiration. '*Wunderbar*. I mean she looks very nice.'

'Fancy her, do you, Helga?' Dex asked teasingly. 'She's a bit of all right, sure enough. With your newly acquired liberal outlook, how would you like to get that lady on the massage table for a rub-down? I dare say you would.'

'The first group of patients is assembling in the lecture hall for your opening talk, Herr Doktor,' she reported to Weissbinder, blushing deeply as she ignored Dex's observation. 'Single males and females as instructed. Do you wish me to wheel you there? I left Mrs Starr to welcome them. Each person was given the questionnaire you want them to complete.'

'Is that the one that asks for a complete description of their sexual history?' said Dex.

'Indeed. Let's hope for some enlightening reading,' Weissbinder said. 'No doubt there will be, for people love to confess their indiscretions when they have been given permission to do so. Good juicy revelations form an important and popular page-filler in my published works.'

'And help sell them like crazy,' Dex said. 'The juicier the better.'

'People like to be informed,' Weissbinder insisted. 'It's like opening a window on the world and letting fresh air in, sweeping away taboos. If I receive a little money, that is merely my entitlement. I believe you resent that.'

'Sure, I do,' Dex grinned. 'I'm green with envy at your formula for giving the punters what they want and getting rich. Helga is waiting, Doc. She said your first group of paying patients awaits the master.'

'Myra knows the routine and will keep things rolling until I get there,' Weissbinder said, ignoring the jibes. 'Join her, Helga. That nurse's white uniform adds a medical touch to the proceedings and makes them feel more comfortable. Instruct Myra to stick an instructional video on the big screen – one that she's in. That'll warm them up and show there's no shame in a game anyone with the right attitude can learn to play. Dr Calvert will accompany me to the lecture hall later. I need to continue my observation of this particular female patient.'

'And I can't say I blame you,' Dex had to agree. Their view was of Ailsa closing the empty suitcase as she completed unpacking, the thin material of her robe moulded to her superb figure. She placed the suitcase in the bottom of a wardrobe, the robe parting to the waist and revealing the tantalising sight of her breasts swinging forward as she leaned over. Straightening up, she paused before the long mirror as she closed the wardrobe door.

'How incredibly voluptuous she is.' Weissbinder remarked in admiration, noting the shapely bulge of her breasts and the way the ivory-coloured satin clung to her splendidly formed buttock cheeks. 'What do you think, Dr Calvert?'

'Eminently fuckable and I hope to get the chance,' Dex said. 'It would not be hard to throw a little fuck in that lady's direction. To help her overcome her neurosis regarding sexual matters, of course. That's the number one priority.'

'Again, I do not appreciate your somewhat flippant way of discussing serious objectives,' Weissbinder said, 'but something you said jokingly to Helga may well be of help in Mrs Craig's case. You mentioned how Helga might enjoy having Mrs Craig on her massage table. We must try to arrange that. It would be a start.'

'Yeah, and who knows how it might turn out,' Dex agreed. 'If Helga is that way inclined, as we suspect, and Mrs Craig finds the massage relaxing enough not to complain about some added treatment, that would show the lady's not dead from the neck down.'

'We would tape it, of course, which could prove useful,' Weissbinder said calculatingly. Both men's attention returned to the screen as Ailsa let the robe slide from her shoulders and fall to the carpeted floor. 'I think Helga would find it hard to resist what we see, don't you agree?' Dex was asked.

'It was well worth signing on your team for this trip just to get a load of Mrs Craig,' he said, ogling the naked figure on the screen. 'Those milk-white tits are awesome, standing out full and firm with nipples like thumbs. Look at the sweep of that back, how it curves out to such a magnificent ass.'

'So I see,' Weissbinder said, his attention held. 'Now she's turning around before the mirror. What splendid thighs. Observe the pronounced *mons*, a pubic mound adorned with a veritable forest. Shapely breasts, shapely limbs, she's got the complete set. Ah, she's peering into the mirror to reassure herself of what we've already confirmed. She's a mature beauty just made to receive satisfaction. It's our duty to awaken her sexuality. Note how she's studying herself, this could be most enlightening.'

Ailsa, facing her reflection, hesitantly brought up both hands to clasp each of her weighty breasts. She squeezed them gently as if to test their mass and firmness, lifting and holding them out towards the mirror as she considered their shapely contours. After a thoughtful pause, as if reluctant to allow herself the liberty, she touched and then pulled out her nipples from each breast, plucking and tweaking them between thumbs and forefingers. Her ivory-white breasts became swollen and suffused with a pink radiation, the nipples thickening with arousal.

Weissbinder and Dex exchanged knowing glances as her right hand sidled down over the smooth belly to a conspicuously curvaceous bulge nestled between her thighs. Both men willed her on silently as she remained still before the mirrored image of herself. Tentatively, again as if having to force herself, the momentary pause ended with her fingers stroking the outer lips projecting from their surrounding bush of soft hair.

'Faced with her reflection she can't resist herself,' Weiss-binder stated in his know-all tones. 'Entirely symptomatic of the Narcissus theorem, of course. You concur, Dr Calvert?'

'Who cares?' Dex said irreverently. 'It makes marvellous viewing. Maybe she just feels horny right now and fancies a wank. Who needs a label for what she's doing? Oh, no! She's had second thoughts, and I thought we'd got lucky.'

Ailsa suddenly drew herself up straight and turned quickly from the mirror. 'Her guilt has proved stronger,' Weissbinder said, 'but the urge is still there being repressed. See, she goes determinedly to the bathroom, to take a cold shower, no doubt. Fascinating case, Dr Calvert. Mrs Craig patently needs our help.' His fingers pressed several of the buttons on the remote control of his wheelchair. 'We'll tape her in case she has a change of mind while in the bathroom. Meantime we'll return to see how her daughters are faring.'

The scene in Ailsa's cabin faded as she entered the bath-room, giving a final shot of her bouncy buttock cheeks. Her image on the screen was replaced by Manda and Dorothy sitting together on one of the single beds, heads close together as they studied a magazine. Others of the same kind lay strewn on the floor along with a selection of vibrators and one large realistic-looking dildo complete with straps.

'You don't go in for half-measures, do you?' Dex had to smile at Weissbinder's artfulness. 'Seems they've found the surprise items you left for them, a treasure trove for impressionable girls. I take it that's a porno magazine they're perusing.'

'The very best, chosen by myself for the especially lewd contents,' Weissbinder confirmed. 'I shocked myself pick-ing them. It would seem the Craig girls are interested in their find.'

'Manda certainly is,' Dex said, as she pointed out some-thing on the page before her, going into a fit of giggles while

Dorothy sat stony-faced. Manda dropped the magazine from her lap, picking up the lifelike dildo and striding about the cabin with it held between her thighs, tilted before her like an erect cock as if copying what she had seen in the magazine.

'You really are beyond words,' her sister complained, red in the face. Further words of protest were silenced as both girls froze. A single hasty knock at their door was followed by Gerald walking in on them.

'Caught in the act,' Dex said as Weissbinder growled his annoyance at the interruption. The sisters were caught in a momentary panic. Both were still in their bras and briefs with the incriminating magazines and sex-toys strewn around their feet. 'This will teach them rule numero uno – lock the door. It could have been worse, it could have been their mother. Take a look at Gerald, beaming like he's just woke up in heaven.'

'Not for long though,' Weissbinder noted with satisfaction as the girls' alarm turned to anger. 'How dare you?' they shouted, bundling him backwards with Manda striking him over the head with the plastic imitation penis. As the door was slammed behind him, Gerald's ignominious rejection was complete.

'They certainly saw him off,' said Dex. 'Poor Marsh, with the programme you've got mapped out for reforming his character, this just isn't going to be his cruise. With all this excitement, haven't you forgotten a little something? Shouldn't you get along to the lecture hall? Your public awaits.'

'Keep them waiting, it adds to the mystique,' Weissbinder answered, unwilling to admit he'd forgotten. 'Let's see how they're doing without us.' He brought up the scene in the lecture hall, the hidden camera sweeping over an audience struck dumb in their seats as they watched the action on a wall-sized screen. A touch on the remote control moved the image to the screen itself with Myra and Helga standing either side of it. The video showed two naked females lying among heaped cushions on the floor beside a fireplace, busy attending to an equally naked male lying between them. An

Adonis of a black stud, he was being fed the nipples of one big-breasted woman while at his crotch the other woman – clearly recognisable as Myra – was engaged in avidly sucking a monstrously thick prick.

'You've never met Orville,' Weissbinder remarked, referring to the black man being serviced at both ends. 'He's tied up making a porno flick in the States at present, and I do mean tied up, for it's one of my scripts and being filmed by my own movie company. When he's through filming he'll fly out to join us at one of the islands we're calling at. It will give you a break. He'll take over some of your surrogate duties so you can help me out in the therapy sessions. Orville's very popular. Even the most repressed lady patients get around to asking for him, which proves the efficacy of my treatment. Often the husband watches.'

'Obviously it's nothing to do with these shy ladies wanting to try out a big black dick,' Dex said, hoping he sounded sincere. 'Myra is obviously enjoying it. It's getting near the end of the tape, as I recall. The big-titted one sits on Orville's face while Myra impales herself on his monster cock and rides it like fury. About ten minutes to run, I calculate. You should be making tracks. Your audience look ready to hang on to your pearls of wisdom.'

'Hardly how I would have expressed it, Dr Calvert,' Weissbinder said with dignity. 'I don't appreciate your light-hearted approach. Remember, I may well include your name as a collaborator in the published results of my survey. It could enhance your reputation as an authority on sexuality. Perhaps you would do well to remember that.'

Before them the video ran its course in the silent lecture hall, the watchers rooted to their seats. The spreadeagled black male was engaged in thoroughly tonguing the hair-surrounded cleft poised over his face, Myra was meanwhile grinding herself down on the length of rigid flesh embedded up her cunt. The breasts of both women bobbed and bounced with the agitation of their movements, their mouths locked in a frenzied open-mouthed kiss. The video ended with all three jerking and coming in a tangle of perspiring bodies. They rolled apart only to continue kissing and fondling to demonstrate that a climax should not bring all show of affection to a halt.

'Let's go,' Weissbinder announced, gratified by the burst of applause as the hall lights came up. 'We'll join them in a receptive frame of mind. You may note for future reference how my words will have them worshipping at my feet. It's one of my gifts.'

Chapter Nine

Woman in Need

'Ladies and gentlemen, the film you have just seen was not intended to shock or disgust you,' said Weissbinder to the audience, after the enthusiastic applause for his arrival had at last faded. 'While here you'll learn to appreciate there is nothing shocking or disgusting about consenting adults being sexually active, free from guilt and inhibition. Those of you before me who suffer from such handicaps, take heart. You have nothing to lose but your baseless frustration. Under my tried and tested guidance, you will no longer be prevented from engaging in and knowing the joy of satisfying sex. As proof of this, I invite you to look upon Mrs Myra Starr.'

He indicated Myra who stepped forward to receive an ovation before returning behind Weissbinder's chair. 'You will of course recognise Myra as one of the participants in the instructional video you have just seen. Would you believe,' he continued, allowing a note of pride to creep into his voice, 'would you believe that Myra, now a valued member of my team of surrogates and counsellors, first came to me as a mixed-up and unhappy lady in fear of men and all types of sexual contact? She was terminally depressed, almost suicidal – much worse than any of you, I venture to say. You see before you the end result of her treatment by the Weissbinder method. She is now a happy, free-thinking and free-loving woman with a zest for life, and a natural enjoyment of a full and healthy attitude towards giving and receiving sexual pleasure.' He allowed himself a smile. 'As you all have just witnessed.'

He raised a hand to halt a further burst of applause. 'During the next two weeks of the cruise all of you will be encouraged to have erotic thoughts and yield to your impulses without shame. You will be able to act upon those natural urges, with your partners or with any of the experienced sexual surrogates who form an important part of my team.'

Dex felt a hand slide around his waist to give his prick a suggestive squeeze. 'I know all this spiel by heart,' Myra whispered in his ear. 'He drones on for an hour. Let's get out of here and fuck.'

'No can do,' Dex said sadly. 'I'm expected to take part as his back-up shrink in a question-and-answer session. If you want to see something interesting about your friends the Craigs, look at the tape in the control room. I'll catch up with you later.'

'If I can wait that long,' Myra said, glancing sideways to see Helga watching them suspiciously. 'There's someone wanting to take over from me, by the way,' she added mischievously, taking Helga's hand and placing it on the tented front of Dex's jeans. 'The girl's stuck on you, why not be kind and give her one sometime? I'm off, see you later.'

Weissbinder did not notice Myra leaving the hall by a side door. But someone else had noticed her departure. Out on the sunlit deck she was approached by Gerald Marsh, grinning like a wolf.

'So you caught the film but couldn't stand the master's sermon?' she said. 'I suppose it would be wasted on you anyway, being a well-known lecher and arse-bandit from way back. Or am I doing you an injustice? I think you're really much worse than that.'

'Flattery will get you nowhere, Starr,' Gerald said easily, 'but it's good to know you're on this ship. Sounds like my kind of cruise. Is that Weissbinder character for real? I'd like his job. He's just a salacious old wanker. I wised up to his phoney pseudomedical claptrap about helping the sexually afflicted get their oats. He's just a con artist.'

'Takes one to know one,' Myra answered levelly. 'He could

buy and sell you, and I happen to know that already you're not his favourite person. A word of warning, Gerald – cool it on this cruise. You look quite dapper in that nautical get-up, by the way. Does it come off?'

'In about three seconds flat,' he said affably. 'For you, even in two. I don't suppose a jump is out of the question?'

'I thought you'd never ask,' Myra replied. 'Count this as a gesture of kindness, for you'll be under surveillance this whole trip. The Herr Doktor thinks you are oversexed, a menace to women, and an all-round stinker.'

'He's just being kind,' Gerald said, unperturbed. 'Where's your cabin? I can't use mine, my dopey son Nigel is in there. Shall we proceed?'

Walking together along the deck they saw Dorothy leaning on the ship's rail, staring as if at nothing, lost in thought, unmindful of the dockside activity before her. 'Penny for your thoughts, Dorothy,' Myra said, touching her arm to make her turn wide-eyed. 'Why so glum? We're on a cruise, remember? We're going to have fun. You know what that is?' She smiled to put her at ease. 'Where's your husband?'

'I haven't seen him,' Dorothy said sadly. 'I'm sure he's avoiding me. He didn't want to come on this cruise at all. And my sister Amanda is, is—'

'Playing with your collection of sex toys,' Gerald finished for her. 'Quite an interesting selection it was, as far as I could see. Who brought them on board? You or Amanda?'

'Those disgusting things were left there,' Dorothy stated hotly. 'Seeing them upset me, if you want to know. And you are a pig, a beast, and no gentleman.'

'Goodness, I've never been so insulted,' Gerald joked.

'You should get out more,' Myra suggested, taking Dorothy's arm. 'Come to my cabin, love, and tell me all about your troubles. It's company you need and a brandy to buck you up.'

'Brandy works wonders on Dorothy,' Gerald said. 'I should know. Count me in, I need company.'

'You're out of luck this time, Gerald,' Myra told him,

shutting her cabin door in his face as they reached it. 'This is between girls for now.' She opened the door slightly after closing it, making sure that Dorothy was out of earshot. 'For now,' she whispered. 'Give me long enough to soften her up and walk in on us. By then I'm sure we could use you. Get my drift?'

'Loud and clear,' Gerald said delightedly. 'What a gem you are. Devious, rotten to the core, a scheming bitch – everything I admire in a woman. I wasn't joking about the brandy either. Where Dorothy's concerned, it's undressing liquid. Go for it, Starr, I shall arrive like the Fifth Cavalry later, weapon cocked.'

Myra shut the door on him and poured Dorothy a brandy. 'Drink this, it will cheer you up,' Myra said. 'We can't have such a pretty girl with that long face.' She dabbed at Dorothy's eyes with her handkerchief. 'And real tears too, my goodness. Is life so terrible for you? Tell Myra all about it, dear.' She waited until Dorothy had sipped half the spirit. 'What really is the matter?'

'I'm – I'm – so mixed up inside,' Dorothy said. 'The feelings I get, I'm ashamed to admit. I know Nigel has never – never been a proper husband or lover to me, and I've felt frustration, but now it seems it's all I think about.'

'Sex?' Myra queried, sounding understanding. 'Why shouldn't you think about it, a healthy young woman like you? When you said the pornographic material in your room upset you, don't you really mean it aroused you?' She put an arm around Dorothy, hugging her affectionately. 'Silly you, it's supposed to arouse. Why be ashamed of a natural response? Now, no more tears.' She turned Dorothy's face to hers and kissed her lightly on the mouth. 'I'm going to make love to you. No argument, you want it too.'

'No, no. What are you doing?' Dorothy said anxiously as Myra reached behind to unzip her dress and draw it from her shoulders. '*Please*. Why are you doing this?'

'To get you undressed, of course,' Myra said calmly. 'I shall undress too, it's nicer that way.' She fended off Dorothy's arms as she tried to resist. 'Do you want me to be strict with you?' she warned. 'You want it and that's all there is about it.' She drew off the dress and fluttered it aside. 'I really believe all this pretence about not being that kind of girl arouses you more. Kiss me, you adorable shy creature. For goodness sake let yourself go as you've done with me in the past. Was that so terrible or shameful?'

She crushed her mouth to Dorothy's, who uttered an anguished sigh before responding, accepting Myra's long tongue and rolling lips, unable to resist. She was undressed completely before she knew it, Myra's hands skilfully un-hooking her bra, drawing off her remaining garments and pressing fervent kisses to every naked inch of flesh. Dorothy was lowered to the bed, grasping her breasts as if in an agony of ecstasy, her knees bent and widely parted in an unconditional invitation, her palpitating cunt laid bare to Myra's predatory eyes as she threw off her clothes beside the bed.

Dorothy held up her arms to receive Myra, her eyes lus-trous, welcoming her as she fell across her. Breast to breast, belly to belly, Myra's crotch fitted snugly into Dorothy's cradled thighs, pubic mounds and outer sex lips grinding together. 'Yes – yesss,' Dorothy moaned. 'Love me, love me, do things I like. Suck my nipples, rub into me harder, it's heaven. *Ohhh-ahh*, I want to make this lovely feeling last before I come. Kiss me again, kiss my breasts, talk to me, tell me things, dirty things if you like—'

'Of course, of course,' Myra soothed her, her buttock muscles clenching as she thrust against Dorothy. 'What a lovely body you have, your breasts like cushions against mine. You're so aroused your nipples stick into me. You really like it, don't you? Like me rubbing my cunt against yours. Don't you wish there was a prick up you, a real man's prick?'

'Yes, I do,' Dorothy moaned, pushing back against Myra, her legs curled around the other woman's waist, hands grip-ping the plump moons to haul them in harder as Myra ground their pubic mounds together. 'I do like a prick up me, it feels so good I think about it all the time.'

'And what did Gerald mean when he said brandy works wonders with you?' Myra asked beguilingly. 'Did he give you brandy to have his way with you?' She pressed a flurry of kisses to Dorothy's eyes and mouth while increasing the pace of her grinding motions against the girl's cunt.

'He fucked me. I let him fuck me and I wanted him to,' Dorothy groaned, working her hips. 'It was good, he made me come and come.'

'And would you let him fuck you if he were here now?' Myra said. 'The way you feel this moment, could you refuse him?'

'No, I couldn't,' Dorothy admitted. 'It isn't right but my feelings get the better of me. I can't say no, I think I'd let anyone fuck me.'

'Well, I'm not just anyone, but I'm here ready and willing,' Dorothy heard Gerald say as he crossed from the cabin door. As the girl sat up in alarm, Myra drew her back down on the bed, holding her there, kissing her mouth and breasts fiercely. 'How charming,' he said, throwing off his clothes. 'Two women in a loving embrace, naked and unashamed.' Divested of his last shred of clothing, he crossed to stand before their feet at the foot of the bed, looking down on Myra's back and buttocks as she lay on top of Dorothy. 'The only thing missing is one of these,' he added, his fist gripping the stem of a straining prick.

'Don't!' Myra warned Dorothy as she was about to protest. 'You've just admitted you'd let him fuck you, he's fucked you before. And now he's going to fuck us both, aren't you, Gerald?'

'The thought had crossed my mind,' he admitted. 'How can I resist looking at the pair of you? Don't wake me up if this is a dream.'

As he fell on his knees beside the bed, Myra lifted her bottom, as shiny and round as an apple, and parted her thighs. She groaned as Gerald's tongue lapped at her source, the tip seeking out the hard nub of her clitty. Then he lowered his face between her thighs, seeking out the crisp auburn bush of Dorothy's cunt. He kissed the pussy mouth passionately, then probed it deeply, getting the response he desired, a momentary stiffening of her body before she began working her thighs to meet his inward thrusts. Satisfied he had taken her over the edge, he withdrew and stood behind Myra's plump arse, separating the cheeks prior to easing the plum-head of his prick a tantalising inch or two into the gaping purse of her cunt. He stood still, hands forcing wide her cheeks, awaiting her reaction.

It came immediately as Myra thrust her bottom against his belly, swallowing his swollen length to the balls. In her agitation to feel it shunting up and down, convulsions swept violently through her frame. Her fully plugged sex bore down upon Dorothy's cunt and all three bodies writhed and jerked in unison. Crying out that she was *there*, her spasms wild as the climax shook her bodily, Myra rolled aside. Still quivering with delight, she urged Gerald on. 'Now fuck her. Let me see you fuck her, Gerald. Give her what she wants.'

In no need of encouragement, Gerald dexterously thrust his glistening prick into Dorothy's receptive cunt channel. Shivering and bucking to his thrusts, Dorothy tilted her pelvis to take all of him on his forward lunges, her legs entwined around his waist, hands hauling on his flanks to draw him closer. 'Yes, yes,' she muttered fiercely. 'Do me – I don't care. Let her watch us. Fuck me all you want. I love it, love it.'

Raging with lust, her breath came in a series of *ugh, ugh, ughs*, as she thrashed out of control under the effect of the big prick poking her cunt so vigorously. Her climax was announced with a long shuddering cry of joy and even as it faded she continued to writhe against Gerald as wildly as ever as if once was not enough. He in turn exploded, the flurry of his heaving flanks gradually decreasing as he shot the last spurts of his hot emission into her. Then he disengaged from her arms and rolled aside next to Myra, exhausted.

'We have here,' he said at last, 'a veritable fucking machine. I fancy Dorothy would fuck all day and all night. I had to struggle to get off her. What a ball-breaker.'

'He's paying you a compliment, Dorothy,' Myra told her. 'You really do go at it. You can hardly say now that it's not your thing, can you?'

'I believe you both contrived to get me in here – to do to me what you did,' Dorothy said. She got off the bed to retrieve her clothes. 'You know my weakness and took advantage. I'm ashamed of myself for letting you.'

'What nonsense,' Myra said. 'You just enjoyed a harmless romp so don't make out that you'll burn in hell for it. The only unnatural sexual behaviour, my dear, is none at all. Get that through your head.'

'Sure,' Gerald agreed. 'Sex is a beautiful thing between two people, between three or more it's fantastic.' He sat up on the bed watching his daughter-in-law dressing. 'You've got many wonderful years of fornicating to look forward to,' he told her kindly. 'Just lie back and enjoy it.'

After Dorothy and Gerald's departure, Myra showered, dressed and went to the control room to find Dex. He was running the tape of Ailsa sitting before her dressing table adding a little make-up to her pretty face. She wore a dress and a light jacket, her hair was immaculately brushed into a neat fringe. 'I fancy her,' Myra said meaningfully. 'Always have. Good-looking, isn't she? Maybe on this trip I'll get lucky.'

'That's what we're here for, to satisfy the customers,' Dex said, unbuckling his belt. 'What kept you? I've been sitting here waiting for that fuck you promised. Did something come up?'

'You could say that,' Myra agreed, thinking of Gerald's prick. 'Where do you intend to have me, the floor?'

'In the master's chair,' Dex said, pushing down his jeans and indicating Weissbinder's empty wheelchair. 'This one's on him.'

'Where is he?' Myra asked, starting to undress. 'I always thought he came with his arse glued to that chair, sitting there with all his electronic gizmos like the captain of the Starship Enterprise.'

'Helga's giving him a rub-down, or a rub-up,' Dex said,

'I'm not sure which. I paused outside her massage parlour on my way here and could plainly hear the slapping of flesh. I wondered if he goes in for bottom smacking. Anyway, let's put his chair to use.' He sat back in it with his erection straining upright as Myra finished undressing. She went on her knees before him, one hand cupping his balls and the other grasping the thick stem of his prick as she covered it with her mouth.

'That's good,' he acknowledged, 'but you won't see the tape from down there. I'm rewinding it.'

Myra looked up and saw on the screen Gerald's ejection from Dorothy and Manda's cabin. Her breasts jiggled as she laughed at his undignified exit. 'You've got to give him full marks for effort. After that he came along to Weissbinder's lecture. The old man didn't fool him. He knows he's ripping off the frustrated who consider him their sex saviour and guru. What about that line he came out with about me being one of his patients? I was horny long before I'd ever heard of the Weissbinder method.'

'It's the old faith-healer's con of telling a stooge to throw away his crutches,' Dex laughed. 'We'll have to be up early to catch Weissbinder out, and make this trip worthwhile for us.' A touch on the wheelchair's console switched the scene to Ailsa's cabin at the moment she'd shed her robe to stand majestically naked. Myra's laughter died in her throat, her attention immediately caught by the ripeness of the female beauty revealed on the banks of screens before her. 'Your honest opinion now,' she heard Dex say, 'is she or is she not a hell of a sexy woman?'

'My God,' Myra muttered, watching Ailsa fondling her breasts and touching up her cunt before the long mirror. 'What wouldn't I give to do that to her. You can see she wants to give herself a thrill, yet stops herself. Fuck me now, Dex, I'm so aroused.'

'The best is yet to come,' Dex assured her as she climbed onto his lap, her back to his chest and legs parted to hang outside his. 'She broke off playing with herself to enter the bathroom, so the camera followed her,' Dex went on.

101

'It was simply swivelled around by Weissbinder from this chair, continuing to video from an air-duct in the bathroom set opposite to the one in the cabin. So now we see the delectable Mrs Craig taking a shower. Soaping her lovely big tits rather more lingeringly than necessary, wouldn't you agree? Playing with them while all nice and sudsy, pinching her swollen nipples too, naughty woman. This time she'll go all the way.'

'This is torture,' Ailsa moaned, pulling Dex's rampant prick to the parted lips of her cunt. 'I'll have that woman yet,' she vowed, squirming down to impale herself fully on the cylindrical rod of rigid flesh, then jogging on it and taking Dex's hands to grasp her bobbing tits while her eyes were glued to the screen. 'Fuck it into me,' she ordered. 'If I can't have her, I'll have you. Look at the bitch, damn her, I should be doing that. She's fingering herself.'

On the screen, while Dex worked his hips and Myra thrust her bottom down on the thick stalk, Ailsa leant back against the tiled shower wall, her thrust-out breasts wobbling in the spray while her wrist worked energetically in her self-pleasuring. With eyes closed, head thrown back, feet planted firmly apart, her viewers knew she was lost to all but the ecstasy being created by her hand. Her opened mouth, stretched neck, the shudders rippling from her shoulders to her crotch told of the approaching climax.

'No!' cried Myra in disappointment, seeing Ailsa's hand move away from between her legs. 'She can't – not at that stage. A few more seconds and she'd have made herself come storming.' In her amazement at Ailsa's unaccountable halt while on the brink, she remained still over Dex, bolt upright with the long stalk inside up to her belly. 'How could she?'

'Wait and see,' Dex told her. They saw Ailsa reach for the shower head and aim its spray directly on to her cunt. Her hips and pelvis immediately resumed squirming and jerking. She leaned farther back against the tiles with just her shoulders in contact, pelvis thrust forward and feet splayed as she held open the lips of her cunt with her free hand. The distended nub of her clitoris was fully exposed between her spread fingers and she held the shower head close to it to get the full force of the needle-like spray.

'The horny slut. So much for being the prim and proper schoolmarm,' Myra said enviously, watching Ailsa targeting the jets of water directly on the supersensitive clitty. 'I've never tried that one myself. Look at her go now.'

With mouth agape, uttering abandoned cries as she continued playing the needles of spray on her clitoris, Ailsa brought herself off in a series of climaxes that shook her whole frame and made her breasts bounce wildly. Myra resumed her frantic jerking over Dex, grinding her bottom against the prick lodged up her as he matched each downward thrust with an upward heave, her tits held tight in his hands to give him leverage. On screen Ailsa gave a final drawn-out groan and slid down the tiled wall, ending up in a squatting position, drained and momentarily stupified.

In time with Ailsa's frenzied climax, Myra jerked in her own final spasms as Dex shot his load into her. 'Four or five, I'd say,' she said, getting off his lap on recovering and in answer to his asking how many times she had come. 'Who's counting? They were all good. Watching Ailsa was fantastic. Just look at her.'

'She's fucked to a frazzle,' Dex observed, 'but she's making the effort to recover. No doubt she's wondering what hit her.' Together they watched the screen as Ailsa roused herself in a daze and reached for a towel. The tape followed her as she left the bathroom and fell across her bed. The towel dropped to the floor, and she lay naked on her back, her magnificent breasts splayed and legs parted to reveal a hair-surrounded cleft still gaping puffily. 'Now there's a sight,' Dex said admiringly. 'She must have given herself the mother and father of all comes.'

'That wasn't the first time she's used a shower spray to bring herself off, you can bet your life,' Myra said maliciously. 'And all the time the bitch pretends that sex doesn't figure in her life.'

'You're only piqued because you didn't make out with her,' Dex grinned. 'In my professional opinion you have the hots to get into that lady's panties. Join the club.' He held out his hand to her. 'Shake on a little side-bet. Fifty dollars. Who'll be the first to have her.'

'You have a wager,' Myra agreed, accepting his grip. 'Ailsa doesn't know it, but her luck has changed. With what we know about her secret nature, she should welcome outside help. Mine, of course. Whatever makes you think you can win, buster?'

'I come armed with a superior weapon,' Dex told her glibly. 'Who should know better, you've just been squatting on it. And what have you to offer her – the head of a shower spray?'

'The thought had occurred,' Myra said, 'with myself directing the jets of water. There are many other things that are possible between two women. Tongue, fingers, you name it, including a certain realistic strap-on dildo I keep in reserve. She's mine. You haven't a prayer once I start on her.'

'I like a challenge,' Dex claimed, pulling on his jeans. 'This is proving one hell of a cruise and we haven't even set sail yet. Tell you what, since you are so confident, let's make it a hundred bucks to see who bags all three Craig females first.'

'That would hardly be fair,' Myra smiled. 'I'm way ahead of you. I've had both daughters already. Let's just settle for their mother. I take it there are no holds barred and dirty tricks are permissible?'

'I wouldn't have it any other way,' Dex agreed readily, stopping the tape and running it back. 'It's a crime to take your money. You've got as much chance as a one-legged guy in an ass-kicking contest.'

'Keep the bet at a hundred dollars,' Myra said confidently. 'And never under-estimate a sexed-up woman.'

Chapter Ten

In the Swim

'We're at sea, Dorothy,' Manda said excitedly, shaking her sister awake. 'Come on, sleepyhead, I've been out on deck exploring and it's a lovely day. Some early birds are already about and there's a swimming pool at the stern of the ship. Let's get in our bikinis and have a dip before breakfast.'

Dorothy looked up bemused, roused from a deep sleep. The first thought that entered her mind was of her inexcusable lapse of the previous day in allowing both Myra and Gerald to make free with her body. 'Please,' she mumbled, 'give me a chance to wake up at least. Must you be so bouncy this early in the morning.' She sat up, stretching her arms in a long yawn, reluctantly admitting to herself that such a restful sleep was a benefit of retiring sexually satisfied. But at what price, she reminded herself. Fancy giving in to such a depraved pair of wantons so easily!

'How your big boobs stick out when you do that,' Manda said as her sister stretched, her breasts moulding their firmly rounded contours against her nightgown. 'I don't know why you insist on wearing a nightie. It's so nice and sexy to sleep in just your skin. I always will – especially when I'm married. I bet you never get into bed with Nigel in the buff. What does *he* wear – flannelette pyjamas?'

'Actually he does in winter,' Dorothy said angrily, deciding to offload the major share of the blame for her promiscuous behaviour on the neglectful Nigel's shoulders. 'If he were a real husband, he'd be here beside me and I wouldn't have to put up with your misplaced exuberance. He ought to wake me up with a kiss and a cuddle. Is that too much to ask? I've never had that and now I'm discovering I'm the kind of wife who wants more.'

'More than a kiss and a cuddle, I bet,' Manda giggled. 'You could always do it yourself if you feel that way, sis. I already have, when I woke up feeling horny. I looked at those magazines again and tried out one of the vibrators. It was great. I fairly made the bed rattle,' her wicked giggle continued. 'You were dead to the world. Fucked out.'

'What do you mean?' Dorothy asked, cringing. 'Why did you say that?'

'It's just an expression, isn't it?' Manda laughed. 'You're so touchy. I bet you wish you had been fucked this morning, going on about Nigel not giving it to you. At least you've been fucked by his father, which is more than I can say. It looks like I'm stuck with being a virgin.'

'I doubt that,' Dorothy said, sliding her feet to the floor. 'You really are the limit but it seems *I'm* stuck with you. What do you want me do?'

'Cheer up for starters,' Manda said, hugging her. 'Then let's go and swim and sunbathe and check out the available males. What do you say?'

'After I shower and see what they serve for breakfast,' Dorothy said. 'I'm starving. It's quite exciting being on a cruise, isn't it?'

'There are no end of possibilities,' Manda enthused, 'and I intend taking advantage of every one. We'll eat first if you must but then I insist we use the pool and flaunt ourselves in our itsy-bitsy bikinis. It's the first chance I've ever had to show myself off. I'm going to do it, whatever mother might think.'

She sat before the angled mirrors of the dressing table, studiously making up her face, using far more than her mother would allow. The glass reflected Dorothy emerging from the bathroom, wet from a shower.

'Don't stare at me like that, Manda,' she protested, reddening as her sister turned in her seat to admire her superbly

106

developed curves. 'You embarrass me. You're looking at me like a man.'

'Like the men are going to,' Manda corrected her, 'when they see your body by the pool. Hurry and dress, time is wasting.'

Wearing pretty print frocks that accentuated their shapely figures, they peeped into the spacious dining hall and saw the tables were still being laid by stewards. They stood undecided as two young men in loose floral shirts and cut-off jeans came up behind them. The new arrivals were youths of no more than twenty, handsome in a rugged way, tanned and with longish hair and earrings.

'Excuse us, girls,' one of them said politely. 'Are you going in, or just standing there looking gorgeous?'

'It seems we're too early,' Manda said, immediately liking the lads' looks while Dorothy considered their open admiration to be rather too obvious. She just watched as her sister prattled on. 'We thought we'd get breakfast over so that we could go swimming. I suppose we'll have to come back.'

'No need for that,' the boy said. 'Be our guests. We're part of the ship's entertainment crew. I'm Martin, and this excuse for a drummer is my young brother Graham. At this early hour it's feeding time for the off-duty officers and the hired hands like us. If you eat with us then you girls can go off and improve the view at the pool. Gray and I have been known to take a morning dip ourselves.'

'Like this morning,' his brother put in cheekily. 'Definitely this morning.'

'So join us at our table,' Martin invited. 'Don't let Graham put you off. He's sixteen and his hormones are acting up. I can keep him in check.'

But who can keep you in check? Dorothy thought, avoiding his admiring gaze, looking at the expanse of bronzed chest revealed by the unbuttoned shirt. 'As passengers, would we be allowed to eat with you?' she said, seeking an excuse. 'We don't wish to intrude.'

'No problem,' Martin assured her, leading the way to a

table with a view of the sparkling sea. He drew back a chair, inviting her to sit while his brother did the same for Manda. At once a waiter approached and handed over menu cards decorated with leaping dolphins. 'There,' Martin said. 'He probably thinks you two are the exotic dancers. You look better than the real ones. How about you girls introducing yourselves?'

Manda spoke up quickly in case Dorothy let slip that she was married. 'I'm Amanda but all my friends call me Manda. This is my big sister Dorothy, known as Dorrie. She tries to act old and wise but don't let that fool you, Martin. We're here to enjoy ourselves.'

'We'll make sure that you do,' Graham promised eagerly, his eyes on the swell of Manda's breasts, thinking that here was a girl with promise. 'You must come and see us play. We're in Mort Titian and The Shrouds. I play drums and Marty's lead guitar.'

'A group,' Manda said excitedly. 'Are you famous? Have you been on *Top of the Pops*?'

'Don't let my brother kid you,' Martin said modestly. 'We were lucky to get this gig. The group was formed when we were at school. We've been The Islanders, Barton's Boneheads, you name it. We won't make it big until we have a hit record.'

'And Marty's going to write it,' his brother said proudly. 'He's the clever member of the group. His stuff's really good.'

'I'm sure he will,' Dorothy found herself saying, impressed by Martin's modesty. 'I hope you do.' Suddenly shy, she averted her eyes, thankful the waiter was arriving with their food. She concentrated on eating her bacon and eggs. The dining hall was now busy with off-duty officers and staff. They were approached at their table by the assistant purser Ellen Jackson wearing a leotard moulded to her slim figure, her pretty face sheened with perspiration.

'Good morning, boys,' she said smiling, her eyes fixed on the sisters. 'You have guests, I see.'

'We got lucky,' Martin replied easily. 'The girls arrived

early, so we did the gentlemanly thing and invited them to join us. Is that a capital offence?'

'Not if it keeps our paying customers happy,' Ellen said, noting Dorothy's worried look. 'If these young ladies can stand having breakfast with you. There's no accounting for taste.' She gave the sisters a warm smile to show she had their interests at heart. 'It's too lovely a day to waste, there's so much to do: an aerobics class, a sauna and jacuzzi, educational film shows and lectures. I've just jogged around the deck before it gets crowded. What plans have you girls got? If you are ever at a loose end, do call on me or leave a note at the purser's office.'

'We're going to use the pool and get a tan,' Manda said, deliberately demure. 'I'm afraid the bikinis we brought have turned out rather skimpier than we thought. I hope no one will be offended if we wear them, will they?'

'I've just jogged by the pool and there's an interesting bunch using it right now,' Ellen laughed. 'You may even appear overdressed.' She prepared to turn away, giving the girls a final long look. 'Don't be stuck for things to do,' she told them. 'Let me help make it a memorable cruise for you.'

'She's really lovely,' Manda remarked as Ellen departed. 'So friendly too.'

'Friendly like a cobra, unless you're her way inclined,' Martin warned. 'Far be it for me to knock anyone's sexual preference, but Ms Jackson is renowned as a seducer of unsuspecting girls. It's said she keeps their knickers as trophies. She was chatting you two up.'

'To think such women exist,' Manda said, acting as if she were shocked. 'You never know, do you? We're strictly into boys ourselves – musicians especially.'

'Behave, Manda,' her sister rebuked her as they all left the dining hall together. 'What did that women mean when she said we may appear over-dressed?'

'Who cares? I want to laze in the sun and swim,' Manda said. 'You promised, so let's get into our bikinis and enjoy ourselves.'

'You could use our cabin to change in,' Martin suggested. 'The entertainment staff quarters are just yards from the pool. Gray and I would give you privacy, of course. Then you could dress in there after your swim.'

They accepted the brothers' offer and collected their bikinis and towels. 'I don't know if this is such a good idea,' Dorothy said anxiously to her eager sister. 'We may be letting ourselves in for more than we know with those boys. You saw how they looked at us.'

'Don't be such a party-pooper, Dorrie,' Manda complained. 'I'm not passing up the chance to have fun with two such hunks. They're gorgeous. Martin really fancies you, and Graham couldn't keep his eyes off my boobs. Is that so terrible? I'd like him to suck my nipples. I'll let him, if we get the chance.'

'Over my dead body,' Dorothy swore. She drew up, seeing the hunks in question waiting for them seated on sun-loungers outside an open cabin door.

From around a corner of the deck-housing the shouts, laughter and splashing of people enjoying themselves could be plainly heard. Martin and his brother rose politely to their feet to receive the girls. Both wore the briefest swimming pouches, bulging with promise, causing Manda to giggle approvingly and Dorothy to stare unbelievingly.

'They may as well be wearing nothing,' she said worriedly. 'Apart from that lewd bit at the front their bottoms are as good as bare.'

'What lovely tight bums,' Manda enthused. 'They're wearing what's known as thongs, stupid. Get with it, Dorrie, we'll be showing them as much. More, in fact, 'cos we've got tits as well.' She greeted the boys merrily. 'My sister says you must wait out here while we undress. Don't worry though, you'll see just about all we've got.'

'You're asking for trouble,' Dorothy warned Manda as they stripped. 'I shouldn't be here, anyway. I'm a married woman.' She studied herself anxiously in front of a mirror fixed to the door of a built-in wardrobe. 'My God, I overflow. They're

110

bound to get ideas with us revealing so much. Why do I let you get me into these situations?'

'Because you like it, if you'd only admit it,' Manda said. 'I'm going out. You can hide in here if you wish.'

Their appearance together brought low whistles of appreciation from the brothers. 'Definitely *Baywatch* class,' the younger one said, highly impressed. 'Promise you'll let me see more of you on this voyage, Manda,' he asked.

'You could hardly see more of her than you do now, Graham,' Dorothy said, uneasily aware of an unbidden spark of lust flaring in her loins. 'Martin, please don't stare at me. Let's go and swim now. I'll feel more at ease in the water. I know I shouldn't have agreed to wear a bikini.'

'I've never seen a girl who suited one better,' Martin said genuinely, taking her hand and leading the way around the deck housing to the pool. He stopped in his tracks with Dorothy standing aghast beside him. Graham and Manda coming up behind greeted the sight before them with a whoop of joy. Laid out on sun-loungers, talking in groups or frolicking in the pool, everyone present was entirely nude.

'This is why Ellen Jackson said you two would appear overdressed,' Graham said, unable to disguise his delight seeing the flesh on display. Before them bobbed big breasts and small breasts, bottoms of all shapes and males with varying sizes of dicks. 'We've nothing to fear here,' he added cheerfully to Manda. 'You and your sis make these chicks look like boys, and Marty and I can measure up to any of the men. When in Rome, they say. Are you ready for some skinny-dipping, Manda?' Before she could reply, he lowered his thong and presented himself entirely nude. 'Who said I'm the little brother?' he asked cheekily.

'Not so little from where I'm standing,' Manda giggled, her eyes fixed on his impressively developed prick and balls. She unclipped her bikini top, giving her firm big breasts an enticing jiggle as she freed them from the cups. 'Anything you can do, I can do better,' she teased, draping the discarded bra over his shoulders, turning away to slowly ease her briefs down her over curvy bottom cheeks. She turned to face him again, proudly displaying her naked body and striking a pose with arms held out from her sides. 'Taa-raah!' she announced gaily. 'What you see is what you get. I can see my sister is about to have kittens, but she should have the nerve. Do you approve?'

'Oh, wow!' Graham crowed, mesmerised by the size of her uptilted boobs, the taut pink nipples, the fork of her supple thighs and the soft nest of hair surmounting her plump girlish cunt. His prick pulsed and twitched, the thickening and lifting of the stalk noted with alarm by Dorothy. Shouting above the noise of the naked revellers around, Graham took Manda's hand as it seemed on the point of clasping his prick. 'Let's join 'em,' he hollered, deciding it timely to submerge his straining cockstand. 'Jump!'

Together, they hit the water, bobbing up with hair and faces streaming, hugging each other chest to chest. Dorothy watched with alarm, imagining Graham's fully erect prick pressing against her sister's cunt, Manda's squeals of delight as good as confirming the fact. The pair sank down and popped up again, locked close together, their mouths fused in a long clinging kiss. No doubt his tongue was deep in her mouth, Dorothy concluded bitterly.

'My sister is shameless,' she said angrily to Martin. 'I'm supposed to see that she doesn't get into trouble. And your brother is encouraging her. Why is everyone here naked?' Her eyes widened as she saw Martin had discarded his pouch, his prick still flaccid but hanging thick and long over heavy balls like two ripe plums. 'You too,' she said hoarsely. 'I can't believe this. It – it's just an excuse for people to flaunt themselves. Won't the captain or whoever runs this cruise put a stop to it when they find out?'

'They already know,' Martin said, wishing to placate her. 'The naked people are members of a nudist group. They've booked as passengers on the understanding they be allowed to do what comes naturally for them. Why are you so upset? It's harmless, surely?'

'Perhaps for them,' Dorothy said unwilling to appear completely disapproving, 'but it makes me uncomfortable. I'm sorry, but I'm going back to your cabin to get dressed.'

'What's up?' Manda called to Martin, seeing Dorothy leave. She swam to the side of the pool with Graham beside her. 'Why is she bolting? We're just having fun.'

'She took fright,' Martin said disappointedly. 'Evidently it's not her idea of a good time. I'm going back to the cabin to see if she's okay. Where has your sister been living – in a nunnery?'

'As good as,' Manda agreed, 'but it's her thing to make out she's so easily shocked. I could tell you what she's really like underneath.' Both she and Graham got out of the pool, dripping water. 'We'll all try to make her see sense. Really, she justs needs careful handling.'

'I'd volunteer for that,' Martin said, the three of them gathering up their swimming things and returning naked to the cabin. As they entered, Dorothy squealed in alarm, caught with her bikini discarded and as naked as the others. She blushed furiously as the brothers gazed at her figure: her breasts proud and firm, the velvet-smooth skin offset by unusually big strawberry-coloured nipples; the tangle of curling hair covering a prominent cunt mound at the base of her gently domed belly.

'You've got nothing to hide,' Martin said respectfully as she tried to cover her breasts and crotch with her hands. 'It's a crime to cover up what you've got, Dorothy. You – you're beautiful.'

'Yes, come off it, Dorrie,' Manda said impatiently. 'We're all in the buff so why shouldn't you be? I remember you telling me you secretly fancied showing off your body. This is your chance. Stop acting like mother. The boys want us to have fun.'

Dorothy's eyes brimmed with tears as she tried a brave smile. 'Don't blame me, there's a good reason why I shouldn't. Let me get dressed now.'

This brought a chorus of 'No!' shouted in unison by the

three others. Dorothy stopped. She saw Manda and Graham with their arms around each other's waists and Martin gazing at her beauty in a way she could never recall her husband doing. Suddenly she began to tremble and Martin led her unresisting to one of the beds, sitting her down with gentleness and placing a consoling arm around her waist.

'I – I've been so unhappy, my life is so mixed up,' she began. 'I don't wish to be like this, it's just that I can't help myself.'

'You don't need to explain a thing,' he reassured her, sensing her resistance weakening and awaiting his chance. He drew her head to his shoulder, the soft feel of her flesh against his. Two big-nippled breasts thrust out, the right one within easy cupping reach of the hand around her waist. His prick was as erect as a poker as he held her. With her face pressed against his neck hidden in the long chestnut tresses of her hair, she remained unaware of such blatant evidence of his arousal.

'What's my sister doing?' she asked hesitantly. To answer her own question she turned her head and saw Manda on the other bed sharing a long lewd kiss with Graham. Sitting side by side, with his hands fondling her breasts, Manda's fingers were clasped around the engorged girth of the boy's cock, her wrist moving rhythmically as she manipulated the upright stalk. As the kiss proceeded, Graham lowered her under him to the bed.

Unable to tear her eyes away, Dorothy turned on Martin's lap to face them. In doing so the rounded cheeks of her buttocks brushed across the bulbous knob of Martin's erection. 'Please, *no*,' she muttered, attempting to rise but he held firmly with the arm around her waist. 'I've got to stop her. She doesn't know what she's doing.'

'I think she does,' Martin said, enjoying the sensations brought on by the feel of Dorothy's bottom rubbing against his dick. 'I've never seen anyone more aware of what she's doing. She wouldn't thank you to stop her. Not now.'

Together they saw Graham lower his face to Manda's

breasts as she proffered them for him to suck on the raspberry-red nipples. He plied his mouth from one to the other, suctioning ardently as Manda's low moans and sighs increased in her mounting pleasure. He withdrew his lips leaving her nipples thickly erect and saliva-glistened, moving down over her. She guessed his intention and raised her knees, parting them to receive him. Her hands drew his face between her open thighs, and guided his lips to her uptilted cunt.

'Yes, oh *yesss*,' Dorothy and Martin heard her whimper as Graham went in with his tongue, probing deeply as she lifted her bottom to his face.

'The – the little bitch,' Dorothy said, exchanging a glance with Martin that said it all – things had gone beyond the point of no return. 'Just listen to her,' she complained, as her sister became demanding, grunting out commands as her wantonness increased.

'Don't you dare stop!' they heard Manda cry, too engrossed in her rapture even to allow Graham a pause to gasp in air, the grip on his head tightening. 'Lick me out, I say! Lick me clean! Make me come! Go on, harder and deeper.' Her bottom jerked furiously from the bed, buffeting his face. 'I'm coming!' she cried out at last in triumph. 'I love it, love it!'

'There's no doubt about that,' Martin whispered in Dorothy's ear. In his excitement at the scene before them and suspecting from her agitated movements that the girl in his lap was likewise affected, he shifted a fraction and guided his erect prong snugly into the warm damp cleave of her bottom. At the same time he raised his hand around to clasp the under-curve of a large pliant breast. As her body stiffened he whispered to her that he could not help himself. 'Doesn't seeing those two at it make you want to do something?' he said suggestively. 'I'm dying to fuck you, Dorothy, more than I've wanted to with anyone.' His free hand stole down between her thighs, stroking the soft hair and projecting lips. She gave what he considered was a submissive moan as he insinuated a finger into the lubricated inner flesh of her cunt. 'You're really moist in there,' he charged her. 'You want it as much as I.'

'I'm a married woman,' she protested, unable to prevent squirming as his finger lightly stroked her clitoris, now projecting stiffly from its hood. She held his wrist in a futile attempt to still his hand but the sensations coursing through her cunt were hard to resist. 'Don't, Martin,' she begged. 'You're going to make me want it. Think of my husband.'

'I can't think of anything but fucking you,' Martin said, his arousal too great to be considerate of her plea. 'I'm sorry, but fuck him—'

'No, Martin, fuck his wife!' Manda urged him wickedly from the adjacent bed. 'Go on, give it to her, she needs a really good screwing. Don't let her stop you, she's had it off before with another man.'

'Is that true?' Martin asked, tickled to know that the shy Dorothy had lapsed before. 'Has someone else fucked you, Dorothy? Since you were married?'

'He took advantage of me, just like you,' she whined, the hard cylinder of flesh between her cushiony cheeks nudging the lips of her cunt. 'I know I'm weak when these feelings come over me.'

'Me too, it's a natural reaction,' Martin said, easing her bottom from his groin until it was poised above his upright stalk. With a forward jiggle of his hips, the knob pushed aside her cunt lips and an inch or so slipped inside. He kept it there to tempt her. 'It's up to you,' he whispered softly into her ear, her back against his chest. 'Sit down on it. Let me fill you up. You can keep an eye on your sister in this position.'

'That's an awful thing to say,' Dorothy protested, giving the first tentative little wriggle of her bottom to get the feel of the plum-sized knob lodged in the mouth of her cunt. 'Good Lord, what are they doing now?' she said, her eyes unable to look away from the couple on the nearby bed.

'It's known as a sixty-nine,' Martin informed her, easing a further inch in, gratified by hearing the soft pleasurable moan she gave. Across the cabin, Manda and Graham lay head to tail, the girl on top and cheeks hollowing as she sucked avidly on the stalk rearing between his thighs. At her nether end,

116

Graham's hands had parted the cheeks of her bottom hovering over his face, most of which was hidden deep within the cleave. Bowing to the inevitable, Dorothy thrust her crotch down to receive the remaining length of Martin's tormenting prick. The thick stalk penetrated her juiced-up cunt with ease and she began to ride it, unable to deny the delicious sensations the big cock produced.

'It's still not right,' Dorothy whined though she was fully embedded, her hips working to match his upward thrusts. The sense of being so deeply and thickly entered, feeling the thrusts of the prick inside her, brought on a growing frenzy in her mind and body. The pace of the fucking increased and her first climax was achieved with a scream.

With her feet firmly planted on the floor, Dorothy lifted and ground down her arse as she sought a second coming.

In her frenzy Dorothy cried out for Martin to squeeze her breasts harder and pull her nipples. Twisting her face to his, she kissed him with abandon, her mouth clamped to his. Breaking from the kiss, Martin fell back on the bed, gripping her hips and jerking wildly as his spurts of come filled her deepest recess and she matched him with a simultaneous climax.

They recovered their senses gradually. Lying back with her eyes closed, Dorothy sensed Martin looming over her, a hand going to her breast, a kiss pressed to her lips. Aware that he desired to continue the bout, she hurriedly got off the bed.

'No, we've gone too far, Martin,' she said, attempting to be firm with him. 'Further than I ever intended. I trust that what happened won't become known outside this cabin. My sister and I are going to dress now and leave. I'd prefer if you and Graham would give us privacy to do that. Come on, Manda, do as I say. I'm sure mother will be wondering where we've got to.'

'We could have stayed longer, I was enjoying myself,' Manda grumbled, dressing beside Dorothy after the brothers had left them. 'And why did you make them leave while we dress? They saw all of us there is and Martin fucked you. I

117

didn't know people did it in that position and I can't wait to try.' Again she could not contain her girlish giggle. 'The way you came off sitting up on his big cock! You went berserk.'

'And you were just as bad,' Dorothy responded. 'I saw how you were behaving with Graham, sucking his thing like a glutton. How could you?'

'Too bloody well, it seems,' Manda admitted ruefully. 'He came off while he was in my mouth. Before he could get it up again, you'd had your fuck and put a stop to it. Bother you and bother mummy. I don't care if she's been looking for us. I'm still a virgin, thanks to you. Next time I'll let Martin fuck me.'

'No doubt he'll be glad to oblige,' Dorothy said bitterly. 'Can't you see what we've become?'

'Yes, normal young women with sexual needs,' Manda told her, her tone serious for once. 'For someone who acts like a prude, you're doing better than anyone I know. From now on, I'm going to make sure I get my turn.'

Chapter Eleven

Doctor's Orders

Ailsa treated herself to a rare lie-in, lulled by the movement of the ship as it sailed down-Channel. She arose and enjoyed a leisurely bath then found a table under a sun umbrella on one of the upper decks and ordered coffee. She was surprised to be approached by a young woman in a nurse's cap and white dress.

'Mrs Craig?' the woman asked. When Ailsa nodded to confirm the fact, the woman smiled and studied the clipboard she carried. 'I'm Nurse Dietrich. Would you like to use the beauty parlour, the hairdressing salon or any of the other treatment centres on board? There's also a daily aerobics class and lectures on healthy living. I can have the details sent to your cabin if you like.'

'How kind, I would appreciate that,' Ailsa said, thinking what a wholesomely attractive young woman she was. 'I shall have to think hard about doing anything too strenuous,' she joked. 'This is the first break I've had for years and relaxing in the sun and sea air is all I care to do at present.'

'Is your work so stressful?' Helga Dietrich enquired solicitously. 'There's a very good massage facility on board with a trained masseuse. The treatment is guaranteed to soothe away all aches and stresses.'

'That sounds heavenly,' Ailsa said. 'I may well be tempted. You did say masseuse?'

'Myself,' Helga said proudly. 'Fully trained at the Munchen Health Spa. I have no appointments this afternoon. Come any

119

time after lunch and it will be my pleasure to give you the full treatment without hurry.'

'It's really very kind of you to offer,' said Ailsa, 'but I don't know. I have two daughters on the ship I should spend some time with.'

'I shall be there in case you change your mind,' Helga said firmly. She turned to leave, adding a parting shot. 'You would enjoy. Believe me, you would enjoy.'

Intrigued by the thought of another woman's hands on her body, Ailsa sat with her coffee considering Helga's offer, deciding against it in favour of finding out how Dorothy and Manda were passing their time. She went back to their cabin, discovering that they had been and gone, as evidenced by the towel untidily thrown across Manda's bed. Ailsa took it to the bathroom to hang it up, pausing at the sight of the bikini tops and bottoms tied to the shower rail to dry. How positively indecent, she thought, inspecting the flimsy items, surprised that one of the costumes could have been worn by Dorothy. She held one of the bras up to her chest, wondering how they had dared wear so little.

Beside the soap on the hand-basin she saw Manda's watch and shook her head at her younger daughter's carelessness. She took it through to the cabin. To teach Manda a lesson she decided to put it somewhere out of sight. Ailsa opened the top drawer of the dressing table, intending to place it under whatever was in there, and froze to the spot. With a trembling hand she drew out a magazine. Its cover depicted a kneeling woman sucking on the huge penis of a black giant who stood over her.

One by one she lifted out the magazines, each cover seemingly lewder than the others. One showed a girl on hands and knees being penetrated at one end by a man, with her face buried in the shaven crotch of a woman. One showed a girl sandwiched between two men, leaving no doubt that both of her nether orifices were being plugged. The last showed an older woman spanking a slim girl across her knees while a man watched them with a rearing erection.

Ailsa's shock increased when she discovered the dildo and vibrators beneath the final magazine. Crossing to one of the beds, she sat trembling with the books in her lap. Unable to resist, she looked at page after page of the obscene illustrations, marvelling at the permutations and previously unimagined sexual activities revealed in the photographs.

It was heady stuff, enough to set her pulse racing. On reaching the last page she leafed through the magazines again to look at certain pictures that had stimulated her. She returned the books to the dressing table drawer a shaken woman, wondering how her daughters could explain its contents, wondering too if she dare ask. She returned to her own cabin, greatly perturbed by the experience. A knock on her door roused her from a dreamlike trance and she rose unsteadily to answer it. A white-jacketed steward faced her. But for his arrival she would have undoubtedly resorted to masturbating to quell the demanding throb in her cunt.

'Mrs Craig,' he said. 'I have been sent by Nurse Dietrich to take you to your appointment. She was afraid the consultation may have slipped your mind.'

'Thank you,' was all Ailsa could say and she followed him as if in a daze. He led her to the massage room. A beaming Helga ushered her into a large tiled area with a massage table at its centre. It stood on metal legs, at least three feet wide and covered with a thin white rubber sheet stretched tight. In a corner of the room was an object like a large square box, made of gleaming white enamel with a door at the front and a round hole at the top. All was spotless, including the white-painted shelves full of bottles and an open-fronted shower cubicle.

Ailsa wished she were back in the privacy of her cabin so she could alleviate the insistent itch in her cunt. 'What is it you want me to do?' she said.

'Take off all your clothes, of course,' Helga directed, going to the box-like object and turning a numbered dial on its side. 'Hurry up, Mrs Craig.'

'Isn't there a screen to undress behind?' Ailsa asked, her mind still distracted. 'Is this necessary?'

'Of course, I have to shower you. But first the steamer to cleanse your pores, and remove the poisons.' She opened the door at the front of the sweat box, indicating the inside with its flat wooden slat for a seat. 'You cannot go in there in your clothes, Mrs Craig. Do not be reserved. I will be the same as you when I wash you under the shower. Then you will see that women all have the same attributes.'

Some more than others, Ailsa could not help thinking, looking at the bulge of Helga's bosom under her white coat. She took off her clothes in silence, each item received by Helga and folded neatly over a chair. 'You have nothing to be modest about with your lovely figure,' said the nurse and Ailsa blushed to hear herself being praised. Soon she stood naked, self-conscious under Helga's scrutiny.

She entered the box and sat on the wooden slat, her head projecting through the hole in the top. To prevent the heat escaping, a thick fluffy towel was tucked around her neck.

Helga stood back and smiled.

'Now I shall leave you for a short while to let you relax, to think your thoughts whatever they may be,' she said, as if aware of Ailsa's raging erotic thoughts. 'The temperature is set at a comfortable degree and timed for five minutes. When I return it will be the hose.'

Whatever that might be, Ailsa could not imagine. Already the dry heat was causing rivulets of perspiration to run down her neck and shoulders. The moisture dropped from her chin onto her breasts, dripping from her erect nipples tormentingly. The sweat filled her navel, soaked her stomach and pooled between her buttocks and the seat. The hairs on her mound grew sodden and her pulsating cunt itched the more demandingly. Unable to resist, Ailsa rubbed herself in the slippery moisture, two fingers penetrating easily and going for the enlarged clitoral nub. On the verge of a mind-numbing climax, she was interrupted by the reappearance of Helga, swathed in a towelling robe and eager to continue the treatment.

'Enough for now, I think, Mrs Craig,' the formidable

masseuse smiled, opening the front of the box. Ailsa hated her for returning when she did. 'Sadist,' she muttered under her breath as she was helped out and led stumbling towards the open-fronted shower. Standing in the centre of the cubicle, she felt her arms being raised by Helga and her wrists securely held by soft leather clamps attached to a metal bar above her head. The restraining was accomplished so suddenly and with such expertise that Ailsa was strung up before she could resist. Her fear and shock, the angry protest that followed, was accepted by Helga with a knowing smile.

'Don't go on so, it is normal procedure,' she said matter-of-factly, picking up the end of a flexible rubber hose of the type used to water gardens. 'No one is going to harm you – in fact you will find it most pleasurable.'

'You have no right,' Ailsa began, feeling extremely vulnerable in her naked state. She looked up to see her wrists pinioned some two feet apart, the effect making her breasts thrust out from her chest. Below, she was almost on tiptoe. 'Why did you do this?'

'Would you have allowed me if I had asked?' Helga said. 'I think not in your stressed condition. You are so uptight. Believe me I have treated similar women before. They have all been sexually repressed and afterwards they thanked me for helping them.' She directed the hose at Ailsa's helpless body. 'I do this for your own good. You will thank me too.'

'How dare you?' Ailsa began to object as a fine spray of pleasantly refreshing water showered her from head to foot. Helga played the hose up and down to sluice away the sweat glistening on Ailsa's body, ordering her to turn to the side and present her back for sluicing.

'Is that not enjoyable?' Helga said as rivulets of water streamed over the curve of Ailsa's spine, finding a natural outlet between the cleft of the ample cheeks of her buttocks. The infiltrating flow swirled over her arsehole and coursed around the rear-hanging split of her cunt tantalisingly, making Ailsa's bottom squirm and her legs part involuntarily. Her agitation was not lost upon Helga, who concentrated the spray exclusively onto the base of Ailsa's spine, making her twist on her toes and scream out for mercy.

'Do you not like our water treatment?' Helga asked as if surprised. 'Turn again then. Just a few moments more and I will release you.' Swivelling round to face her as ordered, Ailsa saw the spray cut out to a dribble. The next moment Ailsa was struck by a powerful jet of water, a stream as accurate as a laser beam targeted on to each of her naked breasts. For long moments Helga played the hose across the sensitive spheres of flesh while Ailsa pleaded for the torrent to stop. The sensations in her breasts were of a nature she had never experienced before: tingling, throbbing, aching all at once. Glancing down as Helga lowered the jet, Ailsa thought her bosom had never thrust out so conspicuously, the nipples thick and proud.

'No!' she begged a moment later as the jet honed in with deadly accuracy on her pussy, striking above, around and on the outer lips until Ailsa found it too provoking to fight. Hanging from the captive clamps, she became abandoned to all else but the urge to respond and achieve the climax she'd been denied. With her thighs splayed and her cunt mound thrust forward to meet the oncoming stream, she howled in protest as Helga abruptly cut off the supply. Tossing the hose into the cubicle, she came forward to unshackle Ailsa's wrists.

'Sadist,' was all Ailsa could mumble as she was released, of necessity slumping into Helga's strong arms for support. 'You – you *knew* what you were doing to me. Why did you stop when – when—?'

'You were so near to having the climax you want?' Helga finished for her, hugging Ailsa to her ample bosom and leading her to the massage table. 'Don't fret, the best is yet to come, my dear Mrs Craig. First, I will dry you.'

She left Ailsa clinging to the massage table to steady the tremble in her legs and produced a large towel which she draped around her. 'You do make things difficult for yourself with your foolish pride,' Helga said. 'Who needs dignity at all times? All you have to do is leave yourself in my hands for complete satisfaction. Be a sensible woman.' Dabbing Ailsa's face gently, she gave her a reassuring smile. 'Surely it is nice to be pampered?' She patted the towelling over both breasts in turn, lifting each one in her hands to dry the flesh beneath with elaborate care. 'How big and beautiful they are,' she murmured as Ailsa stood as if mesmerised, allowing her to proceed. 'You haven't answered me. Is it not nice to be pampered for once? To let someone else take care of your needs?'

'If you say so,' Ailsa said weakly, her breasts rising and falling as her breathlessness increased by the moment. 'It – it's just that I did not expect *this*.' She could not suppress a gasp as Helga dropped to her knees and began drying between her thighs, concentrating on rubbing the towel over her sex. Ailsa moaned and undulated her pubic mound, no longer caring about modesty in her need to gain relief. But once again Helga frustrated her. She stopped the towelling and got to her feet.

'On the table with you now,' Helga said sharply. 'Face down to start with. Up you get.' To add impetus to her words, Helga gave her a resounding smack on the backside. Face down on the rubberised sheet, Ailsa's maddening arousal increased as her breasts and inner thighs pressed against the smooth surface. 'This is oil of almonds and peach,' she heard Helga say as liquid dripped onto her back, a liberal dollop landing between her buttocks. Then she was slapped, pummelled and pounded from her neck to her ankles, all the time in growing agitation at the feel of other hands on her body and the cloying sensation of the oil seeping into the crevices of her bottom and cunt. With Helga's massaging fingers constantly brushing over both orifices, Ailsa could have begged for her to go on and finger her, to give her the orgasm she so badly desired.

Instead Helga merely asked Ailsa to turn over, helping her roll onto her back and pouring oil over her breasts, belly and the forest of hair on her mound. Suddenly Ailsa cried out in alarm as she saw, beside the massage table, a small bespectacled man in a wheelchair. As she tried to sit up he reached out to grasp her wrist, stopping Helga in the act of rising and pressing her back.

'Don't be embarrassed by my presence, dear lady,' said the newcomer. 'Nurse Dietrich told me about your treatment and I've come to assist. Just lie back again and relax.'

'Who's *he*?' Ailsa demanded. 'Nobody said anything about a man being here. It – it's scandalous!'

'I'll handle this,' the man said as Helga made to answer. 'My name is Dr Weissbinder, Mrs Craig, and I am an acknowledged authority on the stresses and trauma from which you undoubtedly suffer. Rarely have I met a person so in need of sensual release. As a sexologist and qualified psychotherapist, I clearly recognise a sexually repressed woman. Be sensible now, both Nurse Dietrich and I realise your baseless sense of propriety is denying you a life. You desire an orgasm, so why not say so? Instead, out of a misplaced sense of decorum, you allowed Nurse Dietrich to frustrate you without ordering her to give you one. She would have done. Do you wish to come now?'

After a long silence and in a small voice, Ailsa muttered a shy 'Yes, I do.'

At once Helga placed her hands over Ailsa's breasts and began circular massaging movement, between times drawing up her fingers and pulling out the nipples. They grew even tighter and longer under the treatment, with Ailsa's breasts responding by tilting to the titillating touch. She looked at Weissbinder in mute appeal, a look which said: please don't think too badly of me. I can't help myself.

Leo Weissbinder nodded affably as if able to read her mind. 'My dear Mrs Craig,' he said to put her at ease, 'there is no need to excuse how you feel. And if you still feel some semblance of shame and remorse, just accept that it's part of your psyche. Humiliation is bitter-sweet, indeed it's a potent aphrodisiac which can make a woman wanton . . .'

'That's how you two are making me feel,' Ailsa admitted, groaning out the words as Helga expertly massaged her breasts, pulling them and kneading them, all the time returning to pinch and stretch the taut nipples. 'For once I feel marvellously used and abused. What a relief it is to let go of the respectable front I've put on for all these years.'

'More women should own up to those feelings,' Weissbinder said, pleased with his progress as Ailsa's voluptuous body quivered on the table. 'The respectable front women adopt for a conventional life is the supreme reason for their stress and frustration. I'm happy you recognise that. Your body is in very good condition, I can see. You're the expert on the female form, Helga. What do you say?'

'Look,' said the eager masseuse, squeezing Ailsa's bosom with relish. 'These breasts are so full and firm they retain their lift and shape even when she is lying down. Such fine nipples too, standing up so big. The flat stomach is good and the strong thighs. Her vagina is like a rose in bloom – I suspect she was masturbating in the sweat box. I could give her the hand massage, but do you think she would prefer the special?'

'The special definitely,' Weissbinder agreed. 'She would undoubtedly like that. Proceed, nurse. I shall observe.'

'What – what are you going to do to me?' Ailsa asked nervously, again finding herself rolled over. She felt several sharp smacks on her upraised buttocks, then the cheeks were parted and a finger stroked the length of the outer lips, going in to probe the well-oiled channel of her sex. As Ailsa moved her pelvis to get the finger where she desired it most, it was withdrawn, moving up the short distance to thrust the first knuckle past the serrated ridge of her bottom hole. Ailsa, too aroused to protest, moaned with pleasure, squirming her rear back against the hand as if finding it impossible to resist.

'Oh, yes,' she muttered throatily. 'Oh, go on, push it up some more.'

'She's had it there before,' Helga declared to the interested Weissbinder. 'I can always tell if a woman has been buggered or would like to be. It's how it is with this one. If she hasn't, she's thought about it.'

'Naughty Mrs Craig,' Weissbinder chided her gently. 'But why not? We all have such thoughts, it's perfectly natural.' He smiled as Ailsa's bottom quivered on the end of Helga's probing finger. 'Time to employ the vibrators, I think. She'll get a double treat today.' He handed Helga two plastic models of the male penis, both realistic in length and girth. 'On her back,' he told his nurse, handing her the dummy pricks. 'I chose the normal-sized ones for this session. If the lady proves amenable we can progress to bigger things another time.'

'Of course, Herr Doktor,' Helga agreed, rolling a bemused Ailsa over to lie on her back. 'She's well oiled to take them both.' Before Ailsa was aware of what was happening, a prick-like object was inserted deep into her cunt, sliding in effortlessly. It was gratefully received after her prolonged torment. Ailsa worked her hips and tightened the walls of her cunt around the intruder. Her knees rose and her feet went over Helga's shoulders, bottom bumping on the massage table as she strove to satisfy herself. The second vibrator entered her back passage and caused her to jerk even more violently. The two dummy cocks were so close together they felt like one.

'What have you done to me?' Ailsa cried out, bucking madly and looking down between her spread legs to see the ends of the vibrators projecting lewdly from cunt and arsehole. A click and a buzzing sound followed as Helga switched on the power. At once Ailsa's body thrashed and flailed out of control. Both vibrator heads bored into her, turning and twisting, sending sensations she had never known coursing through her body. Now past caring as a surge of unstoppable orgasms shook her from head to toes, she screamed out that she was *coming*, repeating the word over and over in her throes.

'Is that not the most incredible feeling, dear Mrs Craig?' Weissbinder said, his words unheard as Ailsa, with both her cunt and rear passage on fire, was lost in a frenzied world of her own. Persistent vibrations sent waves of unending climaxes rippling up to her heaving belly and flying breasts. She thrashed and rolled around in such agitation that Helga was forced to hold her down by the shoulders.

'This proves she can have multiple orgasms naturally under the right circumstances,' the nurse observed. 'I have counted six or seven at least. Shall we continue the treatment? She could have twenty or more.'

'Just for a few more minutes. We mustn't overtax her strength the first time,' Weissbinder decided, watching Ailsa surfing on a constant peak of carnal ecstasy, one sapping spasm following another. At last he gave the sign and as Helga withdrew the vibrators Ailsa lay twitching, the dying pulsations tingling in her cunt and arse. She was reduced to a feeble, whimpering shell of a woman, drained and dazed. Helga loomed over her smiling. As if in need of holding on to someone after a complete loss of control, Ailsa reached out for her.

'There, there, all is well,' Helga said soothingly, opening the front of the towelling robe she wore to reveal her impressive bosom. 'You've been away, but now you've returned safely.' Ailsa's garbled reply might have been more but she found an arm cradling her head, a warm weighty breast against her face and a thick nipple pressed to her lips. She sobbed, clutching at Helga like a distraught child and gratefully nestled her face in the mounds of pliant flesh.

'Was this the usual practice at the Munchen Health Spa?' Weissbinder asked Helga. 'It would seem very effective, the way Mrs Craig is being comforted by suckling your breast. It's an intriguing phenomenon. I shall have to write a paper on the subject.'

'It is not unknown for female clients to nurse on my breasts while recovering after treatment,' Helga told him, offering her other nipple to Ailsa's lips. 'In their weakened state even the strongest woman has a need to be comforted. Mrs Craig will recover in a while. I would appreciate your leaving us, Herr Doktor, so that we can be alone, woman to woman, when she is fully aware again.'

'Very well. I leave it to your experienced judgement,' Weissbinder said, turning his wheelchair towards the door, satisfied that what he might miss would be captured on tape.

'Well done, Nurse Dietrich, an excellent start has been made. With further treatment, Mrs Craig will accept herself as a woman with a need for sexual fulfilment.'

'What did he say?' Ailsa asked, gradually regaining her senses from being so thoroughly dildoed back and front. With Weissbinder gone, she felt more at ease to speak. 'I feel I must have made a fine spectacle of myself. Apart from what it must have looked like having all those orgasms, imagine me a grown woman being nursed by you as if I were a baby.'

'I quite envied you having all those lovely comes,' Helga smiled. 'Of all the women I have treated, never have I known so many climaxes in one session. Dr Weissbinder is right, you must accept yourself as a woman with a need for sexual fulfilment. No more denying yourself in future.'

'I do accept it,' Ailsa agreed. 'I never knew how it could be before, with men or with women,' she added returning Helga's smile. 'And now I know, what a lot of time I have to make up.'

Chapter Twelve

Iron Mistress

'What did I tell you?' Myra Starr said to Ellen Jackson. 'Didn't I say that woman has marvellous tits?' Myra and the young purser's assistant sat before the banks of television screens in the control room sipping coffee. Before them were multiple images of Ailsa laid out on the massage table, clutching her breasts sensuously while Helga stood over her, stroking the hair-covered mound between her outstretched legs. With amazement, they saw Ailsa release her right breast and reach for Helga's hand to work it harder against her cunt.

'Haven't you had enough, Mrs Craig?' they heard Helga saying, smiling down at Ailsa as she withdrew her hand. 'That's enough for the first time, I think, and then you will look forward to further sessions.'

Ailsa slipped off the massage table and yawned luxuriously, stretching her arms wide, her superb breasts heaving, her body glistening with oil. 'I've never felt so wonderful. It's such a relief and I have you and Dr Weissbinder to thank for it.'

'Under the shower with you, Mrs Craig,' Helga said, giving one of Ailsa's bottom cheeks a noisy smack. 'Remember I'm in charge and you will do as you are told.'

'I'm in your hands,' she replied. 'I think – after what has happened this afternoon – you should call me Ailsa.'

The watching women gasped as Helga slipped off her towelling robe. The two voluptuous women were an incredible sight naked. Helga took Ailsa by the hand and led her under the shower. They stood face to face and breast to breast, exchanging a long passionate kiss under the spray. Ailsa stood obediently still while Helga soaped her shoulders and bosom, the sudsy foam dripping from her nipples and coursing over her belly into the fork of her thighs.

'You can see why I fancy her so much, Ellen,' Myra said in a hush. 'No doubt a fully paid-up lesbo like yourself wouldn't throw her out of bed either.'

'Not since seeing her in that shower,' Ellen said intensely. 'I thought she was hung-up about sex? Helga's got it made with her, she's just a randy amateur waiting to be brought out.'

'Are you complaining?' Myra asked, laughing. 'It makes it easier for us. She's sought after. You'd better get in line.'

'You and Dr Dex are not the only ones to want her,' Ellen said determinedly. 'We'll see who waits in line.' She glanced at her wristwatch and frowned. 'Damn it, I'm due for that session Weissbinder's arranged – obedience training for Gerald Marsh and his son. Why me, I'd like to know?'

'Because nobody does it better, dear,' Myra said sweetly sarcastic. 'A mean man-hating bitch was called for and that means you. Think of the fun you'll have with not one but two victims to vent your spleen on. You can go to town and emasculate the poor bastards.'

'Just get them to my cabin,' Ellen said, rising to leave. 'Oh, what a delicious bottom,' she could not help saying as, on screen, Ailsa turned in the shower. 'I shouldn't look at such a sight at this time of day.'

'You *are* in rut for Mrs Craig,' Myra teased. 'Come on any stronger and your knickers will catch fire. Look at the sweep of her back and those magnificent buttocks, she's getting hornier by the minute with that German bitch's hands on her. You should be so lucky – you get the Marsh boys, father and son.'

'Which won't improve their chances,' Ellen promised.

'I almost pity them,' Myra said. 'Let's go.'

Myra found Gerald eyeing the women on deck with a predatory eye. Nearby, his son Nigel was at the ship's rail looking wistfully out to sea. Myra approached as if delighted to see an old friend, and he greeted her warmly.

'My cabin or yours?' he asked for openers.

'Not this time, you've another admirer,' she began, beaming as if about to bestow an unmissable opportunity. 'I refer to that pretty female purser, Ellen Jackson. She reckons you're the most macho male on board and she wants to do something about it.'

'Tell me more,' he said delightedly. 'Where is she?'

'Waiting in her cabin,' Myra said. 'I'm to take you there.'

'Then I'll dump Nigel,' Gerald offered. 'Preferably overboard. The sad bastard follows me around like a lost soul. Missing his mummy, I shouldn't wonder.'

'He's to come along too,' Myra insisted. 'Ellen is under orders to cut the pair of you down to size and find out what gives with Nigel. It's Weissbinder's idea of straightening the pair of you out. You for having too much going for you, Gerald you old ram, and your son because he seems a lost cause. It's one of Weissbinder's experiments in his sex survey.'

'Then include me out,' Gerald laughed. 'I'm no guinea-pig.'

'You'd better go along,' Myra warned, 'and do as Ellen orders without too much fuss. Who knows, you might find it fun? Trust me, there will be pay-back time. I can assure you of that.'

'I'll take your word for it,' Gerald agreed, 'since you seem to have some scheme in mind. For the time being you're on their side, are you?'

'Just to give them enough rope to hang themselves,' Myra concurred. 'Dr Calvert and I have an old score to settle with Weissbinder but we'll all benefit if you and the Craigs play a part. Brace yourself to meet a mean machine.'

'I'll be suitably contrite,' Gerald promised, ordering his surprised son to follow as Myra led them off through a passageway to a cabin door. She told Gerald and the docile Nigel to wait outside while she announced their arrival and closed the door firmly behind her.

'They're here,' Myra said. 'Lambs to the slaughter. I'm to stay with you in case you need help.'

'I won't,' Ellen said decisively. 'Rest assured.'

'This is just your thing, isn't it?' Myra smiled. 'Two prize specimens to train in rigid obedience await your commands. The way you feel about men I can't wait to see you operate.'

As he entered, Gerald studied Ellen with interest while Nigel followed nervously, sniffing at the heavily perfumed atmosphere of the cabin. The purser, Gerald noted, wore a loose satin robe which would be easy to discard before getting down to business. Intrigued, he did not notice Myra locking the door behind him, something Nigel observed with a growing feeling of unease. He looked questioningly at Myra. She in turn added to his disquiet by giving a long suggestive wink and puckering her lips in a kiss.

'So you're the so-called Casanova who thinks he's come here to fuck me,' Ellen began, referring to Gerald but making Nigel quake. 'Think again, buster. To me you're the pits, a slimeball from way back. Get the picture, scumbag?'

'I think we'd better leave, father,' Nigel suggested meekly while Gerald pondered his reply. 'Ask them to unlock the door.'

'Yes,' Gerald said, deciding to appear outraged. 'I didn't come here to be insulted.'

'I'll insult you wherever I like,' Ellen threatened. 'I'll spread the word and make you a social outcast.' She gave him a mirthless smile. 'That is, unless you repent your chauvinist outlook toward women. Starting now.'

'Stuff yourself,' replied Gerald. 'I'm quite happy as I am and not all women are ball-breakers like you. I could supply numerous references from satisfied females. I suggest you unlock the door. My son and I wish to leave this charade.'

'This is no game,' Ellen purred menacingly, slipping the loose robe from her arms and letting it slide dramatically to the floor. She stood in just a black satin corselet which pushed up her pointed pear-shaped breasts, the exposed nipples rouged a striking dark vermilion. The lace-frilled garment barely reached the fork of her thighs, revealing a profuse growth of softly curling dark hair on the curve of her mound. Her suspenders were clipped to sheer black stockings, above which gleamed her supple white thighs. The ensemble was completed by shining black high-heeled shoes.

Hands on hips, she regarded Gerald and Nigel with menace, her legs spread wide. Myra, already naked, handed Ellen a short whippy cane. 'Strip off,' the purser ordered.

'No chance,' Gerald said, though with less bravado in his voice. 'Let my son and I leave now and we'll say no more about it.' He watched anxiously as Ellen swished the cane through the air to test its flexibility, sensing Nigel cowering behind him. 'Not a word, I promise. I'm too set in my ways to change.'

'You'll change and like it, the pair of you,' Ellen said. 'I told you both to strip; that should be up your street, Marsh.' She raised the cane. 'Clothes off or it will be much the worse for you. You too, Nigel. I won't repeat myself.'

Gerald began shedding his clothes, never averse to doing so with unclad women around, giving Nigel a look that warned him to follow suit. Soon both men stood naked, Nigel with his hands covering his crotch while Gerald remained defiant, his long, thick cock on display, threatening to grow longer by the moment. Aware of that possibility, Ellen strolled behind him and, without warning, cracked the cane across his bared buttocks. Gerald howled in pain and anger while Nigel cried out in anguish, as if he too had been struck.

'Bitch!' hollered Gerald, getting another hard swipe across the arse for his defiance. Seeing Myra flash him a warning glance, he fell silent. His cheeks stinging, he attempted to rub them with his hand only to have it pulled away sharply by Ellen.

'Stand still. If you give one sign of gaining a disgusting erection you can be sure of a severe caning,' she promised tersely. 'What's more, you'll gratefully accept every stroke. Your conduct in the time you've spent on board has resulted in serious complaints from a number of women passengers. I hold written statements of sexual harassment, signed by witnesses and held in my office safe. These will be used against you unless you comply with my training demands.'

'This is a set-up,' Gerald protested, his outrage genuine. 'I was only being sociable to the women I've talked to. Okay, chatted up, if you insist, that's my style. But harassment? You got to be kidding.'

'Don't tell *me* what I've got to be,' Ellen said harshly, giving Gerald another taste of her cane. 'We're talking real trouble here, buster. Dr Weissbinder has been informed of the written statements and has given me discretion to act as I see fit. In a word, you're *mine*.'

'Well, do your bloody worst, I deny everything,' Gerald said, incensed and forgetting he had promised Myra he would play along. 'What can you do?'

'A word in the right ear,' Ellen said, the cane poised and Gerald clenching his buttocks at an expected strike, 'the ship's captain for instance, could get you confined to your cabin for the rest of the cruise or even worse. I mean having the *Aphrodite* turn around to heave-to off Plymouth for the purpose of putting you ashore. That would be an expensive inconvenience. Rest assured Dr Weissbinder as cruise director would sue the pants off you to recoup the cost.'

'Thousands of pounds at least,' Myra chipped in gaily. 'It would ruin you. So from here on in, Geraldo you old fornicator, you'd better take the cure. To keep you company, nerdy Nigel will join you. I'm told it's for your own good.'

'I've nothing to do with any harassment,' Nigel bleated. 'It wasn't me – it was *him*.'

'Thanks a bunch, son,' Gerald said curtly. 'It seems we've got to go along with this blackmail, without any choice.'

'None whatsoever,' Ellen agreed. 'The rules are simple. You both do as I command without question.'

'Let's see if it's sunk in,' Myra said impatiently. 'We have two nude specimens of the male sex before us. What have you in mind, Ms Jackson? We don't want them behaving rudely, do we? As you say, getting a disgusting erection and flaunting it as us poor females is a punishable offence.'

'I doubt if even the threat of the cane will prevent a salacious reprobate like Marsh senior controlling himself. But he will learn,' Ellen said. 'Tempt him a little, Myra, please. I'll allow that. Remember, Marsh, you do have a choice. Restrain yourself and your base feelings if you don't want to increase my displeasure. Think pure thoughts, think of the amount of money you will owe if this ship has to turn back, think of anything but being excited by what Myra might do.'

Myra approached Gerald with her breasts cupped in her hands. Steadying himself, he felt the sharp nipples pressed to his chest, tracing circular movements around his own nipples as Myra gyrated her tits. Almost face to face, he gave her a wry grin. 'You really know how to hurt a guy,' he whispered jokingly. 'I shall get a dirty great hard-on if you keep that up and Miss Whiplash will have a ball whacking my arse. I've caned and spanked a few female botties in my time, so I guess it's my turn.'

'This is torture for me too,' she said, whispering her reply. 'It only makes me want to fuck. Play along, remember? All will be made clear later.' She sank to her knees. Finding Gerald already stiffening up to a full erection, she covered the engorged stalk with her mouth and sucked greedily in her own excitement. She felt Ellen's hand pulling her back to leave Gerald standing with a stout prick rearing up to his belly.

'So much for his control,' Ellen said testily. 'I didn't expect otherwise. Bend over that chair and present your rear, Marsh. I keep my promises.'

She gave him six of the best and was disappointed that he remained silent. She was even more annoyed, when he straightened up, to see his erection rearing as prominently as before. She pushed him towards a corner of the cabin. 'Remain there until that beastly thing goes down,' she ordered, turning to an apprehensive Nigel. 'Now what have we here? Is he a man? I wonder. Myra, under the pillows on my bed you'll find my nightdress. Bring it to me.' She fixed her gaze on Nigel. 'For goodness sake stop cowering, you wimp. Put on my nightdress, see how it suits you.'

'No!' Nigel cried. 'I refuse. Why are you doing this to me?'

'Do as they say,' Gerald called out from his corner.

'Father knows best,' Myra chipped in wickedly, holding up the nightdress which was a white shortie type and almost transparent. 'Or do I have to put it on you myself? Any further resistance, young man, and you'll go across my knee for a good bottom spanking. There, that wasn't too bad,' she said as Nigel reluctantly donned the nightie. 'In fact it suits you. You make quite a nice girl.'

Nigel groaned, covering his crotch with his hands, jamming his knees together and crouching over. 'That's not allowed,' Ellen told him sharply. 'Straighten up, chest out, shoulders back. Goodness, what have we here?' Standing before him, she used the tip of the cane to lift his prick. 'Do I detect that the wicked young man has started to get an erection?' she taunted. 'Did Auntie Myra threatening to take you over her knee and smack your bottom turn you on? Or was it wearing my nightie? I think that's what it is. We've discovered your secret fetish, haven't we? Does your wife know how naughty you are?'

'Please, *please*,' Nigel begged miserably.

'Please *what*?' Ellen taunted. 'Please, you like to wear women's clothes? Or, please, you'd like your bottom smacked? You'll only have that pleasure if you are very good, won't he, Myra? I think he's staring at my breasts now, the bad boy. Do you like them?' She held them out before his face. 'Do you want to suck on them and have mummy nurse you like the baby you are? That's only allowed if you are very very obedient. You must behave and not let that unruly penis show what wicked thoughts you have. Would you like to suck Aunt Myra's titties? They're much bigger than mine. Show him, Myra.'

'Look, the dirty little beast has got an erection,' Myra declared. 'How could he let it stick out like that in front of two ladies? Shame on you, Nigel. He doesn't deserve to suck my titties if he can't control the repulsive thing. What are you going to do with him?'

'To be *very* strict,' Ellen promised while Nigel quaked. 'Down, Nigel, on your knees,' she ordered. With head bowed he sank slowly before her and she seized his head in her hands and pulled it forward. Watching her, her eyes half-closed and mouth pursed, Myra knew that Nigel's face was now pressed to Ellen's cunt. She held Nigel's nose and mouth gripped between her thighs, buried in her most intimate part. Slowly she began to gyrate her hips, her face flushed, the hand at the back of his head drawing him closer. A low moan sounded as Nigel responded, making her stiffen and slap at his head.

'No, not that, not your tongue, you dirty beast!' she exclaimed. 'Keep your tongue inside your mouth. Control yourself or I shall cane you. Remain still, that's all you have to do.'

Myra noted the look of pleasure on Ellen's face and watched the shudder of her hips as Nigel's gasps grew louder. Suppressing a groan, Ellen pushed Nigel's head from her. 'Get up,' she ordered, as Nigel sank back on his knees. 'You disobeyed me, didn't you? You couldn't restrain yourself even after I'd ordered you not to use the tongue. As it was your first trial I shall overlook it this time.'

As well you might, Myra thought, at least one of us got to climax and it wasn't me. She heard Nigel being ordered to stand up, his prick in full erection. 'It was too much for him,' Ellen said. 'He obviously liked the taste of me. I wonder if he's done it to his wife. Have you, Nigel?'

'No, never,' Nigel said. 'I – I didn't like to suggest it.'

'Then you should,' Ellen said. 'The object of this exercise is to discover just what preferences you have. Get dressed now and keep my nightdress as a souvenir of the occasion. You won't be required to attend me anymore.'

'What about me?' Gerald called from his corner. 'Does that let me off the hook as well? I give good head if that's what you're after.'

Ellen shook her head. 'You've got a one-track mind,' she said pityingly. She used her cane to lift his prick. 'I haven't done with you. This is the foul object that rules your life. Until we can tame it, you'll return for my kind of treatment. Your orders are not to approach any female passenger for any reason. That goes double for the Craig women, whom I hear you have pestered enough. Dress now and consider yourself let off lightly this time. Any repeat of your previous behaviour and I shall ask Dr Weissbinder to put you ashore.'

Gerald dressed and left without a further word to Ellen. A few doors along the corridor Myra beckoned him in to her cabin, shutting the door behind him and holding out a large whisky. 'What did you think of all that?' she asked him cheerfully. 'I was proud of you, you played along very well.'

'That girl and her nutty professor are up a gum tree if they think they can change me,' he grinned, swallowing the drink. 'Whatever they've supposedly got on me, I'd have told her to get knotted but for you telling me to go along with it. Are you going to let me in on the secret?'

'Later,' Myra promised. 'All will be revealed. They've got nothing on you that would stick, but let them think you believe them, it suits our plan. Blackmail is a serious charge, and that won't be half of what we'll have on Weissbinder. How's your poor backside, by the way?'

'Smarting,' he said. 'The bitch enjoyed laying it on. One day I hope to return the favour. What kind of sadist is she? Did you note the cunning way she made Nigel bring her off?' He let Myra lead him to her bed and lower his trousers. He lay across it as she rubbed soothing cream into his reddened cheeks. 'I've been ordered to leave the female passengers alone, that's the worst of it.'

'I'm not a passenger,' Myra reminded him slyly. 'You'll just have to content yourself with fucking me for the duration of the voyage. Would you call that a hardship?' She began to pull off her clothes. 'Like right now, for instance. That so-called obedience training of Ellen's only got me randy. What effect did it have on you?'

'This,' Gerald said meaningfully, rolling over on the bed and showing her a stupendously erect prick. 'Whatever that bloody girl has in mind for me, it isn't going to work. Get your arse on this bed, Myra, and I'll prove it.'

Chapter Thirteen

Feelings

Leaving a glum Dorothy mulling her recent shipboard lapses with Myra, Gerald and Martin, Manda ventured on deck seeking more congenial company. 'I should be so lucky,' Manda thought resentfully, irked by her continuing virginity and her sister's hypocrisy.

Every chance she was offered, Dorothy conveniently forgot her morals and the fact that she was Nigel's wife. What would it take, Manda wondered, to make her accept she was highly sexed and able to enjoy herself without guilt? That was the kind of soul-mate sister Manda wanted, one who was happy with her own sexual nature.

Looking older than her seventeen years, in a figure-hugging mini-dress without underwear, Manda went out ripe for an adventure. Uncertain about the layout of the ship, she entered a passageway looking for a bar or lounge with some company. She opened a door and entered a long cabin with empty chairs placed in a semi-circle in front of a desk and a large television screen. A group of men crowded around an open door which led out of the lecture cabin. Something was holding their attention. They were a mixed bunch, all around middle-age, looking well-preserved and prosperous.

As Manda approached one of the men held a finger up to his lips for silence. The crowd of bodies prevented her seeing what they were watching but from the other cabin came the unmistakable sounds of a woman being sexually pleasured. The low moans and mumblings, ecstatic cries and whimpers triggered Manda's own sensations of arousal. She looked questioningly at the man who had warned her to be silent, trying to edge her way into the group to see what was going on.

'This isn't for you, young lady,' he whispered in an American accent, his handsome face flushed with excitement at what they were witnessing. 'This is a therapy session for men. I think you had better leave.'

'Aren't I allowed one little peep?' Manda whispered back mischievously. 'From what I'm hearing, I'm sure I'd learn something. Do let me see. What kind of therapy is it?'

'It's for impotent males. Those of us who have difficulty satisfying their partners,' he said openly. 'It's not something to be ashamed of, strange as it might seem. I don't know how you got in here but this hardly applies to you.'

'Why did you have to tell her, Andrew?' complained the man beside him. 'She probably just thinks it's funny.'

'Dr Weissbinder advised us to face our inadequacy and admit it as part of overcoming the problem,' the American argued. 'Hell, so I can't get it up, but I'm going to get over it. Have faith, Lester. Didn't you get anything from Dr Calvert's counselling session? Now he's showing us how to overcome the fear of failure, to take our time about it as a necessary first step to—'

'Getting it up again?' Manda continued for him, finding it all terribly amusing but trying to appear solicitous. 'I do not think being impotent is a joke at all. It must be very frustrating for you.' The men looked at her, unsure her sympathy was genuine. 'How did it happen?' she asked, feeling more was expected of her. 'Was it the fault of the ladies in your lives? Maybe you were trying too hard, that's the way with you men, I'm sure. You want to make the earth move every time, but we women don't expect miracles.' Manda wondered from where she had conjured up such words, but they seemed appropriate to the company by their nods of agreement. She gave them her sweetest smile. 'Remember, the women you are with must help you. We females have our ways and means.'

'This young lady makes a lot of sense,' Andrew said.

'Sounds like she's one of Weissbinder's therapy team, or if she isn't then she ought to be. If she wants to observe the action, why not? Let's get her opinion.'

Manda found herself given space to stand directly in the doorway, surrounded by the men. In front of her, and heightening her aroused state, she saw a naked young man strenuously fucking a naked woman on a bed. His flanks hollowed as he thrust deep into her, each forward lunge producing pleasurable cries and grunts from the woman on the receiving end. From where Manda stood, looking down on the broad back, tapering waist and firm buttocks of the male, she had an clear view of his big balls swinging and the thick stem of a massive prick shunting in and out.

She saw the woman's cunt lips clasped around the intruding stalk like a hungry mouth, her ample bottom heaving up from the bed to swallow in every inch inside her. Her legs were locked around his waist, hands clasping and hauling on his buttock cheeks to draw him closer. A nude man stood beside the bed, viewing the couple closely, holding an erect penis in his hand.

Envious of the woman being so thoroughly pleasured, Manda saw with some shock and surprise it was Dr Calvert doing the thrusting. She recognised him as the attractive man who had welcomed her aboard with her mother and sister. 'That's Dr Calvert,' she said, turning with questioning eyes to the large American who stood watching from over her shoulder.

'It's all part of the therapy,' he said. 'Following Dex Calvert's lecture and counselling this session, he's giving us a practical demonstration. The lady acting as his partner is Ed Salvatori's wife, Maria, and the guy eye-balling it from close range is Ed himself. He's no doubt hopeful of retaining that hard-on until Dex is through with his wife.'

'Doesn't he mind his wife being – demonstrated – on?' Manda giggled quietly. 'Obviously she doesn't care. I don't think she's aware her husband is beside them, the way Dr Calvert has her going.'

'She's loving it,' Andrew agreed, 'and why should Ed object? He volunteered his wife for the part. The way she's taking every inch, I can see why. You came in late, you missed the explicit examples of foreplay Dex demonstrated to show how to turn a woman on. He took his time, doing things that had Mrs Salvatori sitting up and begging for it. She was desperate to be screwed.'

'No wonder, if her husband hasn't been able to do the necessary,' Manda agreed, the hot throb in her cunt increasing. She was suddenly sticky between her thighs.

With a cry of protest from Maria, Dex withdrew from her, disengaging only long enough to roll her over on the bed. He's demonstrating the rear position, Manda observed, thinking what an excellent position it must be. It was definitely something she intended to try. A moment later Dex was curled over his partner's back, his prick glistening with her juices as it slid up to the hilt in her receptive cunt. Manda noticed how the penetrating stalk was accepted, Mrs S thrusting her plump backside against her fucker's belly and jerking and gyrating her arse as if demented. Her pendulous breasts swung as she raised herself on both elbows, back dipped to present her rear at the desired angle.

'The way Maria's going at it, she'll be too pooped to take anything her old man might have to give,' Andrew whispered in Manda's ear. 'I figure she's come more times today than she has in years with him.'

'Don't bank on it,' Manda whispered back, liking the big American and his sense of humour. 'You don't know how much some women want.' She felt very adult, exchanging sexy comments with an obviously sophisticated older man while watching a wanton exhibition of fucking. 'The more we get, the more we need,' she added teasingly, knowing it would be true in her case.

'Not any of my wives,' he replied with amusement. 'All four of them. Beautiful but cold bitches every one, with dollar signs in their eyes. You wouldn't believe the settlements and alimony, an arm and a leg. And all I got out of it was

144

impotence. That's why I'm on this cruise, to restore my faith in the opposite sex and be able to get it up again.'

'As I'm sure you will,' Manda said genuinely. 'You're big, strong and very handsome. What's stopping you?'

'You're a kind girl but I've paid the best psychiatrists in the States to tell me that,' he said without rancour. 'Another arm and a leg but nothing worked. Maybe sea air and Weissbinder's therapy will do the job. Even seeing those two fucking like it's going out of fashion hasn't done the business. Sure, I'm enjoying the show, but though the spirit is willing I guess the flesh is still weak.'

'Poor you,' Manda commiserated, her attention held by the spectacle of Mrs Salvatori's plush bottom being pounded and the sound of her squeals of delight as the dog-fashion coupling became frenzied. 'How nice it must be to feel the way she's feeling.'

Suddenly she felt a hand groping under her dress, moving on up her leg and reaching the warm moistness of her inner thighs. Aroused beyond caring, she shifted her feet to widen her stance, allowing the searching hand to continue its progress between her buttock cheeks. The hand turned over, its thick wrist parting the cushiony divide. Gentle fingers began to caress the down-hanging bulge of her split mound, then traced seductively along the outer lips, swollen and oiled by her excitement, to toy with the hairy growth surrounding her cunt, teasing and tantalising her. Staring ahead and not daring to turn her face, she knew it was the hand of her American friend. She stifled a moan as his finger entered her, probing among the soft velvety inner folds of flesh, the sodden walls and nerve ends highly responsive to the unexpected titillation.

Helpless to resist, she bent slightly at the knees, tilting her bottom rearward to allow the stroking finger better access, biting her lips to maintain some control as the extreme pleasure mounted. The tip of the finger ventured deeper, pushing in and out until Manda's lower torso writhed under the increasing torment, her rear gyrating and squirming on the hand buried between her cheeks. A subtle switch of attention to her taut and distended clitoris made her gasp aloud and she finally lost all control as the finger flicked and swirled around the highly sensitive bud. With a moan she began jerking her bottom wildly, coming in helpless spasms that shook her bodily, accompanying her shattering climax with loud shrieks of pleasure.

As the sensations gradually lessened, Manda lolled back sated and breathless against the chest of the man who had brought her off. She clenched the muscled walls of her cunt around the finger which had given her such pleasure but was unable to prevent its withdrawal. Regaining some sanity, the deathly silence all around brought her back to reality. She stared about her in dire confusion.

On the bed before her Dex Calvert was still embedded up Mrs Salvatori from the rear position, both he and she unmoving as they stared in her direction, as did her husband beside them. On either side of Manda every man stood open-mouthed, faces turned to her with looks of awe.

She broke free and ran from the cabin, pulling down her dress over her divine young bum. Disappearing through the door, she heard a burst of applause for her impromptu performance.

On deck, she considered the event, not blaming herself for the outcome. Her virgin quim still throbbed deliciously from the fingering and she shrugged off her concern about such immodest behaviour. I'm not dreary Dorothy, she reminded herself, who no doubt would have reacted in the same way, unable to resist getting touched up while witnessing a memorable exhibition of fucking. Unlike her sister she felt no remorse. How else was a horny girl expected to behave with a manipulative finger up her cunt? As for the men observing, the applause on her exit showed they'd appreciated her. None more than the tall handsome Yank she'd heard addressed as Andrew. Leaving off her panties had been inspired and she giggled as she imagined his surprise as his hand met her bare bottom.

She thought it time to acknowledge her mother's presence on the ship, but was pleased to find Ailsa's cabin empty. Going through to her own, she discovered Dorothy in bed reading. 'What are you up to sis?' the still-elated Manda said. 'Why don't you dress and we'll go to dinner. After that, who knows? I'm not going to waste a single minute of this cruise. Mother seems to have disappeared, which is all the better for us.'

'I'm not hungry,' Dorothy said petulantly. 'Knowing you, you'll enjoy yourself more without me. I'm hoping Nigel might look in—'

'How you can still be stuck on him, I'll never know,' Manda said, mystified. 'Why don't you go to his cabin and jump on him? That might ease your boring conscience. I haven't got one. Do you know what's just happened to me?'

'I don't want to know,' Dorothy replied coldly. 'I'm glad I wasn't with you if it's what I think.'

'Because *you* can't resist going all the way,' Manda taunted her, undressing to shower. 'That's why you're not coming with me tonight. If we met up with Martin and Graham again you couldn't trust yourself. All the more for me, I'll have both to myself.'

'I believe you would,' Dorothy said disapprovingly, watching her naked sister flounce off to shower with a defiant waggle of her bottom. She studied her book restlessly, watching later as Manda dressed, cautioning her about wearing too short a frock and too much make-up. 'Men will take you for fair game,' she cautioned as Manda went out with a cheerful wave.

At the dining hall, Manda was greeted by a waiting steward.

'Miss Craig?' he enquired. 'Miss Amanda Craig? Are you alone?'

'My mother and sister have disowned me,' she joked, 'so are you going to put me at a table with someone nice? Young and male for preference.'

'I can do better than that,' the steward said. 'Your presence is requested at a private supper party. I was ordered to stand here waiting the arrival of the prettiest girl on the

Aphrodite, so I knew it must be you. Would you care to follow, please?'

'Who's giving this supper party?' Manda asked as she walked beside him.

'All I've been told is to deliver you,' he said, knocking on a door and turning to go before it was answered. Manda was mystified. She stood her ground, apprehensive but as ever game for the unusual. She was surprised to see Dex Calvert open the door and step back to usher her inside. The large cabin was luxuriously furnished with a whole array of drinks lined up on a trolley. There was another person there besides Dex. The older man sat in a wheelchair regarding her through thick spectacles and stroking a wispy beard in obvious approval. Manda was disappointed. She'd rather have the hunky doctor to herself.

'How nice to meet you at last, Miss Craig,' the wheelchair-bound man welcomed her. 'I am Dr Weissbinder, cruise director of this voyage. My young colleague is Dr Calvert, a valued psychotherapist in the field of sexual disability. You may have gathered that from your unwarranted intrusion into his counselling session.'

'Is that what you call it,' Manda said, unabashed. 'I'm very sorry, I didn't mean to intrude, I'd lost my way. One of the men there informed me it was therapy. What I saw was Dr Calvert giving a practical demonstration on somebody's wife.'

'Which did not in any way shock you, young lady,' Weissbinder said. 'Well, in our business we approve of the uninhibited and strive to teach those less liberated to become freer spirits – like you obviously. I take it you approve of counselling and therapy to help the sexually impaired?'

'For those who need it,' Manda agreed, 'but I don't if that's what you're after. I was told I'd been invited to a private supper party. Was that an excuse to get me here?'

'Of course there's a supper party. In your honour,' she was assured.

'Then why the inquisition?' Manda demanded. 'I said I'm sorry I walked in on your therapy session by mistake.'

'I don't think you are,' Weissbinder said knowingly. 'I know you are very glad you did. Watching Dr Calvert demonstrating his sexual prowess turned you on, didn't it? Let's not have any false modesty, Miss Craig. You were observed getting so aroused as to allow one of the men present to bring you to orgasm with his hand. You were being observed but that didn't stop you. What, I wonder, would your mother think of that?'

'She needn't know,' Manda said. 'Why should she?'

'Precisely,' Weissbinder smiled. 'All I ask is your cooperation tonight.'

'Are you trying to frighten me?' Manda said spiritedly. 'You should talk. What was going on in that place wasn't just me getting worked up. A whole bunch of gawping men were watching your valued therapist here fucking one of your patient's wives. Anyway, how do you know so much of what I allowed?' she demanded, giving Dex Calvert a glare. 'Did this creep rush over to give you a full account?'

'Not guilty,' Dex swiftly defended himself. 'No one said a word. Dr Weissbinder was taping the session. That's how he knows about it.'

'Oh!' Manda exclaimed, staring from Dex to Weissbinder. 'That shouldn't surprise me. Did you get a big thrill out of watching it?'

'It was interesting,' Weissbinder said calmly, touching a switch on the arm of his wheelchair, making a television screen across the cabin flicker into life. 'All therapy sessions are taped as a matter of course, Miss Craig, so we may judge their effectiveness and thereby improve our methods. You must agree, no one invited you to arrive and participate—'

'Well, no—'

'—Not that it didn't make fascinating viewing for us professional sexologists,' Weissbinder continued. 'Watch the screen, young lady. Something entirely impromptu and spontaneous, as was your response to the unexpected fondling, is not generally caught on camera. It was a happy accident. See what you think yourself.'

Manda's eyes turned to the screen, seeing Dex and an equally naked Maria Salvatori getting on the bed after undressing each other, her husband watching closely as his wife and Dex began kissing lewdly. As usual Manda felt stirrings in her belly and tremors of arousal were transmitted up to her breasts and nipples, then down to throb in her cunt. Watching the scene as if spellbound, Manda sensed a chair being placed behind her and sat automatically without taking her eyes off the screen. Dex was making free with Mrs Salvatori's plump breasts, burying his face in the cleavage, kissing the ample flesh, his mouth going to each thick nipple in turn. She moaned in pleasure, reaching for his prick, pulling on the engorged stalk, already desperate to guide it between her parted thighs.

'Dr Calvert is giving a demonstration of foreplay,' Weissbinder put in. On screen Dex was spreading the woman's legs and lowering his head between her thighs. Her cunt tilted forward, presenting the hairy split at the desired angle, Maria Salvatori was heard to mutter 'Yes, *Yesss-*' as his face closed in. Transfixed by the sight of Dex clamping his mouth over the profferred pussy and imagining his tongue probing, Manda's bottom squirmed and gyrated into the seat of her chair. Her thighs tightened, squeezing together to respond to the surge in her cunt, desperate to give herself relief. She heard the men conversing as if from a distance, her agitated grinding together of her inner thighs gathering momentum. Not caring how they might think of her, the chair bumped and rocked as she crossed her legs and squeezed her thighs tighter, her bottom thrusting against the seat.

She stifled her moans, concentrating on bringing herself off while watching Dex continuing to arouse Maria, rolling her over and smacking her backside as she attempted to pull him across her. 'I thought she was going to rape me, she was so eager,' Dex said. 'All she wanted was the dick. She was a good fuck though. In the end I had to screw her before she went berserk.'

Manda knew how she must have felt, giving a heartfelt

groan as she came. 'Take note of how you video so splendidly, Miss Craig,' she heard Weissbinder saying as if ignorant of her agitation. When she could focus her eyes again, her image was on the screen with the tall American behind her. It was, Manda recognised, prior to the moment she felt his hand glide up her inner leg.

'Something told me what Andrew Garfield was up to,' Weissbinder said. 'I held the angle of the shot, it was too good to miss. I suspected you wouldn't stop him, Miss Craig, not with the exhibition going on before you. Watch your reaction.'

Manda saw herself alter her stance as Andrew's hand crept under her dress, part her feet and tilt up her bottom to work against the intruding finger. Her hips and pelvis increased their jerking motions as the orgasm made her lose control.

'How fascinating, seeing oneself being made to come,' Weissbinder remarked. 'You're an extremely photogenic girl and a highly sexed one too.' He stopped running the tape. 'Now you have earned that special supper. Do you like caviar and champagne? Andrew Garfield, the gentleman who took advantage of you, wishes to make it up to you.'

'Tell him thanks but no thanks,' Manda said, standing up and straightening her dress. 'What are you, his pimp? Why didn't he ask me himself?'

She walked haughtily out of the door but Dex caught up with her, taking her elbow to slow her down. Manda pulled her arm away, glaring at him. 'Has your lord and master sent his tame lackey to see if I've changed my mind? No way, I'm not that desperate. I've never met such a creepy old man.'

'You were great,' Dex said. 'I think Weissbinder got the message. I don't blame you for walking out.' He led her out on to deck where the velvet sky was spangled with stars, the sea almost luminous.

'I suppose I missed a nice supper,' Manda said, her hunger returning, making them laugh together. 'Would you have been there?'

'I'm not in that league,' Dex grinned. 'It was set up so

that Andrew Garfield got to meet you again. You made a big impression on him for some reason. He's eager to renew your acquaintance.'

'You mean this time he wants to fuck me,' Manda giggled.

'He's undergoing my therapy,' Dex said. 'The guy claims he's impotent.'

'Not when I leaned against him after he'd made me come,' she informed him wickedly. 'I definitely felt something stiff. Very stiff.'

'It was probably the only hard-on he's had for years,' Dex laughed. 'No wonder he's keen to meet you again, you're a better therapist than me. Garfield's into banking, oil, shipping. He owns the *Aphrodite* and other cruise liners as well as a fleet of tankers. Weissbinder was wanting to keep in with the owner. He told me Garfield had some expensive trinket to give you tonight.'

'For services rendered,' Manda joked, 'and here I am worrying about missing a supper. Will dinner have been served by now?'

'Hear the music?' Dex said. 'The dining hall has been cleared for a cabaret. If you're hungry I can arrange our own supper party in my cabin.'

'You can do that?' Manda asked, impressed.

'Rank has its privileges,' he told her. 'I'm a big-shot psychiatrist as well as being Weissbinder's tame lackey. I could have a steward bring us whatever you order from the galley. Will you be my guest, Miss Craig?'

'Are you intending to make love to me as well?' Manda enquired.

'The thought never entered my head,' Dex lied charmingly. 'But if you insist—'

He leant beside her against the ship's rail, sliding his hand around her waist and gliding down over her smooth buttock cheeks. She turned her face to his and they kissed lingeringly, his tongue entering her mouth. Her hand went down to seek his prick, delighting in its feel as it stiffened under her clasp.

'No problem there,' he assured her as their lips parted. 'I'm the therapist.'

'I've seen you giving therapy,' Manda said, excited at the prospect of her virginity being taken. 'Will you give me some, like you did Mrs Salvatori?'

'It will be my pleasure,' murmured Dex in her ear.

They turned from the rail to head for Dex's cabin and came face to face with a smartly dressed Dorothy. 'I thought you were having an early night,' Manda said irritably to the one person beside her mother she did not wish to meet. 'What have you got all dressed up for?'

'I'm allowed to, aren't I?' Dorothy replied defensively, suspecting the worst at finding her sister with the handsome Dr Calvert. 'I decided I would go to dinner, but it seems I'm too late. There's some sort of cabaret going on in the dining hall. I wondered if you were there.'

'This is my sister Dorothy, my married sister,' Manda reluctantly introduced her as Dex stood by expectantly. 'And I'm with Dr Calvert.'

'Are you going to the cabaret?' Dorothy asked, accepting Dex's handshake. 'I didn't want to go by myself. May I join you?'

'We're not attending the cabaret,' Manda said abruptly, unable to keep the annoyance out of her tone. 'We have other plans. You'll have to look after yourself.'

'We're having supper in my cabin,' Dex said graciously, wishing to calm the animosity between the sisters. 'If Dorothy cares to join us, she's more than welcome. As for the other plans we had, there'll be other times.' He looked meaningfully at the irate Manda. 'The cruise has only just started.'

'What were those other plans?' Dorothy asked suspiciously.

'He was going to show me over the ship,' Manda said sullenly, the lie coming readily. 'If you insist on joining us, let's go and eat then.'

'I'm not often fortunate enough to have two beautiful guests at my table,' Dex said as he ushered them towards his cabin.

153

He would get around to fucking Manda soon, he knew, since she was as keen as he was to get at it. The lovely Dorothy might prove a trickier proposition, however, but his invitation for her to join them was a good first step to achieving that goal. And there was still their magnificently built mother to consider, he remembered, enjoying Manda fuming at being denied and glaring hate at her sister, foiled again in losing her unwanted virgin status.

Manda glared at her sister and cursed her inwardly. Was she destined to complete the cruise a virgin?

Chapter Fourteen

Woman to Woman

After the intimate massage session with Helga, her body still tingling from her lewd excess, Ailsa was shaken by her wanton response. She found herself on deck, the cool air calming her, trying to face up to the kind of woman she was behind her outwardly cold and dignified facade. In the fading light of dusk she stood by the ship's rail, unaware of the swish of the sea along the *Aphrodite's* side, her thoughts centred on how readily she submitted when aroused. She recalled her frequent self-pleasuring, the way she had allowed Dr Weissbinder to witness her seduction by Helga, plus her capitulation to the demands of Gerald Marsh. Whatever her puritanical upbringing decreed was wrong, my body inevitably says otherwise, she concluded.

A friendly voice beside her remarked on the array of stars above, interrupting her thoughts. 'Oh, hello, Miss Jackson,' she said, acknowledging the arrival of the pretty assistant purser. 'Yes, I suppose it is a lovely night.'

'Call me Ellen,' the girl said. 'Now why are you looking so gloomy? There's a cabaret starting with a dance to follow.'

'I'd be poor company,' said Ailsa. 'I'm going to my cabin.'

'No,' Ellen insisted. 'If you don't feel like facing people, come to mine. I always allow myself a stiff gin after duty. Join me, perhaps it will cheer you up. You can talk if you wish and I'm a good listener.' She linked arms with Ailsa, leading her off without argument.

Inside her cosy living space, Ellen seated her guest in the one armchair and mixed two generous gin and tonics. 'This is most pleasant having you here,' she said. 'After a strenuous day, I like to relax with good company.'

'Thank you,' said Ailsa, accepting her drink and thinking what a pretty girl Ellen Jackson was. 'You should be at the dance.'

'Not my thing,' Ellen replied, raising her glass. 'Bottoms up,' she ordered, noting that Ailsa swallowed the drink as if in dire need. She refilled the glass, saying, 'Drink up, Mrs Craig.'

'My name is Ailsa, and you'll get me tiddly.'

'Then we'll both get tiddly, Ailsa,' Ellen laughed. 'And why not?'

'Why not?' Ailsa agreed, forcing a smile. 'I need something to take me out of myself.'

'Or someone,' Ellen suggested beguilingly. 'Relax, my dear. In here you can let your hair down. Let's have another.'

'You *will* get me tiddly,' Ailsa said, 'but I don't care.'

'That's the spirit,' Ellen said. 'The first thing I do when I come off duty is take off my uniform. Do you mind? It's lovely to float about free as a bird after a day dressed as an officer.'

'The uniform suits you,' she said, accepting a further gin. 'You look so smart. You're such a pretty thing.'

'Why, thank you,' Ellen said graciously. 'Coming from a lovely woman such as yourself, I accept the compliment.' She unbuttoned the uniform jacket and took it off, shimmied her slim hips to let her skirt fall and kicked it from around her ankles. Sitting down on her bed, she drew off her stockings and frilly suspender-belt, tossing them over the back of a chair with her other discarded clothes, stretching luxuriously as if welcoming the freedom.

'Now,' she said with concern, standing directly before Ailsa dressed solely in miniscule lacy cream bra and panties, her slender body almost boyish apart from the extravagantly pointed pear-shaped breasts, 'why do you want to be alone tonight, Ailsa? We can't have that on a pleasure cruise. Do tell me.'

'It – it's nothing, just something that happened to me,' Ailsa said, forcing a wry smile, glancing around seeking to change the subject. 'What a charming cabin you have. I imagine, as a crew member, you like to make it as homely as you can.'

'You're evading the question,' Ellen said kindly. She reached behind her back to unhook her bra, seemingly indifferent to baring her breasts before Ailsa. It left her in only the briefest of briefs, the transparent material covering the curved mound between her thighs allowing the dark outline of a heavy growth of pubic hair to show through. 'It's to do with a therapy session you've had this evening with Dr Weissbinder and his German masseuse, isn't it? I know all that takes place on this ship.' She noted with pleasure that Ailsa was staring as if mesmerised at her sharply-pointed breasts and long nipples, her face flushed. 'Did old Weissbinder and Helga put you through it?' Ellen repeated. 'Did it distress you? Come on, we're both women, I understand.'

'I – I don't wish to talk about it,' Ailsa said touchily. 'Ever.'

'Why?' Ellen demanded. 'Would you prefer to let it fester inside?'

'Because I let it go beyond the bounds of decency. At least what I've always considered the bounds of decency,' Ailsa said wretchedly. 'I accepted the offer of a massage from Helga in all innocence.'

'Yes,' Ellen nodded eagerly. 'Then what happened?'

'She aroused me, then this Dr Weissbinder arrived unexpectedly. Or so I thought, but it was planned.'

'And what was going on?'

'I was laid out on the padded table being massaged, being fondled actually. Without a stitch on. I demanded Weissbinder left at once, but he refused and said I was uptight, suffering from a complex about nudity and sex. He insisted he could help.'

'That's his profession,' Ellen said. 'But you were unsure. You must have had mixed feelings about the situation. You did say you were aroused but I expect that old guilt and shame reared its ugly head.' She crossed to Ailsa to slide a comforting arm around her shoulder and hug her, the bare pear-shaped

157

tits swinging enticingly before her eyes. 'They meant well, I'm sure. Weissbinder is a world-renowned sexologist, concerned for you, no doubt. Helga is experienced too. And it's plain even to me you *are* mixed up about your sexuality, which is the real shame. You know you could have put your clothes on and left.'

'I – I couldn't, even if I'd wanted to,' Ailsa admitted, disconcerted by Ellen's breasts, the nipples erect and in line with her mouth. 'I found myself submitting against my nature.'

'Or what you believe is your nature,' Ellen said with concern. She stifled a smile at the other woman's discomfiture, adding, 'So they gave you their brand of therapy. For your sake, I hope it helped. Did they question you on your past sexual hisory?'

'Yes, while I was aroused and that woman was doing things to me,' Ailsa said. 'I'm to go for further sessions. I was even glad they said I must. They claimed it was for my own peace of mind, to become a whole person. I suppose they're right, but it was too much too soon.'

'There, there,' Ellen said consolingly, giving Ailsa a hug and pressing a kiss to her inflamed cheek. 'Admitting what you are is a good start. Confessing your sexual problems helps too.'

She sat on the arm of Ailsa's chair and cuddled her. 'No woman should be tortured by suppressing her feelings. It can be most harmful. Didn't you feel good after the session?'

'For a while I felt wonderful. But I told them intimate things, private things,' Ailsa whimpered, her emotional turmoil made more complicated by the nearness of the practically naked girl. Her eyes brimmed with hot tears as she said, 'I had the feeling they were enjoying worming secrets out of me when I was so aroused. Fantasies, I can't admit to myself without shame. What I think about when I masturbate. Even that I masturbate at all. That should be kept private. And all the time Helga was – well – using things and touching me intimately.'

'Which you adored at the time,' Ellen stated. 'I presume you climaxed?'

'I couldn't help myself,' Ailsa pleaded. 'So many times and in front of that man. He watched me in the very act of climaxing. It was humiliating.'

'Not at the time, one can only enjoy orgasms,' Ellen reasoned. 'Recognise it, you really must, my dear. It's your nature, don't fight it. Deep down you want to let your sensual nature free.'

'I don't know what I am,' Ailsa said, sobbing quietly. 'I do know I've been a woman who has suppressed her sexual nature.'

'So think of all the wasted years,' Ellen soothed. 'Think of yourself as a very desirable woman with lost time to make up. Ailsa, you are so sweet. Let me kiss away those tears.' She used gentle fingertips to raise Ailsa's face, noting the wan look of gratitude in her eyes.

'Then you are sweet too,' Ailsa said, smiling. 'Kiss away my tears indeed. I'm not a child but I somehow felt loved when you said that. Did you really mean it?'

'Of course,' Ellen said, pressing her lips to each tear-brimmed eye in turn, then to both cheeks. She paused a moment before covering Ailsa's mouth with her own. Surprised, Ailsa drew back, but she was held firmly captive in Ellen's arms. Her mouth was kissed again, long and passionately, as Ellen probed with a warm wet tongue. She withdrew her lips and smiled at a bewildered Ailsa. 'I did so want to kiss you,' she whispered tenderly, aware that Ailsa had been on the point of responding. 'Your mouth is so sweet, my darling. Did you mind?'

'I don't know,' Ailsa began hesitantly. 'Please, I'm confused enough. I know you are being kind, and your kiss was lovely, but we're two women—'

'Does that matter? Did it stop you with Helga?' Ellen asked, stroking Ailsa's cheek. 'Come to me and cuddle up.' She kissed Ailsa again, a light touch on the lips to test her reaction, the meeting of mouths growing torrid as it lingered, mouths opening and tongues entwining. 'Yes, oh yes,' Ellen said, reassured by the trembling of the woman in her arms. 'So you do like my kisses. Don't fight what you enjoy. Wait, I have an idea.'

She stood up and pulled off her panties, baring a heavily forested mound with a lipless slit. 'You must learn to be confident. You look a strong woman, so become one. I think a little test in being domineering is called for.'

She produced a slipper. 'I want you to spank me with this,' Ellen said, 'or perhaps you'd prefer to use your hand. Many women do. Don't spare me, beat me as hard as you can. I won't mind, I like it, and it will teach you that you don't always have to be the one that's submissive in a relationship.'

'I don't think I could,' Ailsa said meekly, taking the thin leather shoe. Ellen slipped across her knees, her apple-firm bottom tilted upwards, her breasts hanging.

'You can and you will,' she said. 'You'll find you'll like the feeling of power you get. Go on, Ailsa, I want you to.'

'You've had other women do this to you?' asked a mystified Ailsa, an impatient waggle of Ellen's pert bottom urging her to proceed. Raising the slipper, she brought the sole down across the divide of both cheeks in a feeble smack. Ellen demanded at once she use more force. By the fourth strike Ailsa felt more certain of her task, cracking down the leather sole with a will on Ellen's squirming and reddening cheeks and enjoying hearing her squeal. *Whack, whack*, the sole landed with increasing speed and strength until it was Ellen who begged her to stop.

'You cruel, wicked Ailsa,' Ellen said, clutching her thrashed rear with her hand. 'I told you you'd like doing it. It's so good for letting all the stress flow out of your body – and into mine,' she laughed wickedly. 'It makes you horny too, doesn't it? Now you must be rewarded in a special way, after first letting me adore you.'

She drew Ailsa to her feet, kissing her lingeringly while at the same time drawing down the zip at the back of her dress. 'Naked and unashamed, that's how I want you,' she murmured between more kisses. The dress discarded, her bra unclipped and drawn from her, Ailsa found pride in the way Ellen regarded her uncovered breasts. 'How beautiful,' she heard Ellen murmur in a voice hoarse with arousal. 'Oh, Ailsa, I love them – I love you. Let me touch them, kiss them, suck them. Come, come with me.'

Guided across the cabin, it struck Ailsa that twice within hours she was willingly indulging in wanton intimacy with a member of her own sex. But as Ellen lowered her across the bed, looking down with adoring eyes, she did not care. Ellen lay across her and their breasts kissed, nipple to nipple. Ailsa melted, her excitement instant. Still savouring the sense of power generated by the spanking, she rolled on top of Ellen, kissed her with mouth open, lips roving, tongue extended.

'How sweet,' she muttered between each wracking kiss. Ellen's thighs parted to make a cradle for Ailsa's belly. They fitted together snugly, cunt mound to cunt mound. Automatically, Ailsa began working her buttocks, thrusting hard and fast against Ellen's tilted quim, her movements exactly like a man's. 'You wicked witch,' she grunted, looking down on Ellen's face. 'There are so many rude things I'd like to do to you. This is almost like fucking you.' The pace of her thrusting increased and she cried out, spasming out of control with Ellen jerking and bucking below her, both climaxing together.

For a while they kissed tenderly, fondling and nuzzling each other's breasts. 'You shouldn't do that,' Ailsa said with mock severity as Ellen snuggled down to suck gently on a nipple. 'You don't know what it does to me. I think it's time I left.'

'Why?' Ellen asked. 'Because you're getting turned on again? I don't want you to go. Shall I show you something?'

'I'm not sure you should,' Ailsa said as the throb in her cunt was growing persistent again. 'What is it you want me to see? Something outrageous, I'm sure.'

'Then you'll stay,' Ellen said delightedly, reaching into the drawer of her bedside cabinet. With a flourish she produced an object trailing elasticated straps. 'Ever seen one of these before?' she asked, noting Ailsa's astounded look. 'It's a dildo. This type is double-ended.'

'I've not seen anything like it,' Ailsa admitted as Ellen placed it in her hands. 'A vibrator, yes. If I'm to reveal all my dark secrets, I confess to owning one. But not this.' She examined two plastic replicas of the male penis, fused together at the base at an angle, forming a wide 'V'. Both were exact in detail, the flesh-coloured shafts long and thick with bulbous knobs.

'You can't mean—?' Ailsa left the question unfinished.

She heard a muttered 'yes' as Ellen took Ailsa in her arms and pulled her to her feet, pressing ardent kisses to her lips. Ailsa responded, kissing back fiercely, her tongue thrust deep into her partner's mouth, moving her hips to grind their pubic mounds together. Her hands went down to grip Ellen's buttocks, pulling her in to meet each forward lunge. Eager to continue and loving the feel of soft flesh against her own, she protested as Ellen drew back.

'Please, don't stop,' Ailsa begged. 'It felt so good.'

'I know something better,' Ellen said artfully.

'But it was heaven – what could be better?'

'Have you ever fucked a woman with a dildo?' Ellen asked. 'Let me prepare you.'

Kneeling down, Ellen probed Ailsa's cunt with stiffened tongue and used her fingers to open her up. Her hands circled her partner's rear, cupping both cheeks firmly while her tongue worked its magic. A finger was infiltrated into Ailsa's cleave, seeking the wrinkled anal ring, and going in beyond the first knuckle to create even more frenzied writhing of buttocks and hips.

'Oh your finger! You're *killing* me!' Ailsa screamed. 'Do what you want with me. Finish me, let me *come*!'

'I'll slip one half of the dildo inside you and fix the straps in place,' Ellen said, withdrawing from Ailsa's palpitating cunt. 'That way we'll both get all the lovely comes we want.'

She took the dildo and pressed the knob between Ailsa's arousal-swollen labia. Gently but firmly she eased its whole

162

length inside the squirming Ailsa. 'There, you're so wet inside, my darling, it slips in beautifully,' Ellen murmured as her fingers nimbly adjusted the straps around Ailsa's thighs and waist. Then she sat back on her heels. 'How does it feel to be a man?' she asked wickedly. 'To have a cock?'

It made her feel powerful, Ailsa could have told her, glancing down at the dummy prick rearing thick and long from the join of her thighs. A stout cylindrical stalk fully ten inches in length, it thrust out menacingly before her, inclined at an angle purpose-designed for the penetration of another female. Viewed sideways in the long wardrobe mirror, the stout cock looked grotesquely erotic on a well-developed woman with large breasts. It jutted out in front of Ellen's face threateningly.

The girl clasped it between her breasts before lowering her mouth to lubricate the plum-shaped knob with her saliva. 'Yes, suck it, make it wet enough for your hungry cunt, you little slut,' Ailsa commanded harshly, revelling in this feeling of superiority.

'Get it ready for me to fuck you, you dirty bitch. Fuck you better than any man can.' It was words she would never have believed could issue from her mouth. Now she spoke them forcefully, meaning every one.

'Yes, yes,' Ellen agreed eagerly. 'I'll do whatever you say.' On her knees, she shuffled to the edge of her bed, leaning over it with her bottom out-thrust for penetration. There was not a flaw in the ivory-smooth skin and rounded cheeks. 'This is the way I like it most, Ailsa darling,' she purred.

'You have no shame,' Ailsa said, positioning herself behind Ellen. 'But I find it impossible to resist, you immoral creature. You should be thrashed, and so you will be later.' She knelt, enchanted by the sight before her as Ellen's hands reached back to draw apart the twin moons of her buttocks. Between the cleft cheeks the bulging fig of her quim peeped out invitingly in its bed of soft hair. 'Oh, such an irresistible bottom,' Ailsa crooned, mesmerised by the pallor of the rounded flesh, the slight golden hue where the cushiony mounds inrolled. 'I shall die if I don't kiss you there first.'

She leant forward to kiss and then taste Ellen's pungent flesh with her tongue extended, encouraged by the girl's excited murmurs. 'Now fuck me,' Ellen said. 'Shove it right up, fuck me hard as you like. I want it, I need it. *Please*.'

Ailsa raised her knees from the floor, her left hand steadying herself on Ellen's hip, her right hand guiding the knob of the dildo to its target. It plunged in to its full length as Ailsa pushed. A delirious '*Aaaagh*' issued from the girl on the receiving end, the smooth feel of her bottom against Ailsa's belly proof that the dildo was entirely sheathed. This had the effect of agitating the length embedded up Ailsa, making her work her hips with a will as she fucked the girl, thrilling herself by the shunting movement inside her own cunt.

Eyes wild with lust, she thrust her flanks like a man fucking a woman. In her frenzy she slapped hard at the bouncing buttocks beneath her, calling out 'Take that, you little slut, take it all. I'm fucking you, fucking you!'

'Yes, fuck me! Harder, faster!' she heard Ellen shriek out, buffeting her rear back to Ailsa in ecstasy as the big dildo pounded away. A continuing succession of wracking shudders gripped both of them as they climaxed together in an explosion of lust. At last Ailsa slumped forward over her sated partner, both still joined together by the embedded twin cocks.

'I might have guessed what that crafty lesbian cow would get you to do, Mrs Craig,' said a voice from the door.

Ailsa quickly rolled apart from Ellen, the glistening half of the double-dildo she wore rearing up from her crotch. Myra Starr was watching them with amusement. 'Did sweet little Ellen show you her toys? I see she made you have the operation?'

'What do you mean?' Ailsa said, deciding she would not allow her embarrassment to show. 'What operation?'

'A strapadichtomy,' Myra laughed. 'Don't feel bad about it, she got me to wear that thing too. I must say it rather suits you.'

'You interfering whore!' Ellen exploded, leaping from the bed to face Myra defiantly. 'Don't listen to her, Ailsa. She wouldn't know sensitive loving if it kicked her fat arse. Like I feel like doing right now—'

'You and who else?' Myra stated casually.

Instead of curling up in shame and humiliation, Ailsa found the situation highly amusing. Two women were about to come to blows over her and she was not displeased by the thought, finding it strangely flattering.

'Settle down, you two,' she advised. 'So you caught us in a compromising situation, Myra. We were doing nothing more than you've done yourself, it seems.'

'You've changed your tune,' Myra said. 'What's happened to the ice-cold schoolmarm of St Boniface's? Do you find this man-hating dyke irresistible? She certainly plays the field.' As Ellen made to go for her, she held up a warning hand. 'Better not, dear, unless you want a real beating.'

'This is ridiculous,' Ailsa laughed. 'I fucked Ellen because I wanted to.'

'You made a fine job of it from what I could see,' Myra said, shaking her head. 'How often I wanted you myself, but you never noticed.'

'That was the old me,' Ailsa said, getting to her feet and removing the dildo. 'Dr Weissbinder has changed my attitude to sexual matters. I now accept that repressing myself is harmful and I'm getting more used to the fact all the time. Isn't that what you all wanted?'

'This horny slut is just mad because it wasn't her you turned to,' Ellen spat, still furious. 'She told me she's always had a letch for you. Now she's spitting because I've had you first.'

Myra did not reply but suddenly grabbed Ellen by the hair, making her shriek. Ellen lunged back and both women tumbled to the floor. Keeping a safe distance from the wrestling bodies, Ailsa gathered up her clothes and dressed. She judged that the naked Ellen, her body sheened with perspiration from strenuous sex, was difficult for the stronger Myra to pin down.

'Fancy them fighting over me,' Ailsa thought, the idea strangely gratifying as she left them to it. 'That old Weissbinder could be right,' she mused, as she walked back to her cabin in the balmy night air. 'I've wasted years being prejudiced and bitter, all because I had a husband who hadn't the first idea about a woman's needs. Now I've never felt so free. I wanted that fucking. It was *fun*. I'm never going back to how I was. I swear I never shall.'

Chapter Fifteen

Reluctant Lust

The following day Manda and Dorothy could barely tolerate each other and their talk was confined to argument and accusation. Incensed by her sister's sudden appearance when she was all set to surrender her virginity to Dex Calvert, Manda spitefully recounted Dorothy's regular lapses, pointing out that she had no right to appoint herself anyone's protector. Dorothy countered that letting men have their way was humiliating, but Manda shrugged it off by saying she'd welcome the chance.

Manda's horny intentions were now focused on Martin and Graham but the brothers had left by the time the sisters went to breakfast. On Manda's enquiry to a steward, Dorothy was relieved to learn the boys would be rehearsing all day. Barely speaking, they returned to their cabin and Manda announced she was going to the pool intent to show as much of herself as possible.

'And if there's nude bathing again, I'll be joining in,' she stated. Standing naked, unable to decide which bikini to wear, she added, 'With any luck I won't need either of them.'

'That's because you've become a proper little tart,' Dorothy said.

'A virgin tart, which is more than you are,' Manda returned heatedly.

'You love to flaunt yourself,' Dorothy countered. 'It thrills you to have men staring at your – your—'

'Tits and bum?' Manda finished for her. 'I think they're worth looking at and I enjoy it. I bet it thrills you too. And if

167

mummy turns up, too bad. I don't care if Gerald is fucking her as long as she keeps out of the way. She would only spoil the fun.'

'Can you blame her?' Dorothy appealed. 'You know very well how she is. She'd consider such behaviour shocking. The idea of nude swimming, with her daughter shamelessly exhibiting herself, as well as – as—'

'That time with Martin and Graham?' Manda said cruelly. 'You should complain. At least you got fucked.'

'You can be so crude,' Dorothy said, uneasy at the thought. 'It wasn't that I intended to – to let him. Martin took advantage.'

'Exactly,' said Manda. 'I intend to meet those boys after they've finished rehearsing and let them take advantage of me. Then I'll let both of them fuck me. You're such a hypocrite, pretending you don't like anyone seeing you naked. How can you say Martin took advantage when I saw you bonking away like mad? Or claim that you were seduced when your father-in-law fucked you? For someone's wife, you get a hell of a lot on the side. More than me and I'm single and willing.' She challenged Dorothy: 'It *was* good, wasn't it?'

'Yes,' she admitted. 'I just don't feel so good about myself.'

Watching with interest in the control room on the video screen, Dr Weissbinder turned to gauge Dex Calvert's reaction. 'What's your professional opinion?'

'That young Manda has a great pair of boobs,' Dex said with a grin. 'Seriously, in my opinion, Manda is a horny little piece. She was about to let me seduce her last night, when her sister arrived. I'd say the demure Dorothy has a problem with her guilt complex, but evidently that doesn't stop her enjoying herself when the chance is offered. And, looking like she does, that's often.'

'Her husband's indifference explains why she satisfies her sexual needs so readily with others,' Weissbinder said. 'The guilt is a residue of her mother's repressive teaching. We've made progress with Mrs Craig, I'm pleased to report. Her session with Helga proved how vulnerable she is. It turned out to be a highly satisfactory session for both women. I want you, Dr Calvert, to further her enlightenment with a series of therapy appointments. You'll see to that?'

'With pleasure,' Dex agreed. 'That lady is a riper version of her lovely daughters. I'm glad to hear she's responding to treatment. As for Dorothy's guilt problem, I'd count it as a privilege to help straighten it out.'

'In time,' Weissbinder said. 'I've something in mind for her and this misfit of a husband she has. I learned something interesting from Ellen about that young man. Making that couple compatible would provide an interesting case history in my next book. You stick to Mrs Craig. We now know how she is with her own sex, but not with men. Go easy with her to begin with. If she reacts encouragingly to your therapy, leave her wanting more. I don't want her to hold anything back when she's ready. A taped recording of that, with the stuff we've got on her seduction by Helga, will make a very marketable video. Unscripted, unrehearsed, entirely spontaneous caught-in-the-act sexual activity is much sought after by connoisseurs. It would be a bestseller in the underground market.'

'Used without her permission, of course?' Dex asked deliberately.

'What else?' Weissbinder smiled unctuously. 'No matter how liberated we may make her, she'd hardly agree to having her sex romps distributed world-wide. But she's hardly likely to find out and will remain blissfully ignorant. Don't worry, I've got away with it for years.'

'Is it a good little earner?' Dex asked.

'A gold mine,' Weissbinder said. 'This trip will provide a bonanza of good raunchy tapes on the activities of the Craig family.' He wheeled around in his electrified chair to head for the door. 'I shall take breakfast in the dining hall this morning. Why don't you join me. If we see Mrs Craig there, we can arrange a therapy session.'

'I'll be there,' Dex promised, 'after I've changed into something suitable for a serious psychotherapist. Jeans and sweatshirt is hardly appropriate.'

Alone, he swivelled around in his seat as Myra entered the control room holding up a video cassette. 'Got it all,' she announced in triumph. 'The wily Weissbinder is not the only one to make secret tapes. Fixing up that equipment from your cabin to record what he gets up to was a stroke of genius. This time he really put his foot in it, openly admitting he sells tapes of patients engaged in sex. When do we tackle him?'

'Let's give him some more rope to hang himself with,' Dex said. 'Besides, this cruise has lots to offer yet for both of us. Too bad Ellen beat us both to Mrs Craig,' he added with a grin. 'I saw the re-run of the tape this morning, double-dildo and all. Weissbinder's delighted with it. He's got Ailsa Craig on tape masturbating, fucking another woman with a dummy prick and soon, he hopes, in the sack with me. That would be a classic video, especially the part where you and Ellen fight over her. Let's be patient and in time we'll all have her – and take Weissbinder to town in the process. It will be pay-back time, Myra. For all the money and kudos he's cheated us out of. This time the worms will turn. We can ruin him if we choose to.'

'Or he can make me rich and you famous,' Myra added. 'The old swindler has sold tapes of my sexual activities in therapy sessions as porno flicks, and I've never received a penny. That wasn't in my contract, I've got no royalties on sales, so it's time he coughed up. And if this is the time to skin him, there's one other thing I'd like to suggest.'

'Name it,' Dex said amiably. 'He hasn't a leg to stand on. What did you have in mind?'

'Mrs Craig and her school for girls,' Myra said. 'It's bound to close if some money isn't forthcoming. That would be a loss, especially if Ailsa returns with a more relaxed outlook. She's a good woman and her staff are all good teachers. How would you describe Weissbinder filming the Craig family in sexually compromising situations and distributing the tape for sale?'

'Invasion of their privacy at least,' Dex grinned, getting the point. 'Tarnishing their reputation and all sorts of defamatory things. I also know Weissbinder tried to procure Manda

Craig for the sexual gratification of Andrew Garfield, a big-shot tycoon who owns the publishing house which produces Weissbinder's books. Garfield wouldn't be too happy to be dragged into a scandal. When it comes to nailing Weissbinder, I reckon he'd settle out of court for any compensation the Craigs might seek.'

'Enough to keep St Boniface's out of debt at any rate,' Myra said. 'I like it, forcing money-bags Weissbinder to become a benefactor. The only thing is, how can we include the Craigs in our scheme without informing them? You're the shrink, I'll leave that to you.'

'We've time for that yet,' Dex decided. 'A lot depends on how liberated I can make Ailsa in therapy, to minimise any trauma she might have about being a star in Weissbinder's porn collection. The money she'll collect should soften the shock. Let me get to work.'

Alone in her cabin with her thoughts, Dorothy was startled by a tap at her door. She sat up on her bed as her mother entered. 'I thought it time I called,' Ailsa said brightly. 'There's been so much happening on this ship I feel I've been neglecting you and Manda. Where is she, by the way?'

'Out on deck somewhere,' Dorothy said, not wishing her mother to know Manda was at the pool, probably disporting herself naked. 'I don't know where she gets to.'

'You should be out enjoying the sun,' her mother said, concerned by Dorothy's despondent air. 'Hasn't Nigel been keeping you company? Is that what's upsetting you?'

'Oh mummy, I've been unfaithful,' Dorothy blurted suddenly.

'I knew you were unhappy,' Ailsa said kindly. 'I'm not surprised.' She hugged her daughter affectionately. 'It happens, dear. Don't blame yourself.'

'I've never heard you say such things, mother,' Dorothy said in surprise.

'Well, I've learned otherwise,' Ailsa said, pressing a kiss to her daughter's forehead. 'If a husband isn't doing his duty, a wife must look elsewhere. You can't exist starved of affection for ever. Was it good? Did all sorts of lovely sensations send you wild? I know something of that myself now, thank goodness. Was the man a skilled lover?'

'There were three of them,' Dorothy said, blushing deeply. 'One of them was another woman. I couldn't help myself. Once I'm aroused, it seems I'm anybody's. I'm sex mad—'

'No, just a very frustrated young woman,' Ailsa soothed her. 'You have nothing to reproach yourself with. I won't allow yourself to think otherwise. Now, are you going to join me for breakfast?'

'I've already eaten,' Dorothy said, 'but I will go out and enjoy myself. You've made me feel so much better, like a load has shifted from my shoulders.'

Ailsa got up to leave, pausing at the door. 'Naughty Dorothy,' she teased. 'Three indeed.'

Changing into a prettier dress, Dorothy went out on deck feeling a new world had opened up to her with her mother's blessing. Almost at once she experienced a throb in her cunt which signalled the need for sexual satisfaction. Her mind dwelt without guilt on how Martin had fucked her and the lewdness of the session with Myra and Gerald. The memories excited her. Immersed in her reverie, staring blankly out to sea, she felt a hand touch her elbow. Turning, she faced an apologetic little man in a short white jacket and bow tie. Squat but broad of shoulder, his brown skin and oriental features marked him as a Filipino or Thai.

'Miss Craig,' he said, bowing. Dorothy, still in her dream state nodded. 'I was approaching your cabin when I saw you leave. I am Mr Andrew Garfield's valet. He requests your company in his stateroom. If you would care to follow me, please . . .'

Still in a daze, Dorothy obediently let herself be ushered up two decks and shown into a spacious lounge with panoramic windows revealing the sea on both sides. The silk curtains and tasteful modern furniture indicated the wealth of the occupant. Andrew Garfield arose to greet his guest from a deep white leather armchair. Tall, broad and handsome, his face showed his surprise.

'You're not Miss Craig,' he said. 'Though you are a very beautiful substitute. It seems my valet has brought the wrong young lady.'

'I did ask her name, sir,' the valet said. 'I saw her leave the right cabin.'

'Don't blame him, my name is Craig,' Dorothy explained. 'At least it was my name before I married. I was not thinking clearly. No doubt it was my sister Manda you were expecting.' She studied the man before her, thinking him very handsome with his steel-grey hair and the look of a person who took his power for granted. She wondered why he had sent for Manda, not knowing that they had met. She found herself speculating whether her sister and this man had fucked.

She found she no longer thought that wrong or shameful. Manda was eager to be rid of her virginity and the man before her, his broad frame swathed in a silken kimono, looked virile and experienced enough to have made Manda's first experience of male-female penetrative sex memorable. Hence the reason he had sent for her, Dorothy surmised, wanting a repeat performance. She was surprised the elated Manda had not boasted of the loss of her virginity and put it down to them hardly speaking that morning. Even then, she felt Manda could not have kept such a fact to herself.

'Did you fuck her?' she was unable to prevent herself saying.

'Unfortunately, no,' Andrew Garfield said, unperturbed by the directness of her question. 'Didn't she tell you I'm impotent? At least when it matters. It's a temporary ailment, so the experts tell me. Now that you're here, will you join me in drinking champagne?' He nodded at his valet. 'Kim, if you please, a glass for the young lady and one for myself. You do drink, I suppose?' he asked Dorothy. 'I'm Andrew. Won't you tell me your name?'

'Dorothy,' she said, accepting the crystal glass, not wishing to add her married name. 'Why would you want to send for Manda if – if—'

'If I can't keep it up, as the term goes,' he laughed. From the pocket of his kimono he brought out a flat leather case. 'I wanted to give her this. Open it, do you think she'd like it? She was very kind to me.'

'My God, is this gold and are these real diamonds?' Dorothy gasped, opening the case. 'She must have been *very* kind to you. Are they real?'

'The ship's jewellery shop isn't Cartier's, but it's real and a good make of watch,' he said. 'I sent for your sister thinking she might enjoy a jacuzzi. There's one in this stateroom.'

'I've never tried one,' Dorothy said, the champagne bubbles tickling her nose, making her head light. 'I think it would be rather fun.'

'Excellent,' Garfield laughed. 'Would you object if I joined you? There's room for two and more.' He led the way through a door that led to a tiled room with a sunken round tub already effervescing with bubbling water. Dorothy followed, growing excited at the turn of events, with the valet carrying the champagne in its ice bucket and two tall fluted glasses. 'On the question of what to wear,' the big American said, facing Dorothy. 'I go in as nature intended. How about you?' He allowed the kimono to slide to the carpeted surround, going down the steps and standing chest deep in the agitated water.

'It's the only way,' Dorothy said boldly, encouraged by her mother's advice. In the few moments Andrew Garfield had stood naked before descending into the tub, the sight of his broad chest matted with hair, the large balls and thick flaccid prick hanging between strong upper thighs, had drawn her appreciative gaze. It was with a helpless thrill coursing through her belly to her cunt, she envisaged stripping off before Garfield and his valet. She began to draw her dress over her head.

'There is a dressing room,' he pointed out, watching her with his arms spread along the edge of the tub. 'There's a

174

bath robe you can use.' He stopped as Dorothy unclipped her bra and handed it to the valet. 'My God, what a beauty you are. You know you are beautiful, I suppose? You should be told that a hundred times a day. Just where did you get those marvellous breasts, young woman?'

'From my mother,' Dorothy said, elated by his praise. 'Do you like them?' She cupped them in her hands, holding them out on offer to him. To keep her nerve up, she took a glass of champagne from the valet and drank it down, enjoying the wide-eyed look on his face. She stripped off her panties, draping them over the servant's shoulder, feeling entirely free and frivolous, giving a little twirl and a waggle of her bottom at the man in the tub. She stepped down to join him, delighting in the swirl of tepid bubbles between her thighs, agitating her cunt. As she sank down the foam frothed around her breasts.

'Easy on the champers, it's potent stuff, Dorothy,' Garfield warned as she accepted a further glass from the attentive Kim. 'You have a husband, I presume? What a lucky man.'

'He doesn't want me,' Dorothy said lightly, 'so forget him. This is not the drink talking, he leaves me alone. He won't come near me.'

'Maybe the poor guy's impotent too,' Garfield said sympathetically. 'Maybe the shame of it stops him from approaching you.'

'He doesn't fuck me,' Dorothy said, 'for whatever reason. You'd like to fuck me, wouldn't you?' Her hand reached out under the water to squeeze his balls suggestively, going on to clasp the girth of a thick flaccid prick. 'I'd like you to fuck me with this. Fuck me really hard. It's what I need.' She began an insidious stroking of the outer skin, hoping to feel it throb and stiffen in her hand. 'Let me get it up for you to fuck me.'

'I'd like nothing better,' Garfield said, admiring her breasts floating like spheres of flesh in the uplifting bubbles and enjoying the rub-rub of her soft hand on his prick. His own hand went between her legs, seeking the ridged cleft, a finger probing and making her thighs writhe. She pressed against him, pressing her mouth to his lewdly, infiltrating her tongue, bucking her cunt to his hand. The stalk she clasped thickened and stretched to a rigid bar of flesh. With a sweep of his arms he gathered her up, mounting the steps out of the jacuzzi, brushing past his valet to carry Dorothy off to a sumptuous bedroom. There he almost flung her down on the bed, climbing on top of her as she widened her thighs and drew up her knees. He plunged his face into her crotch, licking her pouting cunt, flicking at her distended clit, arousing her to the brink of an inner explosion. Then he thrust his bursting prick inside her, shooting his load with his first stroke while she clung to him in desperation for a continuation.

He sat up, looking down at her questioningly. 'It's been so long,' he apologised, letting her draw his hand to her cunt. 'The first real erection in God knows how long thanks to you, little lady, and I go off at half-cock. What must you think of me?'

'Never mind that, there'll be other times,' Dorothy said, working his wrist with her hand to increase the sensations in her cunt, thrusting her bottom off the bed as she was finger-fucked. 'Just make me come,' she ordered. 'I've got to come. God, yes, yes! Oh, that's *heaven*.'

Looking beyond him, her excitement mounted to a crescendo as she saw Kim, the valet, watching her from the door. *He'll see me coming*! she told herself, shamelessly elated by the thought, her climax jolting her body like an electric shock, as hoarse cries of ecstatic pleasure burst from her throat.

She fell asleep in Garfield's arms, lulled by his kisses and numbed by the intensity of her climax. Later, she woke with a start to find herself covered with a silk sheet, the valet standing at the foot of the bed holding up her dress on a coathanger with her underwear folded over his arm. She sat up, uncaring that her breasts were bared. She yawned and stretched luxuriously. Beyond the window the sun seemed high in the sky. 'What time is it?' she asked. 'How long have I been here?'

'It is almost three in the afternoon, madam,' the servant said. 'I had orders from Mr Garfield not to disturb you. While you slept I took the liberty to wash and iron your things. Do you desire lunch?'

'Where is Mr Garfield?' Dorothy asked, pondering the situation with a giggle. Waking up in another man's bed made her feel wonderfully wicked. 'Is he here?'

'He has a therapy session with Dr Calvert,' Kim explained, his eyes rooted on her breasts. 'Until four this afternoon,' he said meaningfully, placing her clothes on a chair and advancing to the side of the bed. 'How would you like a real fuck, madam? To be satisfied with a cock instead of with fingers? I can do that for you.'

The unexpectedness of the offer from the smiling little man made Dorothy's belly respond with a churning sensation that penetrated down to her cunt. As if aware of her body's reaction, he flicked back the silk sheet, uncovering her nakedness. Mesmerised, she lay before him awaiting his next move. Nodding and smiling, he slipped off his short white jacket, shirt and tie and stepped out of his black trousers to stand in a bulging jockstrap. His lithe and muscled frame was athletic. Dorothy turned to him, fascinated by the apparent size of his endowment, and drew down his remaining covering.

His prick was long and thick. She moaned her approval at the sight of the rearing stalk on the slim hairless figure. She nursed it between her full breasts, its purplish crown projecting beneath her chin. 'You suck, give nice suck, madam,' he encouraged her. 'Wet head, soon give you plenty nice fuck with it. Long fuck, not like master.'

Dorothy needed no persuading, covering the swollen glans with her lips. Kim rose on his toes, sliding into her mouth as she sucked greedily on the thick inches of rigid flesh. A push on her shoulders made her fall back, then her legs were grasped and her knees held firmly under Kim's armpits. With just her head and shoulders in contact with the bed, her cunt tilted upward, he shafted her to his balls at first thrust, eliciting a gasp from her throat as he filled her aching cunt. She felt utterly lewd as she jerked her hips to meet his forward lunges, her tits bobbing and bouncing with each thrust.

She came violently, screaming out to be fucked *harder*, *deeper*! Unceremoniously he rolled her over on the bed, arse up, and impaled her from the rear. The long prick seemed to reach into her stomach, its great head sliding in deep, withdrawing only to be plunged inside again. She was out of her mind, as if she was having one long continuing climax. She ground her buttocks back to his hard belly, crying out wild commands, encouraging him, welcoming the hard smacks he planted on her cheeks as he rode her to oblivion. The fucking seemed endless as she experienced more climaxes, barely separated from each other, until she felt him stiffen his body and shoot his hot cream deep into her most secret recess. As he withdrew, she collapsed across the bed, sated as never before, the pulsing in her cunt continuing as if he were still inside her.

Recovering slowly, she saw Andrew Garfield sitting on the bed beside her. 'You watched?' she asked in her confusion. 'You were there and saw—'

'That goddamn lucky boy of mine gave you the fuck of a lifetime,' he finished for her good-humouredly. 'He can do the business better than any one I know. I'd change places with the horny little bastard like a shot. Don't worry, he's serviced my women before, it's written into his contract now, I reckon. It's a poor substitute, but I enjoy seeing others doing what I can't these days.'

'We could try again,' Dorothy suggested slyly. 'You almost made it.'

'Bless you for that,' Garfield smiled. 'Will you dine with me tonight, here, in my private stateroom? You can freshen up with a shower. Then we'll have a cocktail or two while Kim is preparing the food. He's also a *cordon bleu* chef as well as a remarkable stud. What do you say?'

'Little Dorothy is coming out of her shell at last,' she said, stretching her arms in a lazy yawn and raising her superb breasts to give him the full effect. 'How was your therapy session?'

'Time and patience is all those shrinks can advise, and

charge big bucks for the information,' Garfield smiled, admiring the glowing nakedness of the well-fucked girl before him and laying a cool palm on her upper thigh. 'If you've got the patience, young lady, I've got the time.'

And a handy valet in case of emergencies, Dorothy thought naughtily, rising from the bed. 'We'll make time,' she promised, relishing the challenge. 'All night if need be.'

Chapter Sixteen

Toyboy Temptation

Bright sunlight sparkled on a flat, calm sea as Ailsa strolled on deck before breakfast. Having slept more soundly than she could remember, she'd woken to an unusual feeling of contentment and well-being. It was due, she conceded, to the session in the massage room with Helga and the sex session with Ellen the previous evening. All the advice, therapy, outright seduction – call it what she may – had obviously been just what she needed. If behaving so sexily made her feel so alive, it couldn't be wrong, could it? She acknowledged the fact and entered the dining hall. Dex Calvert rose to draw back a chair for her. Of Ellen Jackson there was no sign.

'Good morning, my dear Mrs Craig,' Weissbinder greeted her cordially. 'You do look well. You're as pretty as a picture in that charming dress, and positively blooming. Is there a reason, may I ask?'

'You know very well there is, Doctor,' Ailsa replied, the words bringing a blush to her cheeks. 'Doesn't anything go on aboard this ship that you're not aware of?' She flicked a napkin over her lap, braving a smile at the two men. 'You might as well know Miss Jackson and I made love in her cabin last night. It was wonderful and I feel a new woman, just as you claimed would happen. I feel no shame and no regrets, only for the years I've wasted. You and the others may take full credit for that. I suppose you want to say, "I told you so".'

Weissbinder squeezed her hand encouragingly. 'Not at all, the credit is all yours. We merely helped you to come to terms with your true nature and overcome your suppressed sexuality. That's the kind of liberation we aim for. To experience real eroticism is to fulfil a basic need. I presume you achieved that by having sex with Ellen.'

'I'm blushing, but you are correct,' Ailsa admitted with a nervous giggle. 'Where is she this morning? I hope I didn't prove too much for her, poor girl. It did become rather hectic.'

'How splendid that you have experienced such pleasure,' Weissbinder said. 'Keep that feeling in mind, Mrs Craig, and nurture it. Further confidence therapy is recommended so there is no relapse. It would help to talk about your experience of making love to another woman.'

'At breakfast?' Ailsa asked shyly.

'Of course not. But Dr Calvert is free this evening and I advise expert counselling to ensure no guilt feelings occur about participating in sex with Ellen. You will agree to undergo therapy?'

'I think you should,' Dex said. 'Enjoy a relaxing day and I'll have an instructional video sent to your cabin to show our methods. The cool of the evening is a good time for a session on my couch.'

'You could have suggested that rather more subtly, Dr Calvert,' Ailsa smiled. 'If you really think it's necessary—'

'Absolutely,' Weissbinder confirmed. 'In New York he charges patients more than a hundred dollars an hour for a consultation. Here on the *Aphrodite*, he's free. Take full advantage, dear lady.' How could she say no?

That evening Ailsa lay down on the padded leather couch in Dex's consulting office. On her way there she had passed Gerald Marsh and his son, Nigel, being led by Myra to their next therapy session with Ellen in her cabin.

They had looked decidedly unhappy.

She, on the other hand, felt quite the opposite.

Stretched out on the couch, Ailsa thought how handsome Dr Calvert was. He smiled reassuringly at her in the glow of one small lamp beside his armchair. With the curtains drawn it made for an intimate atmosphere, the positioning of the adjustable light bathing Ailsa in a soft pool of warm gold.

'Okay, relax,' he said, 'let all the tension flow out of your body.'

And what a body, Dex considered lewdly, his chair drawn up so that his knees touched the edge of the couch. Under her cotton dress the firm curvaceous spheres swelled enticingly, the open neck of the dress revealing an inch or two of tight creamy cleavage. Her thighs were strong and shapely, the stockinged legs trim to the ankle – *just the kind I'd like wrapped around my back*, Dex decided. He drew off her shoes, letting them fall to the carpet. 'There's nothing to be scared of.' he assured gently. 'I'll just ask a few questions and you say whatever you wish. For instance, how did you spend your day? Remember, you must relax completely.'

'If I were any more relaxed I'd fall asleep,' Ailsa said, finding the subtle aroma of his after-shave pleasant to her lulled senses. 'As for my day, I visited one of my two daughters, ate lunch, and sunbathed in a deckchair in the afternoon. Then I watched that video you provided. Shouldn't we talk about that?'

'Were you shocked?' Dex enquired. 'Seeing yourself with Helga?'

'I was astounded,' Ailsa said. 'I couldn't believe it.'

'Remember, it was a therapy session,' he explained. 'Weissbinder does sometimes tape them to study results and to improve his methods. He had no idea it would become sexual between you two women. You must grant him that.'

'I thought I was just going for a massage,' Ailsa said. 'And when Dr Weissbinder arrived, he encouraged Helga to continue. Not that I'm complaining, you know, I wanted her to continue. Seeing myself on that video was—'

'Arousing?' Dex asked quietly.

'Well, yes, seeing myself like that,' Ailsa agreed hesitantly. 'But it was a shock, to think that it had been filmed.'

'Don't worry, I'm assured Dr Weissbinder wipes the tapes

clean after studying them,' he said. 'It won't be seen by anyone but he and I.'

'You saw it?' Ailsa said uncomfortably. 'My God, what must you think of me?'

'Remember I'm a qualified psychotherapist,' Dex said. 'I was impressed by your – shall we say – compliance.' He smiled to bolster her unease. 'You should be proud of letting go. It was no holds barred, wasn't it?'

'Entirely,' she agreed, again with the nervous laugh.

'You said it was arousing before,' he reminded her. 'While watching the re-run, did you masturbate?'

'How blunt you are,' she said, her eyes lowered. 'If you must know, yes. The feeling came over me and I found myself unable to resist.'

'Good for you,' Dex nodded. 'Why not, if you needed release? You also said you were with Ellen Jackson last evening. Do you want to talk about that? I heard you say it got hectic. Explain that. I know Miss Jackson. She's a lesbian of the submissive type. What role did you play?'

'May I ask a question,' Ailsa said timidly. 'Did Ellen pick me up by chance last evening, or was that arranged by you people? If so, was that recorded and have you watched the things we did?'

'Not me,' Dex lied. 'If Weissbinder thought of arranging your meeting with Ellen as part of a programme beneficial to you, I wasn't in on it. I don't know if it was recorded. I doubt it, but I could enquire.' He thought back to the sight of the enthusiastic woman he'd seen on the tape: a double-dildo strapped about her with half of it up her cunt, using the other half to give an energetic impersonation of a horny male fucking a woman dog-fashion. 'With Ellen, I suppose you acted the man?' he suggested. 'It's her thing. Did you enjoy that?'

'I – I suppose I did,' Ailsa admitted. 'It seemed right with her.'

'Has this made you wonder about your sexuality, preferring women to men?'

'It does,' she admitted. 'I've been married and have two children, but the intensity of the sex with that girl surprised me. It makes me wonder if I'm lesbian.'

'What of your past relationships with men?' Dex enquired. 'How many have there been?' He held up a bright silver disc on a chain, the light reflecting on its surface as it slowly spun around. 'Would you prefer to make your answers under hypnosis?'

'No,' Ailsa said firmly. 'I want to know what I'm saying, and it will be the truth.' She could also have added that she enjoyed discussing sexual matters, as was evident by the throb she felt in her cunt. 'At university I had sex with one of my professors. He was far older, I was inexperienced, and he never brought me to orgasm. I found it disappointing. Then I married and my late husband was not highly sexed, he never made demands. I believed that that was the way of it, though I felt there should be more. I masturbated, which shamed me. The idea I got was that men were no use to me. After yesterday with Helga and Ellen, I do wonder if I'm gay.'

'Would that disturb you if you are?' Dex asked.

'I don't know. It's evident I like making love to other women, but I've never really been with a man,' she admitted. 'One has made me orgasm at times; Gerald Marsh, a tutor at my school. He used his fingers – or his tongue.' She drew in a breath before continuing. 'He was never intimate with me. I wouldn't allow that.'

'You mean he never fucked you,' Dex said matter-of-factly, beginning to massage her foot. 'Let's not be coy. Sex talk is exciting, often the cruder the talk the higher the arousal. I'm sure you discovered that with Ellen. She's very vocal.'

'Yes,' Ailsa nodded, the agitation in her sex making her want to grind her upper thighs together. 'Marsh has never fucked me. But he has done things to my breasts, nipples and vagina. I suppose I should say cunt?'

'Marsh is undergoing therapy too,' Dex said, his hand lightly stroking her left ankle. 'Dr Weissbinder is attempting to change the guy's macho attitude to women. Also to find

185

out why his son Nigel and your daughter Dorothy seem not to have a normal marriage. I'm not involved in that therapy.' The massaging hand moved up almost idly to caress a smooth knee. 'As for you, you're a strong woman. You should be more confident, with men as well as women. I'm sure you can be, as you no doubt showed with the submissive Ellen.'

'I shall try,' she promised. 'I did enjoy being that way with Ellen. Do you know, I smacked her bottom? And I did something else I never believed I could do. The feeling of power thrilled and excited me.' Her eyes lowered again as his hand reached the hem of her dress. 'But that was with another woman.'

'You've been unfortunate with the men in your life,' Dex said. 'By contrast, the sex with Ellen was so good you wonder about your true nature.' The moving hand sidled up to her inner thigh, resting there. The cool touch so near the source of her twitching quim added to the surge of sensations in her lower belly. 'If you are a lesbian, so what? It's acceptable,' he stated. 'But my advice is that you should experiment with a male partner, an experienced one. Should you find you're bi-sexual, that's a bonus – you'll have the best of both worlds.'

'I'd like to think I could obtain satisfaction with a man,' Ailsa said, her voice now a hoarse whisper. 'Do you think I could?'

Dex's cupped hand covered the mound of her cunt, squeezing it suggestively. 'Do you find that objectionable?' he asked, giving further presses to her crotch.

'It feels nice,' Ailsa said weakly, her cunt already palpitating.

'You're lubricating freely,' Dex said still using his professional tone, a bulge forming in his trouser front. 'That's good, it shows arousal, and there's no other woman present. To prove you are not averse to sex with a male, would you agree to any further therapy I wish to conduct?'

'Oh, yes,' she answered, striving to keep her pelvis from writhing and thrusting at the touch of the hand on her cunt.

She hoped he intended to fuck her. 'I'll do whatever you say. What must I do?'

'Show me you are able to present yourself to a member of the opposite sex as naked as nature intended lovers to be.' He gave her curved mound a final squeeze before removing his hand, eagerly anticipating seeing her in the nude. 'Could you do that?'

'I suppose so, with the right man,' Ailsa whispered, disappointed that the hand had been withdrawn. 'Yes, I could.'

'So, pretend I'm your lover,' he said, 'eager to make love to you. I desire to see all of you, every inch. You're keen to show yourself off. Take off all of your clothes.'

'My husband never saw me naked,' Ailsa remembered. 'Do you really want to?'

'Of course,' Dex said. 'I want to admire your splendid breasts, that curvaceous body, gaze on your cunt. Doesn't the thought excite you?' *It bloody well does me*, he could have added. 'Doctor's orders,' he said sternly. 'Strip!'

Ailsa drew her dress over her head and unhooked her bra with trembling hands. She blushed deep red as he stared at her big bare breasts. She pushed her briefs over her thighs, stepping out of them as they dropped to the carpet, until she stood in just a suspender-belt and sheer stockings. Glancing down, it seemed her breasts had never looked large or the hair on her mound so extravagantly thick. Excitement churned her innards alarmingly. She stood erect, turning around slowly as he told her to, her buttocks firmly rounded, until she faced him again, trembling.

'You're gorgeous,' he murmured earnestly. 'Lie back on the couch now. It would be a shame to waste all that beauty exclusively on other women. We can't have that, can we?'

'How can we find out?' Ailsa said, her voice almost a whine in her arousal. She lay down on the couch, showing all she had, the big splayed breasts and cunt nestled between her parted thighs. 'How?'

'By this,' Dex said, his voice as hot with emotion as hers. He returned his hand to her cunt, inserting a curled finger

187

and working it among the soft oily folds of flesh. With a low moan, Ailsa widened her legs, arching her back, bottom jerking from the leather couch. 'And by this,' he added, leaning over to fasten his mouth over each erect nipple in turn, briefly sucking as her body went into convulsions. As he straightened and drew back, she clutched at his hand and moaned in frustration.

'*Please,*' she begged, her bottom still squirming and cunt throbbing. 'You – you – *can't*! Don't leave me like this—'

'You may dress now,' Dex said, grudgingly reminding himself of the restriction placed on him by Weissbinder. *So far and no further,* those were his orders. *Leave her unsatisfied and desiring what she's denied herself for years,* the Doctor had said, *that's the best way of bringing her along.* The way Ailsa sat up on the couch, gathering up her discarded clothes and looking at Dex with pleading eyes, proved him right.

'There will be other sessions of therapy,' Dex said to placate her, wishing he could offer her more than mere words. 'Unfortunately I have other consultations tonight. Rest assured there'll be further appointments—'

'Tomorrow?' she asked hopefully, not caring that her breasts remained bare, standing before him with the bra in her hands.

'We'll see,' he said to keep her in suspense as Weissbinder had ordered. 'Your progress so far is most encouraging,' Dex added, cursing his luck at having to stop, an erection straining up to his belt. 'Meanwhile think about our next session. Become more assertive. Acknowledge your feelings and do as you wish.'

I certainly will, Ailsa vowed, as she left his consulting room with an ache in her cunt. Assertive he'd asked for so assertive he'd get, she determined. Her whole being was trembling with frustration and she regretted not dragging him on top of her, aware of the erection stiffly tenting the fly of his trousers.

Sounds of gaiety and music came from the forward part of the ship as she walked aft attempting to cool her anger.

Her aimless wandering along the deserted deck brought

her to the swimming pool. She arrived just as two young men were climbing out as naked as fish and dripping wet. In the moonlight Ailsa saw they were strapping youths. Her eyes were drawn at once to their thick cocks and heavy balls. They stood startled by her sudden appearance. For a moment they awaited her reaction and were amused to hear her break the silence with gentle laughter.

'How's the water, boys?' Ailsa asked. 'It looks very tempting.'

'Still warm from the day's sun,' said the bigger one, quickly appreciating that this older woman had a lot going for her. Her dress was moulded to her impressive breasts and thighs. 'You've caught us out skinny-dipping after our gig at the disco.'

'I can still hear music,' she said.

'Records,' the young man grinned. 'That's why it sounds so good, the ship's disc jockey takes over from us. One day he'll play ours.'

'I'm sure he will,' Ailsa said. 'Don't let me interfere with your swim.' She laughed again. 'As you two have nothing else to hide, won't you introduce yourselves?'

'I'm Martin and this is my brother, Graham,' said the bigger youth.

'Would you care to join us?' Graham asked hopefully.

'Why not?' Ailsa said. She reached for the zip at the back of her dress, sure it was the boldest thing she'd ever done. The prospect of stripping before the two young men thrilled her. With their eyes glued to her every move, she undressed to the skin, draping her clothes over a chair. Excited tremors pulsed through her breasts and cunt at being so openly admired by the well-hung pair who were young enough to be her sons.

She stepped forward to the edge of the pool, her massive breasts jiggling as she dived forward into the water, showing off her full, round buttocks. The boys leapt in after her, the three surfacing in a close circle, Ailsa's big bosom bobbing enticingly before their eyes. She swam away, well aware of the direction of their gaze, turning with marbled cheeks breaking the surface, her eager escort swimming after her. At the other end of the pool she trod water, smiling as they arrived beside her like obedient subjects.

'This is lovely, swimming naked,' she said to the brothers. 'Such a feeling of utter freedom.'

'We do it every night,' Martin told her. 'The pool's always empty at this time. You're very welcome to join us.'

'I'll remember that,' Ailsa promised. 'How sweet of you. After all,' she added, feeling wicked with their eyes on her, 'I'm a woman old enough to be your mum.'

'Our mum never looked like you,' Graham said seriously, knee to knee with her, the objects of his admiration directly under his nose. 'Haven't you heard good-looking older women are the in-thing with younger men? Especially if they've got what you have.'

'Which is?' she teased him, wanting to hear.

'Everything,' Martin said, taking over. 'The kind of tits – I mean breasts – you don't get on young girls, and the rest of you, wow! You're not looking for a toyboy, are you?'

'Two toyboys,' Graham hurriedly put in. 'Have you a husband on board?'

'I'm a lonely widow,' Ailsa told them to lead them on, a wild thought arousing her. 'I'd better get back to my cabin and dry off.'

'Our cabin is nearby,' Martin offered. 'You could dry off there. We can offer you a cup of coffee too. Would you join us, Mrs—?'

'Just Ailsa,' she said, getting out of the pool, 'and your kind offer is accepted.' She felt she had already let things go too far as they led her the few yards to their cabin but she was unable to resist. In their cabin she was handed a large towel. It proved arousing drying herself in front of the boys. She remained naked, handing the towel back to Martin. Both of the boys had wrapped theirs around their waists.

'Let me make the coffee,' she said to the delighted brothers. 'One of you put on the kettle and leave the rest to me.' She found mugs and bustled about to get coffee, sugar and milk, the brothers watching her as if rooted to the spot. The exhilaration of exhibiting herself, flaunting her full breasts, hairy mound and rounded buttocks, made her wanton. 'Whatever is that I see, you two?' she asked, indicating the rearing erections tenting the towels wrapped around their waists. 'You naughty boys.'

'What else could you expect?' Martin said, his voice hoarse. 'You're – beautiful.'

'Well, I didn't ask you to look,' Ailsa said. 'Or to have wicked thoughts. Shame on you both. What have you got there?' Tugging at Graham's towel, she gave a shriek as it came away in her hand to reveal his prick fully engorged and rearing bolt upright. As if shocked, she put her hand over her mouth and turned away, giving them a cheeky waggle of her bottom in their direction.

Her captivated onlookers were presented with an unobstructed view of the hanging split bulge beneath her rear, the forest of hair and ridged lips tucked snug in the deep cleft of plump buttock cheeks. Standing less than an arm's length from her inclined bottom, Graham stuck out his hand. His middle finger went past the outer lips, going on inwards to penetrate the warm soft folds of her moist cunt.

'Oh! Oh!' moaned Ailsa as the finger stroked on her engorged clit, helpless to pull herself away. As if her strength had weakened, her body fell forward across the table in front of her while Graham continued the unexpected frigging of her cunt. He added a second finger as her low moans and whines increased, her upper torso spread across the table with breasts and stomach pressed to the smooth surface. In this position the broad moons of her buttocks were raised, the fig of her quim jutting rearward for the boy to gain full access. Silenced by the erotic sight, the only sound beside Ailsa's tortured moaning was of fingers squelching in her juice as Graham intently finger-fucked the older woman. Before his jubilant eyes her bottom clenched, writhed and jerked in an agony of ecstatic pleasure.

'No, no, no!' she cried out, lost in the throes of her arousal yet aware she should protest. 'You shouldn't, you wicked boy!' she howled, still thrusting back on the goading hand, losing all control. Her protests and gasps changed into little wracking sobs as the sensations within mounted to a crescendo, her pace of working her bottom to the fingering increasing. With a louder cry, her big bottom rotating and jerking, she screamed 'Yes! I'm *coming*! My God, you're killing me—'

Astounded, the brothers watched her broad creamy buttocks twitching as the spasms gradually decreased and she lay struggling for breath. Graham's hand withdrew, the youth unsure what her reaction would be to his assault. Still speechless at witnessing a mature woman coming so violently on Graham's finger, Martin stood awaiting her response. With relief they saw her turn her face to them looking as astonished as they, her eyes glazed and hair unruly around a flushed face.

'I didn't mean to,' she muttered. 'It just happened, I couldn't help myself. He made me come.'

She remained bent over the table, her pouting cunt and glistening pink interior still on offer while she twitched in the after-throes of the climax. Martin, his prick stiff as never before, moved behind her and pushed his brother aside. His iron-hard shaft slid up her to the hilt until her cheeks nestled snugly against his belly. Gripping her wide hips, he thrust home strongly, rearing on tiptoe to give her every long thick inch of his big cock. In her delight, Ailsa squealed in surprise and pleasure, lowering her head and dipping her back, her buffeted arse grinding to meet his forward lunges.

'Yes, yes, fuck me, Martin!' she exulted, loving the fullness of his prick nudging her deepest recess. 'Oh, it's heaven, I can feel it all the way up. Fuck me as hard as you wish. Don't stop. Go on, fuck me, I love it.'

Martin loved the feeling of being embedded up her too, thrusting in and out savagely in his lust, her pliant cheeks gyrating against his stomach, his balls swinging in the cleave of her buttocks. 'Yes, I'll fuck you!' he swore determinedly.

'Fuck you anytime you like. Fuck you rigid. Fuck your greedy cunt whenever you want a prick. Take it, every inch. Don't worry, I'll fuck you plenty.'

'Tell me more,' Ailsa pleaded in her delirium. 'Say what you like, I want you to.'

'I love your great big tits,' Martin muttered. 'Such fine big tits to grab while I screw the arse off you,' he added crudely. His hands slipped under her to cup them tightly, bucking at her even more strenuously and adding to the force of his inward heaves. 'Tits I'm going to suck on later too, you'll see—'

'Yes, but keep fucking me,' she shouted back excitedly, climaxing wildly but continuing to thrust her arse out for as many as she could get. 'Don't you dare come yet, Martin. Look, look, Graham, see your wicked brother fucking me. He's right up my cunt! Are you going to fuck me next? Tell me you will.'

A glance behind showed Graham standing by impatiently, his stiff dick at the ready as his brother finally gave up trying to hold back his climax. With his flanks pounding into Ailsa, Martin shot jet after jet of hot come into her as she peaked again strongly. As their pace slowed, Graham dragged his brother aside and thrust his rigid prick into her avaricious cunt with a howl of delight. In his excitement he came off at once and collapsed on her back as she quivered in the aftermath of her multiple orgasms.

When she had recovered enough to rise unsteadily from the table, it was to smile reassuringly at two young men. 'Well, you certainly had your wicked way with with me, didn't you?' she admonished them gently. 'Fancy you taking advantage of a poor defenceless widow. Cheer up, boys, I'm sure I was as much to blame. We didn't expect it to go quite that far, did we?'

'To be honest we were hoping it would,' Martin grinned. 'You're not only beautiful, but a good sport as well. Graham and I are hoping now that you'll stay the night. Please.'

'If you promise to be good,' Ailsa said. She went to both

brothers, giving each a fond hug and kiss in turn. 'First I think we should have that coffee.'

I like the new me, she told herself. *Yes, I like going naked with adoring eyes devouring my body.*

Suddenly, for the first time in hours, she remembered her daughters and a momentary feeling of guilt flashed through her mind. No more than a fleeting thought, it was swept away as Martin and Graham closed in on her.

Chapter Seventeen

Hard to Handle

Dawn had lightened the sky before Dorothy returned to her cabin. Finding no sign of Manda there, she wondered where she had spent the night – not in her undisturbed bed, certainly. Dorothy wondered if her sister had finally lost her virginity and with whom. The most likely suspects were the brothers Martin and Graham, with the handsome Dr Calvert the next in line. Even her randy father-in-law Gerald came to mind – he'd welcome the chance to break Manda's duck. She herself had no cause to complain about whoever it was, Dorothy conceded, recalling the previous night spent with the supposedly impotent Andrew Garfield. She had cured him of that, she thought, with her newly-discovered woman's wiles – a hidden talent that had roused him to fuck her several times and proving more effective than any psychiatric lecture.

Dorothy had done things in the night that her fantasies were made of. Her breasts, quim, bottom and mouth had all been brought into play and in return Andrew had risen to the occasion nobly. And when she'd exhausted him temporarily, his tireless servant, Kim, had filled the breach, watched by his master. Still feeling an inner glow from the sexual romping and determined her next meeting with Nigel would produce an ultimatum, she went into the adjacent cabin to greet her mother. Her bed too had been unused, she saw, and she giggled to herself on remembering their last meeting and Ailsa's changed attitude. As to the lucky man, either Dex Calvert or Gerald might be the one. Dorothy had no idea that the two brothers were responsible.

Ailsa meanwhile was making her way back to her cabin in a happy haze of sexual fulfilment. Two pairs of hands, two mouths and two cocks had deliriously pleasured her throughout the night. Three together in a narrow bed had meant, with the ardour and energy of their youth, that the whole night had been one euphoric if exhausting sexual melee. There were groping hands at her even in the wee small hours when she had dozed off, between her thighs, on her breasts as she was rolled onto her back to be suckled with a mouth on each nipple at the same time. She recalled being on her knees, being fucked from the rear while greedily deep-throating at the other end, unaware which brother was where. Her breasts felt tender from the fondling they'd received and the tit-rides they'd given. She supposed she'd been fucked a dozen times or more. Now her mind was on a shower and sleep when she was brought back to reality by the sound of her name being called by Dex Calvert.

He stood grinning at her knowingly, dressed for an early jog around deck. 'You look as if you've taken my advice, Mrs Craig,' he said pleasantly. 'I'm sorry I had to leave you like I did, but you evidently went out and found what you required. May I ask who was the lucky man – or woman?'

'Two very ardent young men,' she said, proud of the fact and knowing that this understanding young therapist would not think worse of her. 'Is it so evident?'

'You look like you've had a good time and I'm jealous,' he said, smiling. 'I did notice that your bed hadn't been slept in. I went there to tell you your daughter Manda is in the ship's infirmary. There's nothing to be worried about,' he assured her quickly as he saw her alarm. 'Heat stroke and a rather painful case of sun-burn. *All over*,' he added to gauge her reaction. 'Evidently young Manda went nude swimming and fell asleep on a lounger in the noonday sun. She'll recover, but right now she's madder than hell about being confined to the infirmary for the next few days.'

'I must go to her at once,' Ailsa said. 'Poor lamb. Did you say nude?'

'Absolutely bare buff, which must have been why she's a nice shade of lobster red from head to toe,' Dex grinned. 'It will keep her out of mischief. That young lady was a temptation to all on board. Are you free at two this afternoon?'

'I could make myself available,' Ailsa said hopefully. 'Do you wish to continue the therapy where we left off?'

'Something like that,' Dex said. 'All will be revealed. At two then. I leave you to visit your daughter. Watch out, she's spitting fire at missing out.'

In the infirmary Ailsa found Dorothy sitting by the bed of a furious Manda, her face and body daubed with a lotion that had dried to a white gloss. At the sight of her mother she burst into anguished sobs. 'It's all right for you two, you're out enjoying yourselves,' she charged. 'I'm in here looking a fright. Nothing exciting will happen to me!'

Like losing your virginity, Dorothy thought, deciding not to hand over the jewelled watch Andrew Garfield had given her to deliver to Manda. To let her think she had spent the night with him would have sent Manda into an even worse tantrum. She left her younger sister to catch up on sleep lost from the night's exertions. Ailsa left soon after to find Gerald Marsh loitering outside her cabin. She looked at him in a kinder light for once, deciding that, with her own sexuality so rampant, she could hardly fault him for his past attempts at having her. He was certainly handsome, attentive and admiring; she ought to have been flattered.

'I hear Manda's unwell,' he began. 'I took her some chocolates to cheer her up and she threw them at me. Par for the course with the Craig females, I guess.'

'That was kind of you, Gerald,' she surprised him by saying. 'How are you enjoying the cruise?'

'Great, if you can call being blackmailed and having my backside caned by a man-hating lesbo,' he said, grinning wryly. 'I guess you can say I deserve it but I'm here to warn you. This ship isn't kosher, all this psychiatric mumbo-jumbo is a ploy to get frustrated people to spill the beans on their sex lives, real or fantasy. They've got Nigel wearing drag and found out it's what turns him on. He's been advised that that's the way he'll find true happiness with your Dorothy.'

'That's for her to decide,' Ailsa said. 'Something's stopped him from being a normal loving husband to her. Maybe they're right. It's thorough therapy, you know. I've benefited from it.' She gave him a sly smile. 'Very definitely.'

'All I've got out of it is raw backside,' Gerald said. 'I'm not even supposed to approach you. Now I suppose when we go home, you'll have to close the school.'

'Regretfully, yes,' Ailsa said, on an impulse kissing his cheek. 'That's for the help you've been. Ungrateful as I may have seemed, I knew you've done everything to keep St Boniface's going.' She went into her cabin, leaving him wondering at her change of attitude.

In his own cabin he found Myra waiting for him.

'No, I'm not here for a fuck,' she said amiably. 'This is important. At two this afternoon you're to go to Dr Calvert's consulting office.'

'More therapy?' he laughed. 'Fucking you would be more fun.'

'Not this time,' she said seriously. 'Ailsa will be there, also that German girl Helga. It's a meeting arranged to get our esteemed Dr Weissbinder on the rack. We've all been conned out of our rights by the little cheat. Dex, Helga and myself.'

'Much as I dislike the slimeball, what's that to do with Ailsa and myself?' he asked. 'Where do we profit by helping you out?'

'By getting Weissbinder to bankroll Ailsa's school,' Myra told him. 'I'm serious. He stole the idea for his sex clinics from Dex Calvert's old professor, cheated him out of his practice and has never looked back. Dex wants him for that. Helga was partners in a health spa in Germany. Weissbinder got hold of that through some legal chicanery, had it closed by the local council then re-opened it. As for me, he owes me plenty and I mean to collect. He'll come across when he sees the evidence we've got against him.'

'Good on you,' Gerald said. 'But why should he cough up to

keep Ailsa's school open? He set me up for sexual harassment. Are you getting him on that?'

'That and much more,' Myra promised. 'He's been secretly taping the Craig family since they've been aboard. The results are hot: masturbation, lesbianism, orgies, all filmed without their consent or knowledge. We know he intends to market the tapes, it's our ace in the hole.'

'Good God, Ailsa too,' Gerald said amused. 'This therapy stuff must work. Is she aware of these films?'

'We're hoping she won't need to be, if you agree to stand in for her when we confront Weissbinder,' Myra said. 'Do that and we'll give you the evidence as a souvenir. The tapes include you being whacked. One other demand we'll make as well is that you get your own back on Queen Ellen – you can put her across your knee. Are you with us?'

'You bet,' Gerald agreed and later presented himself at Dex Calvert's consulting office to find Myra and Helga there as well. 'Enter, friend,' Dex said, offering his hand, his liking for the roguish Gerald founded on recognising a fellow spirit. 'Myra has briefed you, I understand. It's all cut and dried. I've made copies of faxes sent to private sex-collectors by Weissbinder offering videos for big money. We've got him on tape ordering me to seduce and corrupt a female patient, Mrs Craig. Then, there's the little matter of attempting to procure her daughter Amanda for sex with Andrew Garfield, a big wheel who could ruin Doc Weissbinder even better than us. That's recorded too. Will you be with us when we nail Weissbinder? Will you do that for Mrs Craig?'

'I love that woman,' Gerald stated. 'I've put money into her school to keep it solvent and gone without a salary for months. If you can screw the dough out of old chinwhiskers to keep the school going, Doc, I'd lie in my teeth for you.'

'No need, we've got him,' Dex said. 'Have you told Mrs Craig that you love her? It's about time you did, and time she realised she loved you. She'll be here soon. Would you object to my team and I getting you two together?'

Before he could answer, there came a knock at the door. Ailsa walked in. Her face fell seeing others present. 'Your previous session was a one-to-one consultation with myself,' Dex put in as she made to protest. 'That's easy with nobody else present but a trained analyst to encourage you. Let's discover if you can be as co-operative in group therapy. I want you to undress completely as you did before. To make you feel more at ease, we'll disrobe as well.' To start, he took off his white medical jacket, looking at the others for compliance. All of them began to strip except Ailsa. 'Mrs Craig,' he said sternly. 'Don't let me down.'

'Did you think I wouldn't?' Ailsa said defiantly, her fingers at the top button of her dress. Soon she was naked, boldly displaying her large shapely breasts and curvaceous body. In front of her Gerald was sporting a huge erection, with Myra and Helga on either side of him, buxomly bare. Dex, she noted with satisfaction, was also stiffly erect.

'Lie on the couch,' he told her. 'Tell me your reaction to seeing Gerald naked. We can see how it's affected him. Are you tempted? Or do the women appeal to you more? Remember, we discussed sexual preferences and whether you were more inclined towards women because of your negative experiences with men. What are your feelings at this moment with both sexes available?'

'That's what you get paid to find out,' Ailsa said smugly, enjoying being the centre of attention. She reclined on the couch and made herself comfortable. Squirming her bottom into the padded leather, she stretched out her long legs luxuriously, inwardly gratified to hear mutters of admiration from the watchers. 'Well, go on,' she said. 'If none of you can think what to do, after the night I spent, a massage would be most relaxing. Shall we take it from there?'

Helga immediately came forward, hands outstretched, delighted by the suggestion. Looking up, Ailsa saw Myra gazing at her with longing. 'Why not?' Ailsa laughed. 'You too.' She closed her eyes and let herself relax in mind and body. Four hands touched her at once. Helga's strong fingers kneaded her upper arms and moved on to the shoulders until, unable to contain herself longer, she clutched Ailsa's breasts. She massaged each rounded tit together, one in each hand, using a circular movement and feeling Ailsa's nipples swell under her palms. On the other side of the couch Myra delicately smoothed her fingers up and down the insides of Ailsa's legs, at times going above the knee to be rewarded by a widening of the thighs. Helga began to stroke Ailsa's stomach, bending over to insert the tip of her tongue into the hollow of her navel.

'It's a race,' Gerald remarked to Dex. 'A slow motion race to see who gets to her cunt first. I always swore I'd never fuck that woman until she begged for it, but a man can only stand so much. So, what about it, Doc? When do we get in on this therapy?'

Feeling Helga's breath on her belly, and Myra's titillating stroking of her inner thighs, Ailsa gave a low moan and a quiver. She felt Helga's breasts brushing hers, nipple to nipple, the pendulous big teats tracing circles around her own. She drew in her breath sharply as if to prevent signs of her weakening, her nipples being sucked in turn while Myra's mouth suddenly descended on her pussy. First Myra sucked in the outer lips, then began to tongue her deeply, chin buried in her pubic hair. Ailsa, her body undulating on the padded couch, began to moan in anguish, 'Fuck me! Gerald, come and fuck me! You always said I'd beg you, so do it! *Please*, for me this time.'

Both Myra and Helga stepped away from her, nodding their agreement at Gerald. 'Go on, fuck her,' Myra said. 'You've always wanted to. We've warmed her up for you, haven't we, Helga? That's what you call real friendship.'

'Go on and fuck the horny thing,' Helga encouraged the surprised and delighted Gerald. 'She's a man's woman, I know that. Her time with me was because of her frustration. It's a good hard prick she really wants.'

'She's waiting, so give it to her,' Dex advised. 'Make it good, doctor's orders. Isn't it what you've always wanted?'

'What's all the talk, did you lot arrange this?' Ailsa complained. Advancing on her, Gerald lowered her back to the couch as she sat up. 'Put it in, I must have it,' she muttered as he curled over her. 'Damn you, Gerald, you were keen enough before.'

'And still am, my love,' he told her, wasting no time on preliminaries in her aroused state. He felt the moistness of her arousal as he plunged deep. It was an immediate turn-on, her response being to lift her pelvis to his inward thrusts, her cunt gripping his prick as she humped her bottom from the couch. Their bodies blended and joined, calming down after the first impetuousness of the penetration, then fucking steadily and rhythmically. Her legs and arms went around him, ankles locked, hands gripping his buttock cheeks and hauling him ever closer. 'That's the way,' he told her, both oblivious of their audience. 'Fuck to your heart's content. I can keep this up until you've had enough.'

Growing increasingly aroused, Helga turned to see Myra kneeling in front of Dex, sucking avidly at his prick. Turning her face and releasing Dex's thick stalk, Myra gave Helga the nod. 'Now's your chance, Helga. I know you have a letch for him and I've got him ready for you. Go on, it's open season on shrinks. Nail him like he nails everyone else.'

In her urgency Helga pushed Dex back in his chair, positioning herself with her thighs straddled over his upright prick. Guiding it with her hand, she groaned in delight as she bore down to impale herself on its full length. At once she began a wild grinding motion as she squatted over his thighs, his rigid staff pistoning inside her. Breasts swinging like bells in front of his face, Dex clutched her ample buttocks, returning thrust for thrust. It didn't last long and their climaxes coincided, Helga pounding Dex into his chair accompanied by her scream of triumph.

Stretched out on the couch, Ailsa lay dazed and stupified by the intensity of Gerald's expert penetration. It was teasingly slow at times then he'd alter the angle of entrance and increase the pace as she begged to be fucked harder. In the climax her orgasm had been devastating.

Now Gerald stood by the bed, gratified that at last he'd had her and proved his worth, something she acknowledged even in her numbed state by reaching out a hand to give his a squeeze of thanks.

Ailsa heard voices seemingly from far away but was unable to rouse herself and drifted off to sleep. Awakening from a short, refreshing nap, she saw Dex smiling at her from his chair.

'I didn't resist Gerald very satisfactorily, did I?' she said with a wry smile. 'I always swore he'd never have me, but with what Myra and Helga were doing to me, and seeing him there with that – that huge hard thing – I wanted him.'

'It was most satisfactory from where I sat,' Dex assured her. 'It showed where your real feelings lie, and that's not exclusively with women. You're a very sexy and uninhibited lady, in my professional opinion. Gerald's no slouch, he just needs a good woman to keep him in line. An afternoon well spent, I'd say.'

'And what about Helga?' she asked mischievously. 'From what I could see, it looked like you had no choice. I could just see a plump backside bouncing up and down on top of you.'

'I was raped,' Dex agreed, grinning. 'Mounted and stuffed. But I'm not complaining, she was delightful. All the times I've ignored her, I didn't know what I was missing. I intend to make up for lost opportunities.'

'Which is what I've been doing, thankfully,' Ailsa said. 'I've been kept so busy that I haven't had time for my daughters. That would be welcomed by Manda, I'm sure, until the silly creature got taken to the ship's infirmary. I've a good idea how Dorothy has spent her time, she confessed she's taken lovers. With the husband she has, I told her why not? Like mother like daughter, I suppose you'd say.'

'I have something to say about Dorothy and Nigel,' Dex

said, becoming grave. 'It would seem your daughter's husband gets turned on when—'

'He wears female attire,' Ailsa continued for him. 'Gerald told me. Is it serious?'

'Hardly,' Dex laughed. 'Cross-dressing is a harmless way to get your kicks. The problem is, how will his wife accept it? An occasional bit of dressing up privately between them in the house or bedroom could be what their marriage needs. He's too shy to mention it to Dorothy, but I'll guarantee he's dying to. I think you should broach the subject to her and test her reaction. It might be the way to get them together. She might like the idea.'

'She loves him,' Ailsa said. 'She always has. If it means they can enjoy sex together, who cares if he likes to swing from a chandelier?' She gave him her wickedest smile. 'May I have a shower, by the way? You do have one adjoining your consulting room, I believe?'

'I'll join you,' Dex said readily. 'By the way the dance tonight is one of those "Tarts and Vicars" affairs, and no one minds if the women go togged up as men, with their men in drag. Wouldn't it be a good chance for Dorothy to see young Nigel dolled up? It might turn both of them on?'

'I'll see that he's there,' Ailsa vowed, leading the way to the shower. 'If it means Dorothy getting regular sex, I'd dress him up myself. I only hope he's up to standard. I wonder about him. Am I a terribly wicked mother-in-law to think it would be fun finding out?'

Chapter Eighteen

Holy Orders

Dex laughed at Ailsa's suggestion she fuck her son-in-law. Ailsa had stood facing the shower wall as Dex soaped her back and buttocks, her legs spread, awaiting the entry of his big cock. 'You wondering how it would be if Nigel fucked you is not an unusual reaction. You probably think you could improve on the performance of your daughter.'

'Oh, that's unforgivable,' she said, groaning out her pleasure as Dex penetrated her to the hilt, water and suds cascading over them. 'The slightest thought arouses me now. I can't seem to get enough. Am I a nymphomaniac, doctor?'

'No, but you'll do until one comes along,' Dex laughed, his thrusts making her jerk her bottom against his belly. He waited until her contortions grew frenzied, on the brink of orgasm then he shot his volley deep into her. 'Don't forget the drag ball tonight,' he reminded her, as he gave her wet bottom a parting smack. 'Make sure both Dorothy and Nigel attend. Who knows what might come of it?'

'Do I have to leave?' Ailsa asked him, as they returned to his consulting room. She got back on his couch, pouting as she watched him getting back into his clothes, clutching her breasts and parting her thighs provocatively. 'Can't you give me some more therapy?'

'The thought is tempting,' Dex admitted, looking at her reclining lewdly. 'A little matter of a business meeting with the revered Doc Weissbinder prevents me.'

Outside Weissbinder's consulting room he found Myra, Helga and Gerald waiting expectantly. 'Let's make this good,' he told them, his hand on the handle of the door. 'It's our chance to take the old bastard to the cleaners. Let me do the talking and back me up on everything I say.'

They entered and confronted a surprised and annoyed Weissbinder in discussion with Andrew Garfield. 'What's this?' the doctor said. 'Can't you see I'm in conference?'

'This is a delegation,' Dex announced, 'and we're not leaving until we're through with you. It's what's known as pay-back time.' He took a thin folder from Helga and offered it to Weissbinder.

Flicking through the contents, Weissbinder shouted in fury.

'We thought you'd like it,' Dex said coolly. 'We've got the evidence to back up what we say and my colleagues here are witnesses. It's *fait accompli*, Herr Doktor.'

'This list of grievances is preposterous,' Weissbinder began.

'They are demands,' Dex corrected him. 'And you'll meet every one of them. If need be we'll bring the Craig women into this and show them the secret tapes you've made for sale to private customers of yours. Think of the scandal.'

'What the hell is all this?' Andrew Garfield asked, snatching the folder from Weissbinder. 'As owner of this ship and as a shareholder in the Weissbinder Foundation and Clinic, I demand to know.' He studied each page carefully while a hushed silence fell. 'Christ, it says here an attempt was made to procure Amanda Craig for sexual purposes with me!'

'Indeed,' Dex affirmed. 'Those are Weissbinder's very words. He also ordered me to corrupt her mother, Mrs Ailsa Craig, so it could be filmed. The tabloid newspapers would have a field day with that.'

'These conditions must be met,' Garfield decided, glowering at Weissbinder. 'Take my word for it, I'll see that he complies. I don't give a damn about his reputation but I refuse to be dragged into this. In future Dr Calvert will be a full partner in all of the Weissbinder operations, and I expect no more underhand business on the side. Nurse Dietrich will be recompensed for the health spa this sleazeball ripped off. And Mrs Myra Starr will receive the payments she is due on the sale of certain video tapes she appeared in. Then I suggest that Herr Weissbinder retires gracefully. He's lucky to get out of it so lightly.'

'There's also the matter of compensation to Mrs Craig and family for the invasion of their privacy,' Gerald spoke up. 'Destruction of the tapes and an out-of-court settlement will ensure no more need be said. I suggest a suitable cheque is made out to St Boniface's School as a gift from the Weissbinder Foundation.'

'Make it a handsome one,' Garfield ordered Weissbinder. 'In thousands. Shall we say fifty? You won't miss the money.'

'In pounds, not dollars,' Gerald added. 'Send it to the school with a covering letter saying the Weissbinder Foundation makes these grants as regular donations to worthy causes. That way Mrs Craig need have no knowledge of the facts. It will be a nice surprise.'

'That's settled then,' Garfield said. 'I've given you my word and I expect the same guarantee from all of you.' He looked at Weissbinder slumped in his chair. 'Any other business before the shock kills him?'

'One last request,' grinned Gerald. 'He can call Miss Jackson and tell her it's my turn to lay on the therapy. I shall call at her cabin around seven this evening and she'd better be there.'

'You got it,' Garfield said. 'I want Dr Calvert to stay and tie up any loose ends. The rest of you can leave. Rest assured all this will be done.'

Ailsa knocked on Nigel's door and, finding it unlocked, walked in. Nigel lay asleep across his bed, clad only in what Ailsa thought looked suspiciously like a white pair of female briefs. Her attention was drawn to the appreciable bulge at the crotch and how smooth and boyish his bare chest looked.

An open magazine was beside his hand as if he had nodded off while reading.

Two more magazines lay on the floor beside the bed. She picked them up, pausing to note the cover of the top one in her hand. The wording was in German, the words easily translated as 'Massage Parlour Maidens'. Ailsa smiled. The cover illustration featured three naked people. Two buxom women, one black and the other a blonde Nordic type, were getting to grips with a male stretched out on a massage table. The strapping black girl squatted over the man's face, holding wide the cheeks of her hefty buttocks above his nose and mouth. At his other end, the blonde Amazon, huge breasts pendulous as she leant over, had his thick engorged prick embedded in her mouth.

This was the first pornographic magazine Ailsa had ever seen and she studied the lurid story told pictorially in full-colour photographs. Every scene increased her arousal, the spreading dampness at the crotch of her briefs proof of the magazine's effectiveness. She ground her thighs together, the arousal growing unbearable. Suddenly Nigel awoke and sat up.

'Oh my God,' he cried, seeing the magazine lying opened in her lap. 'They're not mine, I assure you,' he blurted out. 'They were left in the drawer of this bedside cabinet. I must have fallen asleep when I was examining them.'

'I didn't think for one moment these magazines were yours,' Ailsa said, still affected by the porn-induced excitement and trying to control her voice. 'When did you discover them, just this afternoon?' Annoyed with him for disturbing her perusal of the frank material, she spoke cuttingly. 'We've been on the Aphrodite almost a week, Nigel, and you've only just looked into your bedside cabinet? Is that the truth?' She shook her head at him pityingly. 'Do you deny getting excited looking at these pictures, like any normal young man? I won't think any the less of you.'

'I – I looked at them out of curiosity,' he mumbled.

'And how did that affect you?' Ailsa asked, warming to her

interrogation. 'What kind of husband are you to Dorothy? Are you afraid of women and sex? She has strong feelings that need fulfilling.'

'I – I'm shy. I can't say the things to her I want to,' Nigel pleaded. 'She would despise me—'

'You won't know until you try,' Ailsa said. She pointed up to a double spread of pictures in the magazine. 'Look at what they are doing,' she ordered, showing him the black girl spanking the man across her knee. On the opposite page he was on his knees with his face buried in the white girl's crotch. 'Does that excite you?' she demanded. 'Imagine you and Dorothy in this situation.'

'I suppose it does,' Nigel admitted miserably. 'But you shouldn't be talking to me this way. It's not decent or proper. I'm only human—'

'I'm glad to hear that,' Ailsa said vindictively, enjoying the feeling of power which was growing inside her and noting with satisfaction the enlarged bulge in Nigel's briefs. 'For goodness sake don't look so embarrassed about a natural thing like getting an erection. Come on, show it to me. Stand up and take off those briefs, I want to see how stiff and ready you are when you are aroused.' Her impatient glare made him get off the bed and hesitantly push down the briefs, trembling as he did so in excitement and fear. 'Young man, do you think I've never seen an erect penis before?' she said. 'If you act like this with my daughter, it's no wonder your marriage is failing.'

'I don't think you should look at me like this,' he said apologetically. 'I'm afraid I can't control it.' He glanced down at the rigidly erect prick thrusting before him. 'It must have been those pictures.'

'And would you like to see me naked like these women?' Ailsa found herself saying, aroused by the situation and the sight of Nigel's stout prick. A sudden unstoppable desire to flaunt herself in front of him forced the words from her lips. She began to undress, throwing her clothes aside, to pose before him, thrusting out her large tilted breasts, an expanse of flat creamy belly with a mass of hair covering the noticable curve at the join of her thighs. Watching his reaction, she laughed at the awe in his face. 'You *are* afraid of being confronted by a naked woman,' she said. 'Isn't this better than any photograph?'

'You – you are beautiful,' he said, stuttering the words.

'Lie on the bed, Nigel,' she ordered unsteadily. 'Do as you're told and no more argument.' Her push sent him sprawling across the bed with his prick upright as she fell over him, the cushiony mounds of her breasts pressed to his face.

Immediately and with a groan of pleasure, Nigel captured a thick nipple between his lips and began sucking greedily. Ailsa grasped his cock and directed to her cunt. The bulbous knob parted her outer lips and penetrated the moist inner flesh as she bore down against him. Embedded on the full length of his rigid stalk, Ailsa moaned in satisfaction, working her hips frenziedly, relishing the up and down sliding of his girth. She came suddenly, in wild undulations, grinding down on Nigel as he thrust up to her manfully. The agitated grunts below her indicated that he had shot off into the honeyed depths of her insatiable cunt. A second climax shook her to the toes.

'That was wonderful,' she heard him say as she rolled off him. 'Did I really make you come?'

'Just make sure you do the same for Dorothy tonight,' Ailsa said, sitting up and deciding to dress, aware that things had gone too far. 'You've shown you've got it in you. Go to her cabin at seven o'clock and take her to the party in the dining hall. Promise me you will.'

He lay watching the sway of her buttocks as she arose. 'I'll be there,' he said, considering the prospect of having the mother and the daughter both in one day.

Meanwhile Dorothy was visiting a morose Manda, who was still an unhappy patient in the ship's infirmary. 'I think mother is having an affair, in fact I'm certain she is. Her whole attitude has changed on this cruise,' Dorothy said to her sister. 'It should make things easier for you when you're up and about again. Doesn't that please you?'

'Why should it?' Manda complained. 'Everybody's having it off but me, it seems. I suppose I should be glad she's having sex with something that doesn't require batteries. As for you, you've been fucked by *everyone*.'

'Not quite everyone,' Dorothy said. 'Not by my husband, he's the one who should be fucking me. I'm going to that dance tonight and I'm going to insist he escorts me. Not Martin or Dex or anyone else. This's Nigel's last chance.' She bent to kiss her sister. 'Wish me luck.'

On returning to her cabin, Dorothy found her mother waiting for her. 'You look positively glowing,' she said. 'Can I guess what you've been up to this afternoon?'

'That's a secret,' Ailsa told her, still amazed at her unexpected bout with Nigel. 'Among other things, however, I ran into your husband. He's going to call for you here at seven tonight to take you to the dance. It's "Tarts and Vicars" you know for those who want to dress up. Have you thought what you'll go as?' She gave her daughter a quizzical look. 'And Nigel? Any ideas?'

'Wait and see,' Dorothy smiled. At seven precisely she answered the door to Nigel, wearing just a bra and briefs. 'Take off your suit,' she told him straight away. 'I need it. I'm going as a clergyman complete with dog collar. I'll need your shirt as well as your socks and shoes. Come on, don't stand there like a dummy, get undressed.'

'I was thinking how good you looked in what you're wearing,' Nigel said. 'Even less would be better,' he added, to her surprise. 'You can have my suit, and everything else, but what do I wear?'

'This,' Dorothy said, holding up one of her mini-dresses. 'You've got the legs for it, once you've put on my stockings and suspender-belt. There's a padded bra too and I've borrowed a blonde wig. You'll make a lovely tart once I've made you up.' She paused, looking at the bulge tenting the front of his trousers. 'The thought of dressing up has turned you on, hasn't it?' she teased him. 'You clot, you should have let me know.' Reaching out, she squeezed the front of his fly. 'It would be a shame to waste it. Who cares if we're a little late?'

It was at that precise moment that Gerald was making his promised visit to Ellen Jackson, suitably dressed in the black mortar-board cap and gown of a schoolteacher. She awaited him suitably dressed as a schoolboy, nervously letting him into her cabin. 'You obviously heard from Weissbinder that the tables have turned,' he told her with pleasure. 'Andrew Garfield pitched in on my side too. As he's the owner of this ship, if you want to continue your seagoing career you'd better play ball. I like the costume, it beats the waist-nipping corselet you wear when whacking my arse. I still bear the scars.'

'It was Dr Weissbinder who ordered me to do it,' Ellen pleaded. 'He made me. Honestly, it was his idea.'

'And didn't you just love it,' Gerald recalled. 'That schoolboy outfit suits you perfectly. It's very apt for what I have in mind. Tell me, Ellen, are you a naughty schoolboy?'

'You intend to punish me anyway,' she said tremulously. 'Must – must it be the cane? I don't think I could bear that.'

'Even though you dished it out to me? Actually, I prefer to use my hand,' Gerald informed her. 'I propose a good old-fashioned bottom spanking. I suggest you drop your shorts and go across my knee.' He sat on the edge of her bed, patting his upper thigh. She removed the blazer, dropped her shorts and tucked up her shirt. As she draped herself face down across his lap, he tut-tutted at her lacy briefs. 'Since when did boys wear these?' he asked, drawing them down over her ankles and gazing with approval at the rounded bottom cheeks thus revealed. 'Nice,' he praised. 'Very nice, young Jackson. There's so many things I can think of to do with this sweet little butt. Pressing kisses into the hot little cleave, for instance.'

'Just smack me,' Ellen warned him. 'I don't allow men to touch me. If you didn't know, I'm a lesbian and proud of it—'

'Such a waste of a sweet arse,' Gerald announced, 'but to each his own. Mrs Craig fucked you, I believe, double-dildo and all.'

'She fucked me, but you won't,' Ellen said, her confidence growing. 'Smack me hard as you like and get it over with. I hate men.'

'Then you won't like this,' Gerald said, raising his arm. His hard palm cracked noisily on the bouncy flesh, bringing a loud '*Owww*' of hurt and surprise from Ellen at the sudden impact. Arm flailing, Gerald spanked the pert bottom with a will, seeing it clench, wriggle and redden to crimson. He noted that, despite her whimpers and moans, her crotch was rubbing against his left knee in her struggles. This bottom warming has got the little bitch randy, he thought with pleasure, stopping smacking her when he had judged her wriggling was not solely because of the spanking. With her cunt pressed hard against his knee, she paused breathing heavily as he denied her the climax.

'Go on – why have you stopped?' she whined. 'Damn you for a sadistic beast.'

'Just resting,' he told her, his hand on the fiery cheeks and the rigid stalk of his erection pressing into her belly. Tempted by the curved spheres under his nose, he drew them apart to look into the dampened cleave and admire the tight crinkle of her rear entrance and the lipless split of her girlish quim. He lowered his face, plying his tongue along the ridged mouth of a cunt parted in arousal and on the inch or so up to her puckered ring.

'No!' she screamed. 'Don't get ideas. You're *not* going to use that disgusting cock of yours. I will not let you—'

'As if I would,' Gerald said genially between lapping and probing her with his tongue. 'Imagine I'm another woman. Just relax. Think of me as Ailsa, working you up to fuck you with that strap-on dildo. Wouldn't you like that?'

'But you're not a woman – and that's a real prick I feel,' she sobbed in her anguish, the sensations created by Gerald's delving tongue overpowering her will. She tottered from his lap to fall face forward across her bed, her bottom tilted in offer. 'Go on then, you beast, you *man*,' she uttered, looking back at him with eyes wild with lust. 'Fuck me, I want you to. Fuck my cunt, fuck my ass. Do it!'

'*Yesss*,' Gerald agreed readily, his arousal matching hers. He curled over her dipped back, spearing a receptively-lubricated cunt channel until his balls nestled in the cleave of her arse. Grasping her breasts for purchase, he rose on tiptoe to penetrate every thick inch. At once she began to rotate her smooth bottom against his belly, jerking and shouting out unintelligible grunts and cries as she came violently, continuing her gyrations for more of the same. *Fuck, fuck*! Gerald heard her squeal to spur him on as he pounded her, giving his all with each mighty forward thrust. With his balls about to boil over, he withdrew and let the plum head of his cock nudge against her arsehole. A push forced the tight ring to give, the first inch followed by several more as he eased his girth into the stretched passage.

'Oh yes, there too!' Ellen screamed. 'Fuck me in the arse! Go on, I've had it there before, I love it!' She felt his shaft dilating her anus as if to split her and she thrust back against the invader as if to prevent its escape, engulfing and surrounding it, working her bottom violently and feeling her outer ring sliding along his taut rod. Gerald, whinnying his pleasure, let his jets flood her innards as her convulsions frenziedly pummelled her bottom against his belly. He fell across her held fast by her tightness. Finally he got to his feet and looked down at her gasping for breath, her buttock cheeks twitching in their final spasms.

'You filthy beast,' she said vehemently. 'You made me come all those times, you swine.'

'There's gratitude,' Gerald laughed. 'You were there too, girl. For a dyed-in-the-wool self-confessed lesbian, you'd better rethink your sexual preferences. If it's any consolation from a mere man, it was a fuck in a million. I guess we can call it quits now: you caning my arse and me fucking yours.' He turned to leave with a final grin, 'Made a change from a dummy cock, didn't it? Why not enjoy the real thing in future?'

He went out into the passageway, making for Ailsa's cabin. He found her dressed in one of Manda's mini-dresses, her face heavily made-up with mascaraed eyes, lip gloss and rouged cheeks. 'You've never looked lovelier, Mrs Craig,' he told her affectionately. 'Just my kind of woman.'

'I'm a tart,' Ailsa laughed. 'I'm going to the dance as a tart.'

'That's what I meant,' Gerald said. 'I love the dress and the way you're bursting out of it. The way it's moulded to you.'

'Moulded to my big breasts and bottom, you mean,' Ailsa said. 'It's one of Manda's. I thought it right for a tart's dance, and as the poor creature can't be there, at least her dress is. Shall we go?'

On their way they met Dex Calvert with Helga and Myra on each arm, both women dolled up as painted strumpets showing inches of cleavage and breast flesh almost to their nipples. Seeing them, Gerald doffed his mortar-board gallantly. 'I'm reminded of a dead-heat in an airship race, looking at you two girls,' he said. 'As for you, Doc, I know your name but can't recognise your faith. What the hell are you supposed to be tonight?'

'Bless you, my children, how does the Archbishop gear grab you?' Dex grinned. 'These are two fallen women I'm saving. Can I save one for you, Gerald?'

'That won't be necessary,' Ailsa said, clinging to Gerald's arm. 'He's booked. Booked to make an honest woman out of me. Doesn't he look the marrying kind?'

'I never saw a more likely candidate,' Dex agreed. 'In that outfit he looks just the sort to help run your school.'

'If there's a school to go back to,' Ailsa said. 'Poor old St Boniface's.'

'Don't give up yet,' Dex advised. 'Miracles do happen. We even met your daughter Dorothy and her husband Nigel heading for the dance. He's had a change of mind as well as a change of clothes, it seems.'

'Not before time,' Gerald said. 'You lot go on to the dance and we'll join you later. Something has just come up I must attend to first.' He turned with Ailsa, leading her back to her cabin. 'It came up looking at you and thinking how drop-dead gorgeous you are, my sweet.'

'Oh, Gerald,' Ailsa said. 'You're not going to fuck me, surely?'

'Get one thing straight from now on, madam,' he told her severely. 'You're my woman and I'll fuck you whenever I want. And wherever I want.'

'Even in the potting shed?' Ailsa giggled. 'Cobwebs and all?'

'Even there,' Gerald swore, leading her back into her cabin and pulling her skirt up over her shapely, swaying rump.

In the infirmary, sounds of music and merriment could be faintly heard. Manda cursed loudly and threw her book onto the floor. It really was too awful to be confined to bed when everyone else was having a wonderful time. And the worst of it was being in bed on her own.

The cabin door burst open.

'Hi, Manda,' said a boy in tight leather trousers and a white T-shirt that clung to his broad chest as if it were painted on.

'Graham!' she squeaked, her depression instantly banished. 'Why aren't you playing at the dance?'

'We're in between sets,' said Martin, appearing at his brother's shoulder.

'We've brought you some fruit,' said Graham, placing a large bunch of grapes on the bedside table.

'And that's not all,' added Martin, his handsome face split by a melon-sized grin. 'That's if you're up to it.'

'Up to what?' They were on either side of the bed and Manda looked from one to the other, her stomach suddenly tumbling with excitement. 'It's something rude, isn't it? Tell me, please.'

The boys said nothing but their hands slipped to their waists and they simultaneously unzipped their pants. Together they pulled their engorged and glistening cocks into view.

'Oh yes,' moaned Manda.

There was a river between her legs as four hands stripped her nightdress from her glowing body and arranged her limbs lewdly on the bed.

'What are you going to do to me?' she whispered.

'Everything,' said Graham and pushed the thick head of his penis into the pouting mouth of her wet sex.

At last, thought Manda as the big prick slid all the way inside her.

It didn't hurt one bit.

A selection of Erotica from Headline

FAIR LADIES OF PEACHAM PLACE	Beryl Ambridge	£5.99 ☐
EROTICON HEAT	Anonymous	£5.99 ☐
SCANDALOUS LIAISONS	Anonymous	£5.99 ☐
FOUR PLAY	Felice Ash	£5.99 ☐
THE TRIAL	Samantha Austen	£5.99 ☐
NAKED INTENT	Becky Bell	£5.99 ☐
VIXENS OF NIGHT	Valentina Cilescu	£5.99 ☐
NEW TERM AT LECHLADE COLLEGE	Lucy Cunningham-Brown	£5.99 ☐
THE PLEASURE RING	Kit Gerrard	£5.99 ☐
SPORTING GIRLS	Faye Rossignol	£5.99 ☐

All Headline books are available at your local bookshop or newsagent, or can be ordered direct from the publisher. Just tick the titles you want and fill in the form below. Prices and availability subject to change without notice.

Headline Book Publishing, Cash Sales Department, Bookpoint, 39 Milton Park, Abingdon, OXON, OX14 4TD, UK. If you have a credit card you may order by telephone – 01235 400400.

Please enclose a cheque or postal order made payable to Bookpoint Ltd to the value of the cover price and allow the following for postage and packing:

UK & BFPO: £1.00 for the first book, 50p for the second book and 30p for each additional book ordered up to a maximum charge of £3.00.

OVERSEAS & EIRE: £2.00 for the first book, £1.00 for the second book and 50p for each additional book.

Name ....

Address ....

....

....

If you would prefer to pay by credit card, please complete:
Please debit my Visa/Access/Diner's Card/American Express (delete as applicable) card no:

Signature .... Expiry Date..............